Selected praise for the men of
HELL'S EIGHT

Caine's Reckoning

"Sarah McCarty's new series is an exciting blend of raw masculinity, spunky, feisty heroines and the wild living in the old west.... *Caine's Reckoning* is an erotic novel with spicy hot love scenes... Ms. McCarty gave us small peeks into each member of the Hell's Eight and I'm looking forward to reading the other men's stories."
—*Erotica Romance Writers*

"Intense, edgy and passionate, this is old-school historical romance at its finest."
—*Romantic Times BOOKreviews* (4.5 stars)

"*Caine's Reckoning* is a can't-put-it-down adventure story.... Superb writing and characterization...This exceptional first-in-series book has this reader eagerly anticipating future stories and earns it the *RRT* Perfect 10 rating...a hands-down winning tale that is not to be missed."
—*Romance Reviews Today*

"Though Caine and Desi alone would have made this a wonderful romance, the many other men of Hell's Eight are an integral part of the series and we are certainly left anxious for the next installment."
—*A Romance Review* (5 roses)

Sam's Creed

"Once again using an erotic backdrop, [McCarty] creates a mythic western hero, protective, dominant, and emotionally distant—but never cruel— who believes he is not worthy of the heroine who loves him... Readers who enjoy erotic romance but haven't found an author who can combine it with an historical setting may discover a new auto-buy author...I have."
—*All About Romance*

"McCarty continues her Hell's Eight series with this solidly plotted tale. There's wonderful chemistry between Sam and Bella, and the witty banter between them makes the story come alive."
—*Romantic Times BOOKreviews* (4 stars)

"The jaunty banter between Sam and Isabella is almost as much fun to read as the sexual tension that develops. I'm definitely looking forward to future [Hell's Eight] stories."
—*A Romance Review* (4½ roses)

Also by

SARAH McCARTY

SAM'S CREED
CAINE'S RECKONING

*And watch for Tracker's story, the next book in
the award-winning Hell's Eight series*

Available in 2010 from Spice Books

SARAH McCARTY

A HELL'S EIGHT EROTIC ADVENTURE

Tucker's Claim

Spice

Recycling programs
for this product may
not exist in your area.

TUCKER'S CLAIM

ISBN-13: 978-0-373-60529-3

www.Spice-Books.com

Printed in U.S.A.

A HELL'S EIGHT EROTIC ADVENTURE

Tucker's Claim

To all the ladies of my yahoo group. No one could ask for a better group of ladies with which to laugh and share life's ups and downs. You are simply the best.

1

Music drifted out of the gaily decorated church into the humid night air, wrapping around Sally Mae in a breath of lilting joy. She shifted her hip on the railing, leaned her head against the rough porch support and let the notes roll through her, not feeling the guilt so strongly this time. She was healing, from the inside out, the way Jonah said she would in what he'd considered a kindness. But then Jonah had been that type of man, always able to put others before him, always able to see God's light with no questions attached to the end of the message. His way had always been clear while hers was always a struggle.

Despite their differences, or maybe because of them, she'd been a good wife to him. Their marriage hadn't been the kind that little girls dreamed up while playing in the yard on a summer's day, but it had been the stable kind an impulsive woman valued. No matter what her inclinations, Sally had always known that if she couldn't find the answer in meditation, she would find it with Jonah. He'd been her rock, her balance, her guiding light, and when he'd been murdered, it had shattered her inner light into a never-ending pitch of black, to the point that she'd stopped feeling anything.

For months, she'd walked around in a daze, going through life as if she hadn't lost a vital part of her faith. And then the townsfolk had started coming to her for healing, seeing her as the next best thing to a doctor, and she'd found solace in being needed. From that solace had come a light that flickered through the darkness. Purpose. Life since Jonah's death hadn't been perfect, but she'd found a reason to get out of bed, a pretense on which to keep functioning, and gradually, that pretense had grown into a calling she'd only assumed was hers before Jonah's death. A calling that distracted her from the emptiness left by her husband's death. An emptiness she'd been able to ignore until six months ago when Tucker McCade had come back to town.

She grimaced and shifted her position, the star-studded vastness of the landscape striking her anew with its beauty, almost as though it was the first time she was seeing it. And maybe it was. Sometimes she felt that Jonah's death had wiped clean her understanding of who she was and left a stranger in its place. A stranger who was familiar in her love of these beautiful nights of endless sky and sparkling stars, yet foreign in her attraction to the big Texas Ranger.

She couldn't pinpoint what drew her to the man. Tucker was too big, too wild, too unpredictable to be described in easy terms. He breathed the violence she abhorred, seemed to believe in nothing but the moment, and the only emotion he let anyone see never made it to his eyes. He was a man of secrets and pain, larger than life, and nothing to which she should be attracted, and yet, somehow, he'd become part of her emerging life.

Laying temptation in front of a man like me is dangerous, pretty thing. The remembered warning rumbled over her nerves in a deep promise. At the time, she hadn't thought she'd been laying anything anywhere, just tending the nasty cut on his arm, but looking back, she *had* stood closer than she'd needed to, and her fingers *had* lingered longer than they'd needed to. She blamed it completely on the utter fascination of the man. His eyes alone would be enough to fascinate most women—a shocking silver-gray in his dark face. But for her, the fascination went much deeper than his heavily muscled frame and harshly exotic good looks. For her, the fascination went to the glimpses of gentleness that he hid beneath a sarcastic wit and a propensity for violence. A gentleness she suspected he wore with the same ease with which he wore his guns and knives. Tucker McCade was a man who was very comfortable with himself, in the same way Jonah had been, but for different reasons. While Jonah had been comfortable with the path God had revealed to him and his ability to stick to it, Tucker was comfortable with the path he had laid out for himself, and comfortable with his ability to hold it where he wanted.

Sally shook her head, breathing deeply of the humid night air, fragrant with the aroma of the roasting pig that had been served up earlier. Tucker fought at the drop of a hat. He'd fought for Cissy Monroe, who'd changed her mind about prostituting herself to make ends meet, fought for a mongrel puppy pinned down after stealing a loaf of bread, and sometimes he just fought for reasons that had no discernible cause other than that he wanted to. It was in those moments that Tucker McCade scared her, because those were the moments when he was everything his reputation held him to be. Everything she feared. The very thing that had taken her husband. A man as lawless and as violent as this land.

But he was also beautiful and compelling in the way of all wild things. And, much like the music she was trying not to break her mourning by enjoying, he had a way of getting under her skin, reaching down to the primal part of her that responded on instinct and didn't give a hoot about logic or her Quaker beliefs. The part of her that wanted him very badly.

Closing her eyes, Sally indulged in a bit of harmless fantasy. Imagined Tucker was before her, so wonderfully tall he made her feel small while those broad shoulders of his blocked her view of anything else. Most of all the past. His silvery eyes, so startling above the high slash of his cheekbones, would stare down at her in that semimocking, farseeing way he had that made her both nervous and breathless at the same time. And that long, shiny black hair he wore parted in the center would fall free about his exotic face as he leaned down, enhancing his Indian ancestry to the point of challenge. Enhancing the power of his personality, the magnetism of his sexuality, the sensual fullness of his mouth… He'd reach for her with his big, callused hands that never touched, but instead lingered a scant breath from her skin, promising so much even as they withheld everything. Passion, pleasure, heaven. Hands that killed as easily as they gave joy. A shiver, half negation, half anticipation, shook her from head to toe.

As a Quaker and a pacifist, she never saw the point of fighting. She also didn't see the point of daring everyone around a body to make something of nothing, but Tucker definitely had a take-me-as-I-am-or-suffer-the-consequences element in his approach to the world. When a woman added the easy confidence with which he did everything to that disregard for convention, it totaled up to a potent combination. One she was finding harder and harder to resist in the bright light of common sense. One she didn't want to resist in the soft cloak of night with the moon shining brightly and her imagination so willing to sketch out a moment between them.

The music slowed to a swirling crescendo. Inside dancers would be gliding to a stop with varying degrees of style, poised for the next beat, the next partner. While for her, here in this dream, hers already waited. All she had to do was take that step toward Tucker, that forbidden, terrifying step she'd never managed in real life, because in many ways she was a coward. Not because he was half-Indian, not because society said that was wrong—in her world all women and men were equal—but because Tucker McCade stood with his feet in blood while she followed a different path. But still, in her dreams, she could have him, and in her dreams she took that step forward into the touch of his hand, into the warmth of his embrace, into the protection of his strong arms. She sighed as desire coursed through her body at the imagined culmination of months of longing.

He was a cruel man, some said. A hard man, others whispered. But, on an instinctive level, she knew the only thing she would find in his arms was joy. She'd seen the promise of it in his marvelous eyes, felt it vibrate between them whenever they got close, knew deep inside that Tucker would take care of her body the same way he took care of her safety. Totally and completely, whether she wanted it or not.

Folding her arms across her chest and balancing her weight, Sally Mae hugged the knowledge to her, letting it weave through the fantasy, granting to Tucker in dreams the access that she couldn't in the daylight. Access to touch, access to pleasure. Through the break between songs, when everything was possible, she gave her fantasy permission to move forward into the forbidden with a sense of inevitability. Tucker was a force to be reckoned with at any time, wearing down his quarry with slow, steady pressure. And when it came to resistance, she was apparently no stronger than the outlaws who inevitably surrendered to his law. She didn't want to fight him anymore. Fighting was draining, especially when what she was resisting was the one thing instinct said could color the darkness that enshrouded her life.

The music inside broke into a merry jig, the rhythm percolating through her blood, picking up her spirits, increasing the tempo of her fantasy, moving from languid to fervored as she imagined his long fingers closing around her wrists, skimming her forearms, her upper arms, her shoulders, the rough calluses abrading her skin in a delicious way that Jonah's smooth hands never had.

The edges of her dream rippled at the disloyalty. Tucker was Jonah's opposite in many ways, and it might be the biggest delusion in the world to believe he could be gentle with a woman, but this was her daydream, her escape, and she wanted to believe Tucker could be gentle enough to bring her to the point where she didn't need gentleness anymore. She forced herself to be honest. Past the point where Jonah had always stopped.

She flinched, shattering the last of her dream, and it was once again just her, the night and the longing that wouldn't go away. For the warmth of a man's embrace, the strength of his arms, the burn of his passion. And not just any man. She'd never been indiscriminate. Jonah had been her only lover and until his death she'd never looked at another man, and in those first weeks, hadn't even been aware that Tucker existed. But one day she'd looked up from the cup of coffee that had been placed in her hand, and there he'd been, his expression solemn, his touch gentle, his eyes reflecting the understanding of the loss she couldn't accept. He'd been there ever since, popping into her life when he came into town, sheltering her from the worst of everything while he was there, making sure she ate, making sure her patients didn't get ideas, making sure she was safe and cared for. Making sure she knew he waited. For her.

Moonlight became Sally Mae. It poured over the paleness of her skin with a lover's tenderness, bringing out the silver gilt in her hair, the smooth perfection of her skin, the mystery of who she was. By day Sally could hide the truth under a bustle of activity, but in the quiet of the night, her secrets escaped. Her loneliness, her hunger, her thirst for adventure. Tucker was a man who'd always preferred night and those things it embraced. Sally was no exception. The woman had integrity, beauty, and an appeal from which he couldn't walk away. Even if he should. She turned ever so slightly and he could just make out the gentle swell of her breast beneath the inevitable gray of her dress. He narrowed his gaze until the tempting curve filled his line of vision. He smiled. Thank God he'd never been much on "shoulds."

He watched her, perched like a fairy against the support, her arms crossed over her chest, her head dropping back. The blond of her hair not covered by the fine lawn cap perched on the back of her head shimmered against the dark wood. Sunshine and shadow. The woman was a mystery. Her shoulders lifted on a slight sigh. That emotion he'd noticed lately and couldn't place shifted over her expression, narrowing her eyes and drawing her upper lip between her teeth.

She'd been in that strange mood a lot lately. Full of a restlessness that teased the edges of his awareness. Made him hard with its potential promise. He'd like nothing better than to step out of the shadows, take her hands in his, uncross her arms and draw them around his neck, accepting the weight of her willowy body against his, her troubles as his. If it were left to him, he'd wrap her in cotton wool and keep her safe from any threat, any worry. But it wasn't up to him. Though it sure as hell should be up to someone. Sally took too many risks. And lately, whenever he came into town from the hunt for Caine's wife's sister, nerves jangled, senses hungry for respite, she'd be watching him with those dark gray eyes that had no idea how they tempted, and he'd forget why he was keeping his distance.

Sally Mae sighed and closed her eyes as the music leaped into the calm of the night. The same moonlight that cast her skin in a silvery glow provided the shadows in which he hid. He knew she wasn't aware of his presence. She'd be strung as tight as a drum if she had any inkling that he watched her. And not because she found him distasteful. He wasn't a fool. He knew Sally Mae wanted him, the same as he knew she'd never get serious about it. A brief affair to see how it would be to lie down with a savage, maybe, but he'd learned the hard way that a white woman did not openly take up with a man with Indian blood—not for love or money. She might enjoy him on the side, if the affair could be safely hidden, but there was too much hate between whites and Indians for any more than that to be tolerated. Already there were rumblings because he stayed in her barn.

Not that he gave a shit. Tucker flexed his fingers, remembering the last time someone had suggested he move. It'd felt good to knock the man's teeth down his throat. Release a bit of that hostility Sally Mae had suggested he pray away. Well, quiet contemplation is what she called it. Tucker shook his head. As if prayer was going to settle the discord caused by a randy wrangler's speculation. He flexed his fingers again, enjoying the response of muscle. He'd never found talk as effective as action. Might was a great equalizer, and he had plenty of that. And if he had to go back and do it again, that would be the one thing he'd thank his father for giving him the muscle to make a place for himself in a world that had never wanted to give him one.

The hem of Sally Mae's dress fluttered, drawing his eye. Beneath the somber gray trim of her skirt, he could make out the top of her sturdy boot. Her toe was tapping.

Tucker had never seen Sally Mae dance, had always assumed it was against her religion, but maybe she'd just been in mourning for her murdered husband. Maybe that tapping toe indicated she was ready to come out and join the living. He straightened, the same surge of anticipation thrumming through his blood as when he closed in on his quarry at the end of a long bounty hunt. With the same cold precision, his senses homed in on Sally Mae. He'd lain awake nights, imagining touching his tongue to the smooth white skin at the hollow of her throat where her pulse beat against her smooth white skin. She always smelled of lemon and vanilla, and he bet the scent was strongest there, heated from her excitement and fear. He'd draw a deep breath and take it into himself right before he unbuttoned her prim dress and eased the flaps aside to reveal the treasure beneath.

Some men liked their women plump and soft, some liked them curvy. He'd decided, about two minutes after Sally Mae touched him, that he liked willowy blondes. He'd been in a rage—angry at life, indulging his temper on an equally big man who was in an equally big snit when she'd walked into the saloon, stepped between them and started to lecture them on the foolishness of fighting. He'd had to deck the bastard when he'd hauled back his arm, ready to flatten her. Then he'd had to listen to her lecture him all the way to her house, half-lit, keeping his steps steady because he knew if he tripped she'd try to catch him, and with her delicate build she'd only end up pancaked beneath him. She'd ranted at him in that quiet way she had as she'd gathered her supplies, as if her wild opinions had weight.

He'd sat and listened, breathed her scent, and as he looked around her cozy kitchen later, the longing had hit him with the force of a blow. Had things been different—his mother white or his father Indian—his blood wouldn't have been mixed and he could have had a home in either the white world or Indian, but as it was, he didn't fit anywhere except Hell's Eight. He certainly didn't fit here, but he'd wanted to. For the first time since his family and town had been wiped out by a Mexican raid when he was sixteen, he'd wanted to fit somewhere other than Hell's Eight. And when Sally Mae's hand had settled on his bare arm in an offer of pure comfort, for that brief moment in time, he'd wanted to fit here.

In the months since that night, the need kept creeping back. Didn't matter how much he told himself Sally Mae was a good woman. Not the kind a man trifled with, he couldn't shake the belief that she was meant for him. For however long he could tickle her fancy. Since that moment she'd touched him, he'd been biding his time. He was good at that. It made him a good Texas Ranger. A good horse trainer. He eyed the gentle thrust of Sally's breasts beneath her demure lace collar. A damn good lover.

The music resumed a lively beat. Sally's toe kept time. He bet she danced with the same inherent grace underlined with an innate sexuality, as she did everything. She was the only woman he knew who could make stitching a wound a sexy event. A smile tugged on the corner of her wide mouth. Probably too wide for beauty, but Tucker liked the generous way she smiled. It reflected the generosity of her spirit. He liked the way her nose wasn't some small bit of nonsense, too. Straight and narrow it complemented the strength in the rest of her features.

Truth was, a moment spent studying Sally's face revealed a lot about the woman's personality. Including how stubborn she was. Just look at the set of her chin. More than one person had tried to get her to move back east after her husband had been shot, but she'd refused politely. When pressed, she'd just ended all argument with a simple statement that she wouldn't be run out of her home. And when the suggestions had started that she needed to remarry, she'd been just as blunt. Her husband had been a good man. She'd mourn him properly.

The town had backed down. Which had been pure foolishness, in Tucker's opinion. Texas wasn't a place for a woman who believed God lived in everyone and turning the other cheek beat a beating when dealing with a threat. Tucker would have put her ass on the next train east, bound and gagged if he'd had to. Sally Mae was too fine for life alone out here. Green to the difficulties she faced, green to the reality that she'd have to marry again. Green to the danger she faced from him. Hell, she'd even pointed out that with a Texas Ranger living in her barn, how much of a threat could there be? Completely missing the connotation people might put on that. Completely missing how right they'd be to speculate on his interest. He did want her and he intended to have her.

On a sensual sigh, she smiled and settled further against the porch wall. Alone in the dark, apart from the town, the way she always was, even though she tended to the townspeople with an evenhandedness a preacher couldn't fault, taking care of good and bad alike, losing all caution under a sense of dedication. Lately, even more so. As if driven to prove something only she understood. Which was another reason he was still here and not out following the latest lead on what had happened to Ari, Caine's wife's sister, why he'd turned down Sam and his new fiancée's invitation to make his home off Hell's Eight at their comfortable ranch. He grimaced. He was a glutton for punishment, that was for sure, but someone had to watch over the widow when her common sense took a hike. Like last week when she'd taken in Lyle Hartsmith after he'd been knifed in a bar fight.

Lyle Hartsmith was a real no account, an outlaw with no morals and no allegiance, and if there was any justice in the world, the wound would have killed him, but there was no convincing Sally Mae of that. In her eyes, the prairie rat was one of God's creatures and entitled to care. And that was the end of it. So Tucker was here cooling his heels, keeping an eye on things, making sure she didn't take on more than she could handle, feeding a hunger that could go nowhere while he paid back a debt she wouldn't acknowledge he owed. He shook his head. Who the hell had said that with age comes wisdom? He was thirty-one, and from all recent signs, getting dumber by the day.

The fiddler dropped into a slow, popular tune and Sally's smile changed, becoming sad and just a little bit lost in the memories the song evoked. No doubt, of her dead husband. Tucker wanted to resent the man for having Sally for his wife, but he couldn't. Jonah had been a good man who'd deserved better than he'd received. And he'd been stolen from Sally the same way Tucker's life had been stolen from him when he'd been sixteen—in a hail of bullets and with no warning. He knew the sense of shock left by that kind of murder, the feeling that there was nothing left to hold on to. His parents might not have been the best, but they'd been better than the nothing that had remained when the Mexican soldiers had finished annihilating his small town.

A thinning of Sally Mae's lower lip told him she was biting it. To hold back sobs? Hell, the night was too beautiful for tears. Especially Sally Mae's. He stepped out of the shadows, drawn by her sorrow and the need to alleviate it. Drawn by his lust and his hunter's instincts. Drawn by the desire to make this moment in her life better than the memory that consumed her. It took only three steps to get to the bottom of the stairs. He held out his hand, looked up and asked, "May I have this dance?"

There was a slight start to reveal her surprise, but Sally Mae didn't move away from the wall, and she didn't open her eyes, but her smile changed. Softened. She really was in a mood tonight.

"That would be scandalous."

He cocked an eyebrow at her. "So was taking a notorious outlaw into your house, but I didn't see you balk at that."

Her right eye cracked open. "In that, I didn't have a choice."

His instincts perked. His blood thickened with the slow course of desire. "And now you do."

He didn't expect her to take his hand, and she didn't, but her other lid opened and the gaze with which she weighed him was as keen as anyone's, even Caine's. And Caine had a wicked ability to take a person's measure. It's what made him the natural leader of the Hell's Eight.

"I find I am at a fork in the road of my life, Ranger McCade."

His heart beat faster and his senses sharpened. "Forks can be good."

She closed her eyes again and took a slow breath. The way a person did when they were thinking. "True, but only if one can discern the difference between an opening and temptation."

She had him there. "An opening?"

"An opportunity provided by God to grow."

"And without this opening you can't dance with me?"

With her eyes closed and the moonlight catching on her hair, she looked like an angel he'd seen in a book he'd stolen as a child.

Her eyes opened and he changed his mind. No angel looked that earthy.

"It means I must decide the source of thy temptation for me."

"As in good or bad?"

"Yes."

Placing his foot on the bottom step, he grazed his finger over her knee. The practical wool of her skirt did nothing to dim the impact on his senses. "Then I vote for bad."

Her lids flickered and her lip slipped between her teeth. "Why?"

He smiled, holding her gaze, his pulse kicking up. She wasn't fighting him. "Because I can make being bad...very, very good."

Her breath caught. Exhaling, she confessed, "Such is what I suspect, which simply makes my decision that much harder."

The flush on her cheeks destroyed the last of his good intentions. Sliding his fingers to the back of her knee, he curved his palm over the point. "Want me to make it easy for you?"

Sally's expression shifted. An element he didn't recognize enriched the speculation as she ran her gaze over him. The glance, rich in feminine knowledge, burned along his desire, as it traveled from the top of his hat to the toes of his boots, neither of which were courting clean. "Would thee be willing?"

The lack of disapproval in her summation only goaded his anger with the message it sent. He'd been here often enough to recognize the signs. She wasn't looking for proper from him, just a few illicit moments in bed that she could hug as her sexy little secret on cold winter nights. He dropped his hand and stepped back. "Is your bed getting so cold that you're lowering yourself to invite a savage into it?"

She blinked and slid off the rail. It was easy to read the emotions chasing across her expression this time. Horror. Affront. Anger. And then pity. "Thee do not think much of thyself."

That wasn't true. He thought a lot of himself, he just didn't think much of how other people saw him. "Thinking on changing me?"

With a cock of her head, she acknowledged his displeasure, then she shrugged. "I've been thinking on many things."

"Like what?" He didn't trust that too-calm way in which she observed him.

"Like the fact that thee are a good man, as well as being a very big temptation."

He might be a temptation, but he wasn't good. And she damn well knew it. "Have you been drinking?"

"I don't believe in drink."

She didn't drink, she didn't dance and she didn't believe in violence. "What do you believe in?"

She didn't answer right away, just studied him with her big gray eyes to the point that he was beginning to feel like a bug under a magnifying glass. And then in that regal way she always moved, which spoke of confidence and commanded respect, she descended the steps. When she reached the bottom one, it was natural to hold out his hand, natural that she place hers in it, natural that he continue to hold it as she took that last step that brought her directly before him. Her fingers curled around his. Her hand was cool and dry. She wasn't nervous about dancing with him. "I believe in choice."

And this close it was easy to determine why. There was a touch of alcohol on her breath. Someone had spiked the punch. Sally Mae probably wasn't in command of all her faculties. A decent man would have escorted her back inside to the dance. But he wasn't a decent man. He was Tucker McCade, known more for his brawling skills than his scruples. In short, he was no better than he had to be.

"Then I'm glad you're choosing me."

Her head cocked to the side as he pulled her in. "Thee are lying."

Yes, he was. What with Sam just having left with Bella, Tucker was more conscious than ever of what would never be his. A woman to love him for what he was. The way Bella loved Sam. The way Desi loved Caine. But tonight, he was in the mood to pretend that it could be, and with Sally Mae. He drew their linked hands up and to the right, guiding her into his arms. The top of her head tucked under his chin as if it belonged there. "Do you care?" he asked against the silk of her hair.

"Not tonight."

"Good."

"Thee are holding me too closely."

She might be protesting, but he noticed she wasn't stepping away.

Would thee be willing?

He was more than willing to give her anything she wanted for whatever reason. A man like him wasn't one for passing up golden opportunities.

"Your husband let you lead when you danced?"

She shook her head. "No, he was like thee. He liked to be in charge."

At least she had one thing right. He was a man who led. "Then you won't have trouble following me."

Her head tipped back. Her eyes were very dark in the shadow of his hold, mysterious with an emotion he couldn't decipher. "No, I don't think I will."

The soft huskiness underlying the statement increased the fire that just being near her ignited. "Good."

He led her into the first steps of the three-count dance. She followed easily. Her free hand slid up his chest to settle on his shoulder and her head snuggled against him. She was as graceful a dancer as she was in everything else, following him easily under the stars. And he came to a decision. This kind of pretending could be good. "I guess you dance after all."

"What made thee think I didn't?"

He smiled at the softness of her tone, as if she, too, didn't want to break the quiet of the moment. "You seem awfully religious."

"Being a Quaker does not mean I abandon joy."

Her hips brushed his as he led her through a turn. His cock

jerked as if her fingers had closed around it. Damn, she made him ache like a green boy.

"Glad to hear it."

Chuckling, she squeezed his hand. "I imagine thee are."

He wanted to close his eyes, as she had, and wallow in the moment, take the pretense to another level. Take advantage of her inebriation. It would be so easy. She was making it easy, but he remembered the gentleness of her touch on his arm when she'd tended him, the softness she gave him so easily, and knew he wouldn't do it. Sally's reputation was a very fragile thing. Nurses weren't held in high regard, often being considered little better than prostitutes. Being seen dancing with him would cost her everything. He'd give her this moment, but he'd make sure it didn't come back to haunt her.

Sally's fingers shifted on his shoulder, moving across, following the line of muscle, testing his strength. His hands did a little testing of their own. The right opened across the small of her back, easily spanning the distance from side to side. She was a very slenderly built woman, to the point that it was hard to believe a body this delicate could house such a backbone of steel.

Her hands slid back up over his biceps to curve over his shoulders.

"Thee are a very strong man."

It came out more of a sigh.

"You are a very beautiful woman."

As she shook her head, the citrus scent of her shampoo teased his senses. "I'm not, but it is very nice of thee to say so."

He debated arguing the point, but there were better ways than words to convince a woman of her beauty, and he'd much rather spend his time indulging them. He led her through another turn, pulling her against him so the press of her hips to the hardness of his cock was more than a brush. More of a lure. Fire raced up his backbone as Sally sighed and relaxed against him, prolonging the moment.

"Thee are also very light on thy feet."

"It comes in handy in my profession."

She stiffened. She'd never made any secret that she hated what he did. He had never made it any secret that her dislike didn't change anything. "Thee will not speak of such things tonight."

"You think that will make them go away?"

"No, but if we do not speak of them for tonight, they cannot exist."

"Interesting way to look at things."

"There is no knowing the future, so I have decided there's value in enjoying the now."

The theory coincided with his own. Except for their opposing views on the necessity for violence, he and Sally were often on the same side of an argument. Testing her, he led her through some intricate steps. She had no trouble following them. If she could follow those steps, she was aware enough to make a decision, and if Sally was ready to take a lover, he wanted to be first in line. He finished in a series of turns, pulling her tightly against him, forcing her with pressure in the small of her back to arch away, until she braced her hands against his chest and looked up at him.

"And now is tonight?"

Her lips parted, and he could see the hint of her teeth, the flick of her tongue. Lust shot deep.

"Yes."

He spun them one last time, before leaning in. "Then let me help you with the enjoying."

2

K issing Sally was as natural as breathing. Tucker bent and she lifted, participating in the discovery as if she were as hungry for the taste of him as he was for her, her lips already parted when they met his. Soft, demanding with feminine hope. She didn't have to worry. He wouldn't let her down in bed. Supporting her with his hand in the small of her back, he arched her closer, not immediately taking advantage of her parted lips, savoring the anticipation, raising it with light nips and easy busses. Grunting as the fire gathered deep inside, built, flashed outward in a near crippling release of pleasure.

"Ah, damn, pretty thing, I knew you'd be like this."

Her fingers dug into his shoulder, gripping tightly as the shock went through her. No shy miss here, just an open, honest woman very sure of what she wanted, which was good because he'd never been so vividly aware of a woman, the press of her nipples against his chest, the soft graze of her hips, the sweet relaxation of her body against his... Never been so vividly aware of his own senses through a kiss to the point that he could feel his blood surging through his veins, feel her breath whispering over his skin as she relaxed against him with the soft sigh of surrender he'd been imagining for the past six months. Her lips were soft, her muscles taut as she rose up on tiptoe, stoking the fire between them. She pulled back. He allowed it, barely.

There was a touch of wonder in her expression. "Thee kiss like an angel."

He caught the words in his mouth, holding them, irrationally making more of them than was wise before letting them go and falling into the game, the seduction. Brushing a few strands of hair away from her temple, he smiled as if he weren't so aroused that he was in danger of simply lifting her, unbuttoning his pants, finding the wet heat of her through the slit in her pantaloons and thrusting deep. "You should see what my devil can do."

"An angel, a devil, a man and a woman. Our bed is going to be crowded tonight."

Laughter caught him by surprise, escaping before he could muffle it. "I suppose we could kick a couple out."

"Good, because I want only thee."

For tonight. As a young man he'd been slow to hear that silent qualification, but he'd soon learned the reality of this exchange. And the benefits of giving a woman what she wanted. Pretty much, his size and muscle, when combined with the forbidden of his ancestry, meant that no matter what town he landed in, his bed was never empty unless he wanted it to be. Since he'd landed in Lindos for the first time a year ago, he'd slept alone because the only woman he wanted was grieving, but now it looked like his luck was turning. Satisfaction spread right along with his smile. "Good."

Sally Mae blinked, reached up and touched the corner of his mouth. "Thee are smiling."

The tenderness, when he expected passion, threw him off balance.

"You've seen me smile before."

She shook her head, leaning back. He liked the way she trusted he'd support her almost as much as he liked the gentle brush of her fingertips over the corner of his lips. "Not a true smile."

"I've got you in my arms with the night in front of me. That's a lot to be happy about."

"Will thee think badly of me if I admit I'm smiling for the same reason?"

He pressed experimentally with his fingertips. She responded by snuggling closer, her breath catching as she felt the extent of his desire. "If I say yes, will you try harder to please me?"

"I would be more likely to find a man less persnickety."

"In that case, absolutely not."

The softening of her smile let him know she understood his teasing. "Ah, good, because I have my heart set on thee."

Inside, the music died off. People would be coming out soon to catch a breath of air. They couldn't stay here.

"What are thee thinking?"

"Where we can go for a little privacy."

"Thee do not have this all planned?"

The question hit him on a raw spot he had thought long since scabbed over. His mother being Indian didn't make him an amoral tomcat with nothing better to do than plan the next skirt to lift. "I've been busy."

Trying to find Desi's sister, Ari, before her uncle's henchman did. Trying to keep Sam and Bella alive against the outlaws that wanted Sam dead and Bella's inheritance in their pockets. Trying to keep his hands off Sally Mae.

Sally winced and sighed, her palms pressing against his chest, stroking the apology into his skin. Her fingers tangled in the cord around his neck, sliding down to nudge the bullet he always wore around his neck as a reminder of what happened to those who were weak. "Thee should know I'm not good at this."

He pulled them away, not liking the thought of her tainted by the memories it harbored. "What exactly is *this?*"

"This is supposed to be me seducing thee." She slanted him a look from under her lashes. "I've been led to believe it doesn't take much."

"To seduce an Indian?"

This time, she slapped his shoulder, the small, painless violence just arousing him more. Pushing back, she glared at him. His hand in the small of her back kept her from putting any real distance between them, but it didn't keep her from trying. A little of his resentment faded as he quelled the rebellion by lifting her just a bit so her struggles snuggled the ridge of his cock into the V of her thighs. On a sharp gasp, she went utterly still. But she didn't back down.

"Any man."

"Your momma tell you that?"

"It was more of a warning, to keep me safe from the base desires of men."

"And yet, here you are, blatantly tempting my baser self."

She frowned. "Who wants to aggravate me."

"Who wants you very much," he corrected, sliding his hands up her back.

"I'm not so sure I want thee anymore."

The little liar. The truth was in the way she cuddled against him and the way her eyes watched his lips shape around the words as if imagining other things. "Even if I promise to be very easy to seduce?"

Her fingers dug into his shoulder as he pressed against her in little pulses. "How easy?"

Trailing his fingers down her cheek, over the slight ledge of her shoulder to her chest, he confessed, "Very."

Biting her lip, she continued to hold still as he found and followed the strap of her camisole beneath her dress. "I could meet thee in the barn."

The confession came out in a breathless rush that touched his tender side and reminded him she was new to this, likely had never been with anyone but the good doctor. That being the case, this was a very big step for her. The least he could do was make it easy. As his finger hit the bodice of the hidden camisole, he kissed her lips for no reason other than that it had been fifteen seconds since the last time he'd placed his mouth on hers, fifteen seconds since he'd taken her breath as his. Fifteen seconds since he'd felt that particular arc of pleasure go through him. It was no different this time. Pleasure arced in a rich unfurling. And when its journey culminated its race down his spine, settling in his balls, pulling them up tight, it was almost like coming home. This time, when their lips parted, he couldn't manage easy. His impatience bit into his drawl, dragging it down to a rough growl.

"The barn's too conspicuous."

She blinked, not with him yet. Her tongue ran over her lips. "I can sneak."

As if sneaking was an option. "The rumors will start before you get to the rose garden."

His staying in her barn when he was in town hadn't raised suspicions when her husband was alive, but now that she was widowed, a hostile edge had invaded his dealings with some of the town's more ornery citizens. Pretty much everyone but Sally Mae held his motives in suspicion. And as the days passed, that suspicion was growing.

She sighed and flicked her fingers in dismissal. "Some people lead very boring lives. They seek something to talk about."

She'd obviously never been on the wrong side of community opinion, otherwise she'd know how much other people's assumptions could ruin a life. He drew his thumb across the remnants of their kiss, the soft, moist flesh clinging to his calluses.

"Bored people could make life very difficult for you."

"If I worried about how others see my choices, my life would be equally boring."

He kind of liked the idea of her life being boring. Predictable. Safe.

"Thankfully, the sacrifice won't be necessary." He let her slide down, his breath hissing between his teeth as her stomach slid along his cock. "The moon's bright enough. I'm thinking that I could meet you down by the pond."

She ran her hand up his back. "Outside?"

She didn't sound put off by the idea. He hadn't really expected her to be. In his experience, being taken outdoors was part of what women expected when they invited him to their bed. "Yes."

Her fingers pressed against his nape in a fleet kiss of excitement. "I'll have to take my leave and then stop by the house. I will meet thee in an hour."

An hour was too damn long. As the only thing he could

figure she needed from the house was a blanket, he offered. "I can take the quilt off my bed."

She stepped back, out of his arms. "Not those kind of things."

He had a gnawing urge to drag her back. "Care to explain?"

She sighed. "Thee must not take this wrong, but I do not wish to become with child."

He wasn't in any particular hurry to be a father, though a part of him couldn't resist toying with the thought of a child. A little bit of him to go on in the future. He wouldn't have one, of course. Caught between the Indian world he'd never known and the white world that wouldn't accept him, there was no place for him, any more than there'd be a place for a child who would no doubt bear his skin color. For him, there were just these stolen moments with different women with no forever on the back end.

"You've got a way of stopping that?"

"Yes. Jonah taught me."

"It works?"

"We were married six years and I do not have a child."

She sounded neither happy nor sad when she said that, which just struck him as wrong. A woman like Sally Mae, who cared for everyone, would have strong maternal urges. Yet she didn't have children because her husband had taught her how to avoid it.

Sally's fingers brushed his, drawing his gaze. "This bothers thee?"

He smiled automatically. "Not a bit."

She didn't smile back.

"I do not want thee to take offense, but…" She licked her lips. "I must ask…."

No doubt she wanted to caution him to be gentle. Women

always seemed obligated to ask that, as if he weren't aware of his size and the harm he could do. "What?"

"It occurs to me that a man like thee might already have a woman."

Shit. He'd rather she'd ask him to be gentle than to be insulting him. "If I did, I wouldn't be out here kissing you."

She shook her head, causing moonlight to dance off the crown of braids wrapped around her head as the strings to her white cap danced about her shoulders. He wanted to pull those hairpins out so that heavy swathe of hair spilled like sunlight, brightening the darkness around them.

"I don't mean to insult thee. It's just not my way to cause another pain."

He knew that about her, but it annoyed the hell out of him that she didn't know the same about him. Then again, why should she? To her, he was a means to an end. "Then you can stop worrying. No one's expecting me anywhere."

Except Ari, Caine's sister-in-law, either dead or held prisoner somewhere out there. But until he received a response to his latest query, he didn't have a lead to follow so he had no choice other than to stay put.

Sally Mae reached up, cuddling the softness of her breasts into the hardness of his chest. His hand fell naturally to the small of her back, supporting her. There were definitely compensations to staying put. "Except me."

"Except you."

He shook his head, feeling her shiver when the ends of his hair flicked across her forearms as her fingers linked behind his neck. She was very sensitive to him. "I'll be waiting for you at the woods straight off the back door."

"But what if someone—"

He put his fingers over her lips. "No one's going to see me unless I want to be seen, but you're not to walk in the woods at night by yourself."

"I have done it many times. Two nights ago, in fact."

"I know."

She frowned. "Thee watched?"

"I kept guard."

Her smile caressed his fingertips. "Thee always watch over me."

"I owe you."

She went still against him again.

"What?"

Her hands slid down to his shoulders. "Thee are not planning on being with me tonight because thee feel obligated?"

Only a woman could come to that conclusion. "Moonbeam, I'm not that nice a guy."

The mischief came back to her smile. "Good."

It was foolish. Someone could come out any second, and the one thing he never was, was foolish. But when Sally looked at him like that—part seductress, part challenge—he lost all sense of civilization. Yanking her into his arms, he kissed her with all the hunger she roused—hard enough to bruise, hard enough to leave an impression. And when he let her go, she swayed, her gray eyes glazed over with the same passion tearing through him. Hell, when he finally got her to himself, they were going to set the grass on fire.

Touching his finger to the kiss-swollen center of her bottom lip, he drew it away from her teeth, revealing the moist inner lining. He licked his lips, savoring her taste. Tonight he'd know what she tasted like all over. Tucking his finger under her chin, he lifted her face to his.

"Don't make me wait too long."

★ ★ ★

Sally stood in front of her mirror, studying her reflection. Tucker McCade was waiting for her out in the woods. The illicit thrill that went through her was very much out of place, but exciting. Staring at the mirror, she wondered what he saw in her. She was a plain woman with plain ways, wearing a plain dress. She had nothing frilly under her dress, such as the saloon girls wore to entice a man. No fancy scents to please his senses. She was just Sally Mae Schermerhorn, widow of Jonah Schermerhorn, mother to none, daughter to none. A woman who'd come west in the hope of finding the sense of belonging that she'd never had, even amidst the accepting arms of the people who had taken her in when she was ten. Even in the arms of her husband.

She touched the demure white cap she always wore over her coronet of braids. Nothing like what was worn by the other women Tucker had known, she was sure. Tucker, with his big bones, big muscles and bold face with the aggressive slash of his cheekbones beneath his incredible silver eyes was a harshly exotic, handsome man. There was nowhere he went that women's eyes didn't follow. A dart of insecurity pierced her anticipation. Which meant he could have his pick.

She pulled the cap off slowly, watching in the mirror as it revealed the tightly pinned braids. Suddenly she hated the hairstyle and all it represented. Conformity. Control. Acceptance. Tonight, she wanted to be the woman that Tucker imagined. Someone as fanciful as a moonbeam. She studied the cap, her image. Tonight, for whatever reason, he wanted her. And tonight she wanted to be more than plain Sally Mae. Tonight she wanted to drown in the attraction between them and just bury the pain that festered inside beneath some sort

37

of joy. Since that horrible night when the sheriff had brought her Jonah's bloody body, along with his last words, she'd been silently screaming. She didn't want to be silent anymore, locked in her mind with her screams. And tonight she didn't have to be. Tonight she could give Tucker what he wanted and take a little for herself. No promises would be made. No one would be hurt. Just two bodies coming together to satisfy separate needs. And when it was over, she'd go back to her silence and plain ways and Tucker would go about his wild ones. There was no worry that he would gossip. The added benefit of taking a man with Indian blood as her lover was that he wouldn't—couldn't—say a word for fear of being strung up. She didn't personally care about his heritage. God created all men and women equally, but societal issues did offer her that guarantee.

Another pause as she considered how selfish she was being, using a man to relieve pain. But then she remembered the look in Tucker's eyes as he'd stood in the back of the cemetery on one of her recent visits. He had stalked over the rise like some wild cougar, his torn-off shirtsleeves and leather vest showcasing his massive chest and powerful muscles, giving him a primitive intimidation, making everyone and everything else seem insignificant. The ever-present bullet hanging on the leather thong around his neck completed the image of a cold, lethal predator. Until his silver gaze met hers. There hadn't been any sympathy there. No pity. But as she stared into his eyes, understanding arced across the distance between them, and she saw the pain he, too, felt.

It would just be one other thing they had in common—an understanding of how pain too great to be borne had to be hidden, because to let it loose would destroy everything they were. At first, that had made her uncomfortable, but as the months passed there was comfort in knowing that her secret was shared. And now their relationship was going forward, down a path that had a predestined feel to it. An opening, Friends called it. An opportunity, presented by God, to grow.

Sighing, she put the cap on the polished vanity top.

She was going to take a lover. A man not of her race, not of her beliefs. A man who, supposedly, was built of nothing but violence and darkness. A man who had such bright, shining moments of goodness that it was very hard to reconcile his reputation with what she knew. A man with whom, tonight, she would share more secrets. Intimate ones in a step she'd accepted was meant to be. She wasn't sure what God had planned for either of them, but tonight was right. Others might point a finger if they found out, but the same way she'd known since she was ten that Jonah was to be her husband, she knew Tucker was what she needed tonight.

The knowledge didn't make her any less nervous. She had an incredible urge to slap the cap back onto her head, to go back into hiding, to let the pain grow until it got too big to fight anymore. To be the coward no one ever let her be. Instead, she unbuttoned her dress and quickly divested herself of her corset. It didn't seem right to go to a tryst wearing one. She didn't look in the mirror as she tossed it on the bed and rebuttoned the fastenings.

Running her hands over her stomach, she sighed. It felt strange to feel her flesh beneath her dress. Wearing a corset always made her feel more in charge, as if she had a second backbone to see her through when her own failed, but tonight, it was just her. Tucker had better appreciate it.

A glance at the clock on the wall showed more than an hour had passed since Tucker had left.

Don't make me wait too long.

Or what? She hadn't asked what, but nothing her imagination came up with made her feel better. He'd leave? She didn't want that. He'd come get her? Even worse. The whole reason she was late was because that cantankerous, lecherous Lyle—her current patient—had proved demanding, wanting food and making insinuations while she'd served it. Thank goodness, by tomorrow he'd be up and about and gone. He made her nervous with his sly glances and free ways. While it was her duty to care for the sick, there were some patients she debated the wisdom of saving. Lyle was one.

Immediately, she felt guilty. All men were capable of change. The prompting came from within and there was every chance this last brush with a knife had opened Lyle's heart. If Jonah was here it wouldn't be so hard to believe that. She likely wouldn't have slipped in the first place. Jonah had believed very strongly in God's power to induce change.

Unlike her. She glanced at her reflection again, noting the high color in her cheeks. The almost wicked anticipation in her eyes. The utterly proper braids above. She reached up and changed her mind halfway to her destination. She couldn't walk out the door with her hair down. It was too brazen, too bold. It would leave her feeling naked.

Sally knew there was a wildness in her that could match the wildness in Tucker, but knowing it and experiencing it were two different things. To complicate matters, she had a tendency to be shy. If she got mad, that fell by the wayside, but she didn't intend to be mad tonight. Raking her teeth across her lips to give them a bit more fullness and color, she turned away from the mirror. She would have to do as she was. Jonah had always enjoyed taking her hair down for her. Maybe Tucker would enjoy it, too. Smoothing her skirts, she headed down the stairs and into the sweetness of the night.

Tucker was waiting for her right where she expected. As soon as she stepped into the shadows of the trees, his hand reached out and snagged her arm, pulling her into him.

"You're late," he growled as his other hand cupped her head, tilting her head back. Before she could answer, his mouth was on hers, swallowing her gasp of surprise as his tongue plunged past her lips, all the wildness she'd ever sensed in him pouring over her in a shocking bath of fire.

Wrapping her arms around his neck, digging her nails into his nape, she let his passion sweep her up. Pulling him to her, opening her mouth wider, she begged for more as he made a rumbling noise in his chest. A growl? Had he really growled? She shivered with the possibility as he lifted her and walked her back until her shoulder blades came up against a tree. His chest came down against hers, holding her prisoner as his mouth continued to ravish hers.

She'd never been wanted like this. Never had a man come at her like he'd starve if he didn't have all she had to give as fast as he could get it. It was surprisingly erotic. His thigh pushed between her legs as her knee came up and met the barrier of the fabric of her skirt. She strained forward. He was so close, so close…

That low rumble surrounded her again. His big hands left her back and reached down. His lips bit at hers. "You're wearing too many clothes."

"Any less and I'd be naked," she moaned as he worked his

knee higher so it just grazed her center. Three yanks on the yards of fabric and he had her right leg free. She wrapped it around his calf, which was as high as she could reach. Another rumble, this one bit off in the middle by frustration. "What the hell's wrong with naked?"

There was no way that he could do anything with her skirts like this, but she could feel how hungry he was, how fevered with need. Because of her. Power and wonder joined desire. "Someone would see."

"Who cares?"

"Thee would." She didn't know how she knew that, but she did.

Fabric ripped and his hands closed over her thigh. Heat seared through her skin. "Yes, I would." He squeezed. "Only I get to see you like this."

"Thee can't see anything."

This time the rumble was anticipation. "Yet."

Yet. Such a powerful word. She shuddered. Bark rasped against her back as he shifted his grip. As if she weighed nothing, he lifted her higher, snuggled her tighter. The muscles of his thighs flexed against hers. He was so different from her. Pure muscle and temptation.

He bent his head. There was no evading his mouth. No wanting to. She loved the way he kissed. The way he tasted. She wanted to taste him more intimately. To feel all that muscle flex at her command. She pressed against his shoulder in a silent request.

He shook his head, his hair tickling the sides of her neck. His hat brim shadowed her face as his denial grated into her mouth. "No."

"Yes." She pressed harder. "Let me go."

For a second she didn't think Tucker heard, but then his chest heaved against hers and he stepped back, his hands settling on the tree beside her head. Still keeping her within the circle of his arms. His mouth was set in a straight line. Beneath the brim of his hat, his eyes slitted. A shiver of awareness swept over her skin. This wasn't the man she knew. This was the man outlaws feared and women desired. He looked like he'd kill to have her back in his arms. Oh, she liked that.

His mouth twisted. "I'm sorry."

Licking her lips, she caught the lingering salt of his kiss. "For what?"

His hands drew up into fists, scraping across the rough bark. "I usually save the rough stuff for a little later in the game."

It took her a minute to understand his meaning. He thought she was afraid? The harsh line of his jaw drew her touch. His skin was smooth without the constant roughness of impending beard that her husband had had. Did Indians not have facial hair? "I like that thee want me like this."

His teeth closed over the tip of her finger. "Good, because I feel like I'm about to go off like a firecracker."

She slid down the tree, the bark pulling at her hair, smiling when his hand automatically came between her head and the tree, protecting her even as his breath came in a hard sigh. "Then maybe we should do something to ease the worst of thy hunger."

She held her breath as she reached for the button fly of his pants. Jonah hadn't liked her to take charge. Tucker merely took a step back, giving her a bit more room. "Sally Mae…"

There was enough light to see the bulge of his erection pressing hard against his pants. She leaned forward. His fingers twined beneath her braids. To pull her away or hold her close? "What?"

"You're living dangerously."

Her smile deepened as she brushed her lips across the broad tip where it rested above his hipbone. His breath hissed in as she opened her mouth and encompassed as much of the broad head as she could through the thick cotton of his pants. "Thee have been telling me that for months."

"You might want to listen."

"Not tonight."

This time when she pushed, he took that step she needed, his eyes shining like silver fire in the new moonlight as she knelt in front of him and unbuttoned his pants. His skin was hot and damp, enabling the slide of her hand down beneath the material. She held his gaze, not bothering to hide how he made her feel. Tonight was about pleasure. "I like knowing I can affect thee like this."

His laugh rumbled softly around them. "Good, because there isn't a chance in he—hades after this that I'll be able to pretend that you don't."

She liked that he modified his language for her. She liked even more that, when she slid his underwear down, his cock fell into her hands. Big, surprisingly thick. She curled her fingers under the head, sliding her hand down, her grip widening as his cock thickened until she got to the base. Hair tickled her fingers. He didn't move as she cupped his balls, rolling his testicles gently between her fingers as she slid her hand back up. Once again as she worked her hand down, her fingers were forced open. She paused, studying his cock—the dark color of the flared head, the sheer size, taking in the enormity of what she was doing.

She was going to sleep with a man other than her husband, going to take him into her body. And once she did, there'd be no going back. She'd no longer just be Jonah's widow, her future defined by her past. She'd be Sally Mae Schermerhorn. A woman whose future stretched…endlessly…in front of her. She closed her eyes. She felt as though she were perched on the edge of a cliff. One way was disaster. One way was safety. She just didn't know which way to go. Forward or back. Life or death.

Dear God, I need a sign.

Tucker's cock flexed in her palm, drawing her attention. His fingertip under her chin pulled her gaze to his. Looking into his eyes was like looking into the vastness of the night sky. It was scary and exciting all at once. "You've got nothing to be afraid of with me, moonbeam."

It was the moonbeam that got her. That silly, fanciful name he called her should have offended, but it didn't. Because it very much fit how she wanted to see herself. She wanted to be silly and fanciful. To be the woman who truly felt as if she could take on anything, especially Tucker's passion.

"Thank thee."

Watching his face as she was, she couldn't miss the smile that twitched his lip at her politeness. She couldn't blame him for the humor, but laughter wasn't going to give her what she needed. She needed passion. A lot of passion. Passion so bright it burned her from the inside out. With a swipe of her thumb across the sensitive head of his cock, she banished the humor. His eyes narrowed and his nostrils flared. His mouth settled into the familiar straight line that gave him that dangerous look. Her pussy flexed and her breath caught. Yes, that was how she wanted him to look. Dangerous and ready.

She opened her mouth, letting him watch as she angled the tip downward, not immediately taking him into her mouth, teasing him with the heat of her breath, the sweet agony of anticipation. Pressure on the back of her head pulled her forward. She resisted, just another second, for no other reason than she could, but there was no fighting Tucker. He was a force as elemental as the night, as unstoppable as the wind. As soon as her lips slid over the crown, a drop of hot liquid coated her tongue. Salty. Earthy. Good.

Tucker groaned and his grip on her skull tightened convulsively. "Shit."

If her mouth hadn't been full of him, Sally would have smiled. She intended for him to lose a lot more control before morning came. Tonight he was her dream come true and she wasn't missing a minute of it.

Bobbing her head up and down the length of his cock, she adjusted to his width by stretching her mouth as far as she could until he hit the back of her throat. It was her turn to moan. No matter how hard she worked, she could only take half of him. It wasn't enough. She wanted all he had to give, wanted to give him everything, more than any other woman ever had. As she caressed his cock, she realized that she wanted to be memorable. To him. Dear heaven, she was breaking her own rules.

His big hand cupped her cheek, his fingers caressing behind her ear as she struggled with the urge to gag.

When she met his gaze, he shook his head. The swaying ends of his hair created slender shadows around them.

"Don't force it. Just let it happen."

Everything in her rejected the suggestion. It couldn't just happen. It had to be right. The way she'd planned. She took him faster, her hands working his balls and the base of his shaft. He didn't protest, but this time his fingers pressed at the nape of her neck, tilting her head back as she withdrew until she held only the heavy tip balanced on her tongue.

"I'm not going to last too long like this."

She drew back. Proof welled between them. A shimmering drop of desire bathed in white light. Pure and tempting. Another sign?

"Are thee only good for one time?" That would require an altering of her plans.

Tucker laughed and shook his head, his hair sliding across his shoulders in a pagan enticement. She'd love to feel that hair brushing over her skin. Her nipples tightened and a shiver went through her as her imagination provided an image to feed her passion. His eyes narrowed.

"I'll be at you so much, you'll be lucky if you can walk come morning."

That sounded good to her. If he was "at her" she couldn't think. Couldn't mourn. Couldn't long. "Prove it."

His expression shifted, lost its neutrality. In its place was lust, passion and a wild emotion she couldn't place. His beautiful lips barely moved as he said, "That was a mistake."

She didn't get a chance to ask why. And in the next breath, she didn't need to. His cock pressed into her mouth, spearing strong and deep as he pinned her with his knees to her shoulders, holding her to the tree a willing prisoner to his desire. Holding her for the thrust of his cock, the pulse of his pleasure.

The passion in his eyes burned over her, finding an answering level in her, jerking it to the fore, causing her to gasp. Lovemaking with her husband had been proper and satisfying, but it hadn't had this wildness. And she wanted it, every primitive wild pulse.

When Tucker tried to pull back, she leaned her head forward, doing a little imprisoning of her own, sucking and licking along the throbbing shaft, urging him on with her tongue and teeth, studying his reaction. Glorying in it. Glorying in him. His hand cupped her head in a subtle command to stay put.

"Unbutton your dress."

She'd never known an order could be so arousing. Clenching her thighs together, watching him watch her, she did. Without being told, she untied her camisole, too, separating both layers until the taut fabric cupped her breasts, pushing them in and up. For a moment, she couldn't breathe, insecurity gnawing at her confidence, stilling her movements. She wanted to please him.

Tucker swore, his eyes glued to the sight, and then with a jerk, he tore his cock from her mouth.

"No." She grabbed for him, finding only the hard muscle of his thighs.

"Hold still."

Angling his cock downward, he pumped it once, twice and then hot come splashed over her breasts, covering her nipples in an erotic bonding.

It wasn't what she wanted. She wanted him in her mouth, a part of her. When he jerked and his cock came within reach, she tucked her tongue under the broad head, held his gaze as she wiggled it lightly, and let him see the final splash of his seed coat her tongue before slowly swallowing. Tucker swore and moaned. His still-hard cock forged into her mouth, filling her the way she wished it filled the place between her legs. She held him as he relaxed, cuddling her tongue to the softer shape, breathing through her nose as desire and satisfaction poured through her.

She thought it was over, but with a simple motion of his

hand behind her head, Tucker took her with him. "I didn't know you wanted my seed."

She blinked at the apology. She wasn't used to such plain speaking. His fingers cherished the curve of her cheekbone, followed the line of her jaw, tucking into the corner of her mouth with the same tenderness with which she cradled his cock. He held her to him as if he couldn't bear to part. He reached down and cupped her breast in his big palm. The heat of his hand joined the lingering warmth of his seed, sending a shiver down her spine. His lips softened into a smile. "Did you like that?"

She nodded. She had and she wanted more. She wanted the whole experience of Tucker, no matter how shocking, how wild.

"Good."

Those pagan eyes of his captured every nuance of her expression as he took a step backward, forcing her to creep along with him, and leaned back and sat down. She caught her weight on her hands as he spread his thighs, making a place for her. He clearly did not want her mouth separated from his cock. She didn't have to wait more than a second to wonder why.

"Get me hard again."

3

It was the first time a woman had ever made him weak in the knees. Not to mention weak in the head. Threading his fingers through Sally's hair, Tucker struggled for control as her mouth worked his cock. Tonight was his one chance to know the splendor of Sally and he'd already wasted enough time being a selfish bastard.

A simple flex of his muscles brought her up over his chest. Her face turned into his shoulder. He felt the graze of her teeth through his shirt. Lust went through him like a bolt of lightning, searing the ragged edges of his control. "I guarantee you, if you bite you'll end up right back where you were."

She looked up at him, her eyes liquid pools of silver in the moonlight. "And thee don't want that?"

He pressed his lips against her forehead, as he fought to hold on to control. "Moonbeam, I'll take you any way I can get you, but I want tonight."

"If that makes me happy, what's wrong with that?"

"It doesn't make me happy."

He felt a smile push against his chest. "Thee realize, of course, that I'm going to disagree."

He stood, taking her with him. Her little gasp as he lifted her left him feeling more manly than he had a right to. After all, he'd just come on her breasts and not given her any pleasure at all. He'd earned a whipping, not bragging rights. Her breasts... A glance down showed them to be small and white, pert and gleaming with his seed. He couldn't resist. He cupped her right breast in his hand, the hard nipple prodding the callus on his thumb as he slicked his seed across the tip, branding her as his. Her forehead grazed his cheek as she watched.

He let his thumb linger. She moaned. A fresh flood of desire whipped through him. "That's a pretty sight, isn't it?"

She looked up, her eyes soft and luminous. "Yes."

He couldn't help himself. He needed another kiss. Her lips parted expectantly. Damn, she was one sexy woman. He breathed into her mouth, "I think we should do it again."

"Yes."

"But this time you come for me."

Her eyes darkened, and a shiver took her from head to toe.

"I see you like that idea."

"Did thee think I wouldn't?"

He laughed, tucked his cock into his pants and fastened the top button, keeping his mouth glued to hers, letting the uniqueness of the passion carry him through the mundane. When her knees sagged, he slipped his arm behind them and scooped her up. Her hands came around his neck and she shivered, making him glad for the years of hard labor that had built the muscles in his body.

"I like this, too," she whispered.

"Good. Give me five minutes and I'll give you something more to like."

"Thee have it, but no more."

The subtle attempt at taking control made him smile as he wove between the trees. He wondered what kind of man her husband had been. Not the doctor, who'd treated all with the same level of competence, but the man who'd lain beside her at night. From the way her fingers were working on the buttons of his shirt, he clearly hadn't left her with a distaste for relations. The tiny brushes of her nails as she undid the first few buttons before slipping her hands beneath burned like hot sparks.

They broke into a small clearing twenty feet from the pond. The bed of quilts tucked into the middle of the area caught the pale gleam of the moonlight. Sally turned her head as they stopped. He felt her gasp in the expansion of her ribs against his chest.

"When did thee find time to do this?"

He released her legs slowly, savoring the feel of her thighs sliding down the outside of his, imagining the same sweet glide without material between them. He stopped the descent when her pussy aligned precisely with his still-hard cock. "Give a man the right incentive, and he can do anything."

Her hands pressed against his chest as he lowered her to her feet. "I'll keep that in mind."

He caught them in his, bringing them up to his mouth, centering a kiss first in her right palm and then the left. "I was serious about this being your turn."

"And this means I can't unbutton thy shirt?"

"I'd much rather see you naked."

She tugged to free her hands. "I'm nowhere near as interesting as thee."

"I'm not wanting to argue on our first night together, but…"
Her head tilted to the side. "But thee will if I force thee?"
"Yes."
"Then I will be quiet."

Her eyes said she intended to be anything but quiet. He smiled. The woman had a fair amount of sass in her. He liked that. Reaching for the pins in her hair, he said, "Not entirely, I hope. There are some things I'd be interested in hearing."

The first pin fell to the ground. "I'd be open to hearing words like 'harder.'" He found the next hairpin holding the end of her coronet in place and pulled it free. "Softer." Five more pins were removed in rapid succession. "Deeper." The braids unrolled, extending past her rear. She cuddled into his chest.

"How about 'faster'?"

He shook his head as he untied the end of the braid. "I intend to enjoy every moment of tonight."

He fluffed her hair out, holding a long, silken strand to the side so that it caught the moonlight. "You have beautiful hair."

She looked at him from beneath her lashes. "If thee let me finish taking off thy shirt, I'll let thee feel it against thy chest." Her nail wiggled between the buttons over his stomach. "And maybe lower, too."

As he turned her, he said, "You're a bold little thing."

"Is that an objection?" she asked over her shoulder.

He went to work on the rest of the buttons on her dress. The buttons were tiny and hard to manage. The frustration just put a finer edge on his hunger.

"Not a bit."

He got six more free, exposing the hollow of her spine. He paused, taking in the view from the delicate point between her shoulder blades to the sultry hollow just above the fine turn of her ass. She was a very finely built woman. Too fine for him, but he'd survived his whole life stealing bits of other people's lives, pretending they were his. It wouldn't hurt to do it one more time. Trailing his finger down the slight bumps of Sally's spine, he enjoyed the smoothness of her skin a minute before he tested that fine-grained perfection with his lips. As she did every time he tried something new, she shivered, paused and then relaxed into his lead.

"I like you just the way you are."

In truth, Sally Mae knew she wasn't giving him much to object to. She was being a different woman for him, letting out the wildness he called forward because, with him, there was no right and wrong. It was simply right that his arms came around her waist. Right that she take his kiss against the side of her neck, right that she feel engulfed, treasured, protected. Right that he hold her. Something that had never felt right before with any other man.

"Thee are a very dangerous man, Tucker McCade."

The touch of his tongue made her jump, right along with the lightning that ripped along her nerves.

"And you're a very tempting woman."

"I think…only for thee."

"Are you going to tell me your husband didn't appreciate you?"

No, she wasn't going to tell him that, because it wouldn't be true. Jonah had been an attentive husband. He'd done his duty by her. But it *had* been a duty, in some respects. There had been warmth. There had been commitment. There had been a deepening of respect for each other, but there'd never been this primitive lust that burned from the inside out, this primal desire to belong only to him. Mostly, there hadn't been the…potential that existed with Tucker. "He was a good husband."

"Well, then, I'll try to be as good a lover as he was."

He pressed another kiss just above the curve of her shoulder, bringing the nerve endings to life, raising a string of goose bumps before nestling his wonderful mouth fully into the curve. She tilted her head, granting him access. His big palm opened over her stomach, his fingers spreading wide, his thumb touching hers.

She turned in his arms, slipping her hands around his sturdy back, pressing her fingers against the hard muscles. He was so warm. His tongue stroked her lips, which tingled and swelled to the touch. Her breasts quickly followed suit. What was it about this man that was like a match to tinder to her senses?

"Now I have a question of my own."

"Yes?"

"I can't help but wonder what brought you to my way of thinking."

Ah, he wanted an answer.

"There's something between us, Tucker, and it occurred to me tonight that I don't want to die without knowing what it is."

He tipped her face up. "I'm not going anywhere."

But he would…someday. Either by God's hand or by the violence that he courted with the challenge he offered in the way he carried himself. He would leave. And she would have to accept it. But not tonight. "Good."

His beautiful eyes crinkled at the corners. "Come here."

She went eagerly, expecting a flood of passion. What she got was something else entirely. Something unexpected. Something that melted her from the inside out and broke

55

loose parts of her that she'd never known existed. Parts that rose to the answer to her question. Tucker didn't take a woman, he savored her. One taste at a time. One tempting sip followed by another. Tiny sips that led a woman past her inhibitions to the total appreciation that lay beyond.

It was completely sexy, completely consuming to be wanted so much. She shivered as Tucker's big hand slid down her back, the tips of his fingers riding her spine until they reached the hollow. Pressure urged her between his spread thighs. She shuffled forward on her knees, unmindful of the hardness of the ground, resenting the impediment of her skirt when it drew her up short.

"Blast!" She caught herself on Tucker's broad shoulders. His chuckle followed her curse.

"You're still overdressed."

His fingers were entirely too deft on the waistband of her skirt, unfastening the buttons with speed.

"I'm not that overdressed."

The waistband gave way and his fingers met the cotton of her pantaloons. "That would be a matter of opinion."

His mouth crooked in that small smile that always sent her heart to pitter-pattering. Tonight was no different. Lit by the moon, hidden by shadow, his expression was visible only in bits and pieces, but what she saw sent shivers down her spine. The white flash of his smile, the shine of his eyes.

Oh, I could love him.

The thought had just popped into her mind. Forbidden. Scary. Intriguing.

"Tucker…" Her whisper, full of longing, filled the space between them.

"Right here, Sally Mae."

Another shiver snaked down her spine. He never called her by her name. That he did so now made it just that much more intimate. Wrapping her arms around his neck she let him draw her against the hard muscles of his big body. Her skirt rustled as it slid down her thighs. She didn't care. She'd waited her whole life for this moment, this man, to take her in his arms. She could feel magic waiting just beyond the next second. It was a sin, but it couldn't be wrong. Nothing between them could be wrong. The knowledge slid into her soul in a swell of enlightenment. Her confidence grew right alongside. Whatever this was, it was meant to be. And it was right. She lifted her mouth, stealing Tucker's smile for herself.

His satisfaction rumbled in his chest.

"Hungry?"

The gruff question set her to shivering again.

"Very."

Another of those sexy growls before Tucker slanted his mouth over hers. The passion in the move rippled across her desire, sparking it higher.

"Yes…"

She wasn't aware that she'd even spoken the word aloud until he reflected it back in his deep baritone.

"Yes."

Yes, this was what she'd needed. The thrust of his tongue, the power of his embrace, the shudder of his big body against hers as she straddled his thighs and settled gently over his groin.

"Goddamn it, Sally."

She shook her head as anticipation blended with pleasure.

She fitted her groin to his, rocking on the hard ridge of his cock, breathing deeply of the humid night air. She spread her fingers across his magnificent chest, touching the tips of her pinkies to the tips of his flat nipples.

Never would she delude herself that this between them wasn't magic.

His hands slid under her thighs, the backs brushing her pussy and he went to work on the buttons of his pants. "Lift up."

Lifting up was the best thing she ever did. Lifting up allowed Tucker the opportunity to free his penis. Lifting up allowed the slick slide of her pussy over his thick cock. His very thick cock.

Instinct had her pulling back from the potent threat. "Oh my."

His big hands settled on her hips, guiding her back into the motion. His cock pressed eagerly. Her breath caught in her lungs. Tension coiled in her stomach, spreading outward. There was the slightest shift in his grip, and then he pressed up. Delicious shivers radiated up from her pussy in hot pulses. Her fingers curled. Something like a growl rumbled in his chest. Her body, still primed from their previous encounter, ignited in a storm of passion.

"Tucker!"

He lifted her, but this time when she came back down, he was waiting for her. His cock wedged into the well of her pussy and her breath exploded from her in a gasp.

"Relax, Sally."

Yes, she needed to relax, otherwise she'd never be able to take him. Biting her lip, she tried again.

"Shh, baby." His hand touched her cheek. "I know it's been a while. We'll take it slow and easy."

It had been more than a while. Jonah had never been this big, stretched her to this point, challenged her so.

"Tucker," she whispered as she took that first little bit.

"Damn, I knew you'd feel like this."

"Like what?"

His eyes narrowed. "Like a fist coated in liquid fire."

She blinked and bit her lips. He wasn't the only one who was burning. "Perfect."

"Perfect," he agreed, thrusting up in tiny pulses, testing, stretching until her tight pussy spread over the head of his cock. Only one pulse of his hips kept her from the shining knowledge of what it would be like to be his. "It's perfect."

He was perfect and she needed him to… "Hurry."

"Some things aren't meant to be hurried, moonbeam, and this is one."

This was the continuation of the tiny pulses of his hips that teased and retreated, promised and denied. She dug her nails into his chest. "Tucker!"

Another not–quite-there nudge. His thumb swept down, slipped between the wet folds of her pussy and found the hard nub of her clitoris. She almost jumped out of her skin. Fire whipped through her womb, spread outward in a sweep of bliss. His cock slid easier, the erotic burn increased. She wanted more. Needed more.

"Please."

His gaze held hers. The silver was darkened by the same desire that was coursing through her. She tangled her fingers in his hair, holding on. "Thinking you can give orders now that you're on top?"

Was she? The answer came to her as he gave her that ghost of possession. "Yes."

He laughed, a deep rumbling sound that was a velvet caress down her spine. Oh, how she loved to hear him laugh. In one smooth move, he rolled them over, his big hands cushioning her from the ground while his hair fell about her face, shielding them in an intimate cocoon. His cock settled between her thighs with the same easy glide that his smile settled across his lips.

With his broad shoulders filling her vision and his big body dominating hers, she took a deep breath, shivering as the bullet he wore around his neck settled between her breasts. It was warm from his skin. Not for the first time she wondered where he'd gotten it, how it'd come to have so much importance to him.

Propping himself on his elbows, he kissed her hard, hot and…sweet? Oh heavens, so sweet. She wrapped her arms around his neck and pulled him closer. The heat from his skin sank into hers, sealing them together. His fingers trailed up her side then along the length of her arm until he'd captured her wrist. She was still shivering when he repeated the procedure on the other side. His eyes crinkled at the corners as he brought both her hands up beside her head, effectively pinning her. A shiver took her from head to toe.

Everything within her melted, but she held onto her fight. The hot cry of pleasure broke past her control.

His lips brushed her cheek, her jaw. "Ah, moonbeam, that was a very sweet sound."

Not nearly as sweet as the buss of his lips against hers. There was so much emotion contained there. So much held back, so much she wanted to unleash. She forced her eyes open. His face was so close she could make out the fine scar on his upper lip, the tightness of his jaw, the need in his eyes. Another shudder shook her. She was going to fulfill that need tonight.

"Love me, Tucker."

Had she really said that aloud?

"I will, Sally Mae. Better than you've ever been loved."

He was talking physical love. She didn't care. She lifted her hips up, begging.

Again that burst of laughter followed by the hot press of his body into hers. His lips nuzzled hers, parted hers, took possession of hers. And this time his cock didn't stop, just kept forging into her body with relentless pressure that grew right along with the burn of desire.

Mine.

The thought whispered into her mind, her soul. Oh God, this was so much more than physical. Pressing her hands against his chest she opened her mouth, straining for the words that would put an end to temptation. They wouldn't come, stolen by the thrust of his tongue, his cock. A silent scream of bliss tore through her as he slid deep.

Her "Tucker" blended with his "Damn, Sally."

Above her his dark face was tight with passion and a battle for control. The night was hot, but he was hotter, all dark muscle and exciting promise. Experimentally, she flexed her inner muscles around the thick intrusion of his cock. Splinters of delight rippled through her pussy, wending their way to her womb. Above her, he jerked and moaned.

His lips met hers in a biting caress. "Keep that up and we'll be done before we start."

"Mmm…" She did it again, holding his gaze, absorbing the passion that was hers, just for the asking. A miracle…

"I dare thee to resist," she whispered as his lips skimmed across her cheek.

His chuckle vibrated against her ear. Within her, his cock flexed, stretching her a delicious bit. Her body quivered. Her muscles contracted.

He whispered back in a low rumble, taking her earlobe

between his teeth and biting gently. "Maybe I should just bring you up to my level."

She suspected she was already there.

"Thee could try."

"Pushing me, moonbeam?"

Was she? The next bite to her ear was a little harder, adding an erotic sting to the hot pleasure whipping through her.

"Oh, yes."

Humid air seeped between them as he levered himself up onto his elbows. She resented its touch, her senses wanting only the feel of his skin on hers.

"Why?"

Strands of his hair tickled her breasts. A silken contrast to the hardness that was the man she'd chosen. "Because this is an opening and should not be missed."

"Can't say that I've ever heard it labeled that way." His cock caught intimately as he withdrew. She gasped. He paused, holding the tension until it stretched so finely between them, it—she—something had to break.

She dug her nails into his shoulders. "Please." Oh God, he had to take it—her. Had to put an end to this fire burning so brightly between them. Had to take them to the fiery satisfaction that she could sense waited just beyond her reach. Because if he didn't, it would be bad. So bad, she'd never stop regretting.

Wrapping her legs around his hips, she pulled herself farther onto his cock, moaning as he stretched her deliciously tight, moaning again as desire whispered a welcoming yes. She groaned with Tucker as that last inch slid home.

"Oh!"

He leaned down, sealing them together knee to chest, so

tightly that she could feel the echo of his heartbeat against her own. The trail of kisses he sprinkled down her neck fell like sparks across her skin, igniting a burning yearning for—

"More?"

"Yes." She needed more.

The tension in Tucker's arms vibrated down her side as he nipped at her neck. The quilt bunched beneath her hips as she twisted closer. She didn't care. All she cared about was the slow, tantalizing brush of his mouth over the slope of her breast, the moist touch of his tongue as he cradled her nipple on the rough surface. The gentle pressure as he caught it between his teeth. The searing pleasure as he bit down.

"Mine."

The claim vibrated against the hard nub, whipping the nerve endings into writhing need.

She made a last grasp at sanity as his cock slid along the ultrasensitive lining of her pussy, tempting the wildness inside her to come forward.

"For tonight," she gasped.

His response was to thrust deep, stealing her breath, repeating the gesture over and over as he took possession of her senses, her will, with every push of his body into hers, and when his hand slipped between them and found the swollen nub of her clitoris, he took possession of her soul. She shattered, falling into the explosion, embracing the joy, embracing him as he stiffened and swore. His cock flooded her pussy with the warmth of his seed.

She kissed his chest, tasting the salt of his sweat, the depth of his satisfaction. His arms came around her. One hand cupped her head as he rolled them over until she lay on top of him. He brought her mouth down to his, running his tongue along her lips until she parted them for him. His dark eyes caught the moonlight, shining up at her with an almost otherworldly beauty. The shadows weren't so kind to his face, casting a feral wildness to the harsh planes. Beautiful. Wild. That was her Tucker.

She kissed his lips, squeezing her pussy around his cock as aftershocks rippled through her. His response was immediate and absolute.

"This," he replied, "is as for as long as we want."

4

Tucker watched Sally Mae from the edge of the woods as she crossed the clearing, her steps a little shorter than normal, her stride not quite so flowing. He'd been hard on her, demanding more, even as she'd given him all, taking him again and again, rising to his touch with soft sighs and eager acceptance. He should have played the gentleman, leaving her alone after the first couple times. She'd been a long time without a man. But he couldn't. He'd been a wild man, cramming the type of loving he'd normally spread over a month into one night. Taking her in ways he knew damned well Jonah hadn't. Staking his claim in the most elemental ways he could, expecting her to turn him away, but she hadn't. She'd given him everything, taken him everywhere, and always with that soft exultant cry that drove him wild. He remembered the first, tight clasp of her pussy around his cock, the resistance as he pushed through the taut muscle of her ass, her gasp as she'd accepted him fully. Her surrender as her body climaxed around his, time after time, without any inhibition, following his lead, letting him take them where he wanted them to go. Over and over. His cock, which should have been worn-out, stirred.

Sally Mae reached the porch and stopped. Though he'd told her not to look back, she did. Not only that, but with lifted chin, she waved. Fool woman. Resignation, pride and the surge of possessiveness that was more than just a simple emotion welled again. Which was ridiculous because, sure as shit, a woman like Sally Mae wasn't for him. He didn't know why she had come to him tonight, but there was no way it would happen again. Hell, he had to pay three times the normal price for most whores to assuage their guilt at lying down with an Indian. It wouldn't be long before the same sense of shame claimed Sally Mae.

Sally entered the house. The door closed. There was no subsequent flare of light. Which was just as well because, if there had been, Tucker would have stood there longer, looking more like a lovesick fool than he already did, lusting after a woman he could never have.

"That's a fool's game, you know."

Tucker sighed and turned to face Tracker. His infatuation with Sally Mae was getting out of control if his senses were so dull that he didn't hear another approach. If it had been anyone but Tracker who had come up on him outside a white woman's house, Tucker'd be dead by now. White men were very rigid on the penalty for a red man lusting after one of their women. While he'd like to think it was doubtful that anyone *but* Tracker could sneak up on him—Tracker and his twin brother, Shadow, were practically ghosts—truth was, he wasn't sure. Sally Mae was the type of woman to play havoc with a man's concentration.

"I know."

The shadows seemed to shift and Tracker stepped into the pale glimmer of dawn. Dressed in his customary black, Tucker couldn't make out much more of Tracker than his tall, broad-shouldered silhouette and the gleam of light off his silver hatband. But he didn't need to see to know what Tracker looked like. He knew the man's face as well as he knew his own. When the Mexicans had ridden out that day so many years ago, only eight residents were still breathing. Eight boys. The weight of the bullet around Tucker's neck seemed to increase the way it always did when he thought back to those days. They'd banded together, to survive. Learned to become meaner and deadlier than anything that tried to take them down, to the point they'd earned the name of Hell's Eight. If they hadn't drawn the attention of the Texas Rangers no telling how they would have ended up. They'd been buck wild, taking their revenge with lethal efficiency, but they had been given the choice to become Rangers and they'd taken it, earning a touch of respectability and gaining a broader purpose. Hell, there were even some who'd probably say the Hell's Eight were downright civilized these days. He smiled. Comparatively.

"After a walk on the wild side, the widow's going to wander back to respectability, and then where are you going to be?"

Where he'd always been—on the outside looking in. "Looking up a new bed partner. What are you doing here?"

"Just passing through. I thought we'd check on you and Sam."

"We?"

"Shadow's here somewhere."

He bet. "Sam is over at Bella Montoya's place."

"So I heard."

He wasn't sure he liked the tone in Tracker's voice. While everyone considered Sam the wild card of Hell's Eight, Tucker had always felt that Tracker and Shadow were the unpredictable ones. "What else did you hear?"

"I heard he married up with a little spitfire."

Tucker smiled. "That's one way to describe Bella. Others would say she's passionate, funny and completely devoted to Sam." He wanted that point made. "And they're not married yet."

"She good enough for Sam?"

"What are you planning on doing if she's not?"

"Steer clear?"

"That would be wise. Sam's a bit touchy about his Bella."

Tracker grunted. "Fell hard, did he?"

"Like a rock slide."

Tracker shifted the bundle. "She make him smile for real?"

Tucker understood what prompted the question. They'd all watched helplessly as Sam's real smile had faded to fake over the years. And they'd all come to the conclusion that what it would take to bring it back would be the *right* woman.

"I don't remember him ever smiling more."

"Good. I'll have to wander over there and see if she's got what it takes to love a man like Sam."

Tucker remembered how Bella had thrown herself after Sam when he'd tumbled over that cliff, how she'd clung and refused to let go, pitting her tiny weight against the force of gravity to keep him here in this world, to the point that she'd almost gone over with him, as she waited for help to arrive. "She's got what it takes."

Tucker's left eyebrow went up. "You sound convinced."

"I am."

"Then there's going to be quite a wedding in a couple months."

"Yup. Bella's an heiress in her own right."

"That must have stuck in Sam's craw. He's an independent SOB."

"Might have, but along with her big ranch came a pack of trouble."

Tracker laughed, the vicious scar on his cheek glaring white in the predawn. "That would have cheered him up."

The only thing Sam loved more than Bella was a challenge. "It did lessen the sting."

"Did he really threaten to kill her mother?"

"Her and the entire crew at the Montoya ranch when Bella went missing." It was Tucker's turn to shrug. "They underestimated his devotion to Bella."

In the shadows, there was a glimmer of Tracker's smile. "People always underestimate Sam."

"Yeah, well, this time it was Sam who underestimated Bella's people. You're going to like them, Tracker. They're almost tough enough to be Hell's Eight."

"Heard that, too." Tracker shifted the bundle he held tucked against his side and took another step forward. The first rays of sunrise touched his face. The jagged scar down his cheek almost glowed red with the light. For a moment, Tucker was thrown back in time to the small town where he'd been born, heard again the battle cry of the invading Mexican army, relived the terror, felt the bullet slam into his chest as his knife slid into the stomach of his opponent. Saw Tracker standing over him, blood pouring down his face, a feral smile on his lips as he tossed aside the man who'd shot Tucker.

Tucker reached up and grazed the bullet hanging on a

rawhide string around his neck. His lucky charm. His impetus to never forget. The smell of blood lingered in his memory long past the fading of the mental image.

Tucker motioned to the bundle Tracker carried. "What's that?"

Tracker grinned. The scar crinkled. He was not a hand-some man, but he was a fierce-looking one, full of strength and power. And his smile definitely had the tendency to put the fear of God into people.

"Desi sent you a present."

The bundle wiggled. "It's not my birthday."

Suddenly, Tracker cursed and held the bundle away. It whimpered.

"What?"

"I think the damn thing peed on me."

It was a puppy. Tucker had a way with animals and was known for his ability to train them. "What'd you expect him to do when you were holding him like that?"

"Not use me as an outhouse."

Tucker could see a red-brown muzzle and long floppy ears. There was no mistaking the pup's heritage.

"Looks like Boone's a daddy." A wave of homesickness washed over him, thinking of the rawboned hound back at the Hell's Eight compound that everyone had written off as lazy and worthless, but had turned into the hero who'd saved Caine's wife's life. "Who'da thought he'd ever work up the energy to court the ladies?"

Boone had always been the laziest hound around. Turned out, he'd just been saving his energy for when it really mattered. Or at least that's the story Desi touted in the aftermath.

Tracker folded his arm across his chest. "Desi's kind of disgusted. The one saving grace for Desi is the only dog Boone wants is Daisy. Won't have any other dog and won't let anybody else near her."

Tucker could imagine the dog's joy and Desi's consternation. "Must be true love."

"Uh-huh. Well." Tracker put the pup on the ground. The similarity to Boone grew as he immediately lay down with a long, drawn-out moan. "Desi saved this one for you. She says he's Boone's best."

"Saved him?" Tucker bent and scooped the pup up. He was big boned, but still not large and he was all gangly puppy wiggles. His ears drooped to his knees and his nose wrinkled back to the bridge. Tucker held him at eye level. "Cute little thing." The pup licked his face. "Why'd she have to 'save him' for me?"

Tracker shook his head, sending his long hair swishing around his shoulders. "There isn't a body in the territory who doesn't want one of Boone's offspring. A dog that'll track with a knife wound to his chest with no direction other than his conviction that his mistress needs him, hell, that's the stuff legends are made of."

There was no doubt the hound had earned his forever place at Hell's Eight. "Just because Boone's that way doesn't mean his kin is."

Tracker shrugged. "You try telling folks that. They pretty much don't want to hear anything but that there's a puppy for them."

"How many were there?"

"Six, and the competition is stiff for every one. People keep raising their offers."

"As in money?" The pup snuggled in a disjointed flop against his shoulder.

"Yup. And Desi keeps turning them down flat, much to Caine's disgust."

"Why?"

"Seems Desi is real particular where she'll let the pups go. Calls them Boone's children."

"Damn." Tucker laughed. He would like to have been there to see Caine's reaction to that. Desi's Eastern ways often clashed with Caine's Western practicality.

"Caine used stronger words." Tracker grimaced and pulled his wet shirt away from his stomach. "He needs the money, and Lord knows the ranch could use it with the pressure those Easterners are putting on us, trying to force Desi out of safety."

"They haven't given up?" Tucker sighed. Desi and her twin sister, Ari, were heiresses, but someone didn't want them to come into their money and was doing his level best to make sure they didn't. It looked like their father's trusted solicitor was the culprit, but who the hell could be sure? This wasn't the kind of battle he was used to. He was used to a straightforward track, hunt and kill. You knew your enemy, and if only for the moment it took to get off a shot, you saw him. But this battle with the threat against Desi and Ari, this was a whole different animal. This took place behind the scenes with whispers and payoffs and well-hidden third parties calling the shots. And the fights were like shooting at ghosts that slipped in and out of the shadows, sniping at Desi and Caine's happiness, but never coming into the light so they could be exorcised.

"Desi is worth a hell of a lot of money."

Tucker grunted. "It'd be easier if Caine would take it."

"A lot of things could be easier, but blood money always comes with a curse."

"So you're siding with Caine on this one?"

"You're not?"

Tracker released his shirt. "It's Desi's money. Just because some cowardly son of a bitch hired Comancheros to kill her family to get it doesn't change that fact."

"It's cursed."

"It's *money*, and if put to use as Desi wants, it would put Hell's Eight in the black."

It was the same argument they'd been having since it became clear Desi was an heiress. "Some things aren't worth the price."

"Desi won't be in any more danger with the money than she is with someone trying to make sure she doesn't get it."

"Money changes things." Might even change Desi to the point she wanted to go home. And if Desi went, so would Caine. Even if he'd die a slow death in the East, he'd go because there would be no life for him without his Desi. Tucker couldn't imagine Hell's Eight without Caine. "And not always for the good."

Tracker sighed and looked into the distance, a disturbing sense of…inevitability in his expression. As if he knew something Tucker didn't. "Everything changes. Even Hell's Eight."

A chill went down Tucker's spine. Tracker had worn that same expression all those years ago when he'd looked at the sunny horizon and said, "Today is going to be a bad day." Eight hours later, the Mexican army had raided, slaughtering everything in their path. He'd thought his life hell before the raid. It was only afterward that Tucker realized he had no idea what hell really was. "Hell's Eight is forever."

Tucker wouldn't believe otherwise.

Tracker smiled. It didn't reach his eyes. "So it is." He motioned to the puppy. "Truth is, placing the puppies has been a good distraction for Desi. She's getting close to her time."

"The pregnancy's going well?"

Tracker's lips settled to a thin line. "She seems awfully swollen to me."

"Is that bad?"

He shot him an exasperated glance. "How the hell would I know?"

Sally Mae would. The thought popped into Tucker's mind. But Sally Mae was here, and Desi was at home at Hell's Eight, a place Sally would never be. Damn. "It will kill Caine to lose Desi."

None of them had had much softness in their lives, but when Desi had swept into Hell's Eight's circle, they'd all gained hope.

Tracker straightened. "He's not going to lose her."

Not if they had anything to do with it, but how much control did a man have over pregnancy? The sense that the world as he knew it was shifting increased.

"From your mouth to whomever's listening's ears." He wouldn't say God. Couldn't. He didn't have Sally's faith. When God had allowed the Mexican army to wipe out his town and everyone he knew except the Eight, when God had allowed them, as boys, to almost starve to death before they'd found Tia, he'd decided God wasn't for him.

The pup grunted and wiggled in his arms. Tucker put him down. With a little whine and a look, the pup squatted a couple feet away. As soon as he finished the rest of his business, he attacked a piece of grass and then came and sat on Tucker's booted foot with a little satisfied squeak.

Tucker slid the toe of his boot side to side, giving the pup an awkward pet. The pup moaned. "He's the spitting image of Boone."

"Which is why everyone wanted him, but Desi said he was for you."

Desi's way of saying thank-you for all she thought he'd done for her. She really didn't understand the bond of Hell's Eight. Between them, there wasn't a need for gratitude. Hell's Eight protected their own. And Desi had earned her place. He bent and petted the little guy's head, catching its ears on his fingertips. They were surprisingly heavy. "There's no need."

"Desi's been trying real hard to fit in."

Tucker looked up. "She doesn't have to fit in. She's already Hell's Eight."

Tracker tipped his black hat back. Everything about the man was dark, including his personality, but there was no one better to be on a man's side in a fight. "She seems to have a need for the formalities when it comes to friendships."

Because she was still afraid her new way of life would be taken away, as it had been before. As if Caine would ever let anyone near enough to disturb a hair on her head. As if Tucker would. He'd gotten real fond of Desi. She had grit, sweetness and a sense of humor. What had happened to her wasn't right and should have broken her, but she'd come out of it head high and courage waving. A man had to respect that. "Then I guess I'll thank her."

"Caine would appreciate that." There was a slight shift in Tracker's stance, a subtle honing of his attention. Tucker knew why. It wasn't like him to stay away from Hell's Eight so long.

"You going to be heading home soon?" Tracker asked.

"I'm waiting on a lead to pan out, but after that, yes." He missed the simple life and acceptance he got at Hell's Eight. And staying here was making him weak, as evidenced by tonight's stupidity. Tracker was right. Lusting after Sally Mae was a fool's game.

Tracker looked toward the house. "Folk get wind of what you're doing with the widow and there won't be much left of you to drag home."

"I'm not doing anything. It was a onetime thing. It's over now."

"That wave she tossed you didn't look like goodbye."

No, it hadn't, and that pricked his conscience.

Mine. Had he really said that to her?

"Sally Mae has some odd views on things."

It's an opening. What in hell had she meant by that?

"From all I've heard, she's a levelheaded woman."

Tucker tossed Tracker a grin. The last thing he needed was Tracker chewing on his love life. "How levelheaded can she be if she took up with me?"

The expected, joking agreement didn't come, but a look that asked who did he think he was fooling did. "The woman has a lot to lose."

No shit. "I won't let her get hurt."

"Good to know. Any ideas how you're going to prevent it?"

"Mind your own business, Tracker."

Ever since they were kids in their small town, Tracker had been treating him to that skeptical lift of the brow. It was as irritating now as it had been the first time he'd seen it twenty-four years ago when Tucker had boasted that he could make a stone skip five times across the pond.

"I could argue that you are my business."

Like hell. "And you'd lose."

Cocking his head, Tracker conceded the point. Tucker changed the subject.

"What else brings you here?"

"I'm supposed to meet up with Shadow."

Tracker and Shadow had volunteered to scout the farthest-out areas for word of Desi's sister. No one had protested. The two men, twins, were perfectly suited to the job. They could move through the most dangerous territories undetected. Part of it was due to their appearance, and the other had to do with their uncanny, deadly ability to work in tandem. Almost as if they knew each other's thoughts without speaking. "Any word on Ari?"

Tucker knew the answer before Tracker spoke. Ari and Desi had been stolen by Comancheros eighteen months ago. As unlikely as it was that Ari was still alive, Caine had promised Desi Hell's Eight would find her. And what one promised, they all honored. No matter if that promise had them chasing a will-o'-the-wisp of hope that Ari was still alive. There were some things a man didn't mind doing. And there wasn't a man at Hell's Eight who minded looking for Ari. Not only because of how they felt about Desi, but because not one of them could stomach the thought that Ari might be alive and trapped in the hell that the Comancheros delivered women into. Maybe it was because Ari was Desi's twin and it was like picturing Desi trapped. Or maybe they just needed to make a difference. The past year or two had been frustrating. Raising horses didn't provide the same day-to-day excitement of bounty hunting. And the reward wasn't as clear-cut.

"No. I keep hearing talk of how, about a year ago, someone dumped a white girl eight hours south of here." He shrugged. "But that could be Ari or someone else. Or complete fiction."

More likely fiction. Made up by someone wanting the reward for information that Hell's Eight had put out. Or there could be a more nefarious reason. "You think maybe it's a lure to a trap?"

Tracker shrugged. "It's unlikely a white woman in those parts wouldn't generate comment."

"Well, if it is an attempt to lure Desi out into the open, it's a fool waste of time." Tucker pulled his hat down against the first bright rays of the rising sun. "Desi isn't moving a foot off Hell's Eight until Caine feels it's safe."

And as careful as Caine was of Desi, that wasn't likely to be anytime soon.

"That's a fact." Tracker stared off into the distance, that peculiar stillness surrounding him.

"What?"

Tracker pulled his hat down with the small jerk that said he'd come to a decision. "I've just got a feeling, and until I check it out, I'm not bringing any news back to Desi. Good or bad."

The hairs on the back of Tucker's neck rose. "You think Ari might be alive?"

"I've just got a feeling is all."

Eerie as it was, Tucker had come to have faith in Tracker's feelings. "When are we going to check it out?"

"We?"

"Figured I'd come with you. It's rough country south of here."

Tracker cast another look at the house. His eyes narrowed. "You sure you want to be leaving now?"

It didn't take much to figure out where his thoughts had traveled. Tucker let his gaze follow Tracker's. The house stood as a small dark fortress bathed in the light of sunrise. Dark surrounded by bright. Despair surrounded by hope. And in the midst of it all, Sally slept, protected by her faith and that will of iron that believed miracles were created by man, not God. Son of a bitch. Tracker was crazy if he thought Tucker didn't understand the reality. The woman did not need a mixed-blood, beat-up bounty hunter messing with her life. It just wasn't as easy to walk away as it should be.

"I'm sure." Tucker slid his toe out from under the pup. "I could use the distraction."

5

S he needed a distraction.

Sally Mae rolled over in the bed three hours later and pulled the pillow on top of her face, as if the act could erase from her mind's eye the pagan beauty of Tucker as he'd loved her. As if it could keep her body from flushing with remembered pleasure, could keep her nipples from peaking, keep her from wanting to do it all over. She'd have to douche again. Just in case. Tucker was a very potent lover. And as much as she'd always wanted a child, she wouldn't want to make one face the stigma of illegitimacy. Between the vinegar sponge she'd used and the vinegar douche after, she should be safe. Jonah had been adamant it would work and she'd never conceived during her marriage. Which shouldn't have surprised her. Jonah had always been right.

A stab of resentment came out of nowhere. The ability to prevent pregnancy had been one area where she'd never wanted him to be so all knowing. And during the last years of her marriage, she'd spent the days of her flow in mourning for the child she'd begun to believe Jonah was never going to want. After six years of marriage, she'd felt the time was right, but her hints had been met with a patronizing caress of her hair, a shake of Jonah's head and an ever-increasingly annoying, "Not yet."

On the heels of resentment came guilt. Jonah had been a great man. Of all the woman he could have selected to wed, he'd chosen her. And he'd never hidden the fact that he wanted to make a difference in the bigger world, wanted to be free to practice more progressive techniques while bringing the benefits of modern medicine to people who needed it. He'd never made a secret that he wanted his wife to be a helpmate. And at first she hadn't minded. She'd been like a sponge soaking up all the knowledge he'd imparted, until she could diagnose illness and perform surgeries as well as he did. But over the years she'd found herself wanting more.

Not that learning what Jonah wanted her to learn had been easy. Jonah had been an exacting teacher, but a very good one and he'd never been short on praise. He'd been very proud of her accomplishments, which just made her disloyal thoughts that much uglier. Especially since in a time when most of her contemporaries longed fruitlessly for more op-portunities, she was being taught everything there was to know in a profession most women could never dream of pursuing. She pressed the pillow against her face. She should have been more grateful. It was her own sense of inadequacy that had left her sometimes feeling that, outside of medicine, she hadn't had a place in Jonah's life. And it wasn't that she didn't enjoy practicing medicine. It was just she'd sometimes longed for the comfort of more traditional roles. Especially that of wife and mother. She'd always wanted a family. Maybe to replace the one she'd lost as Jonah had suggested in one of his rare disapproving moments, or maybe just because she genuinely enjoyed caring for others and being needed.

A pounding came at the front door.

"Miz Sally, Miz Sally! Come quick." The pounding grew louder, more urgent. "Someone's been shot."

Sally pulled the pillow off her face and sighed.

"Hurry, Miz Sally."

The news that someone had been shot was all it should take to get her moving, but the violence in this town assured that someone was always getting shot, and the truth was, she was becoming immune to the panic that announcement used to inspire. Jonah would have called it maturity, but she knew differently. Jonah had been the most brilliant man she knew when it came to medicine, and looked on every case with an eager curiosity. But for her, the constant demands were more wearing and depressing and she was coming to resent the scale of the intrusion into her life. Not a pretty thing to realize about oneself.

She threw back the covers, pulled a dress over her nightgown and hurried to the door, buttoning it as she went. Old Jed stood there, his wrinkled face dotted with perspiration, his breath wheezing in his chest. Shadows of the man he'd been in his youth could still be seen in his face and his lean frame, but so could the battles he'd fought. While his blue eyes were keen with the knowledge of his lifetime, his hands and back were bent with arthritis. And his lungs were almost worn out.

"Thee shouldn't be running, Jed. It's not good for thy lungs."

He shot her an impatient look. "That bullet isn't helping Billy none, neither."

"Billy Hanson is the one shot?" Dear God, he was just a boy. "Are they bringing him over?"

"They don't dare move him."

She grabbed for Jonah's bag and pushed past Jed. She didn't need to ask him where the shooting occurred. It was always at the saloon. She hurried down the street, her heart pounding. Behind her she could hear Jed wheezing as he tried to keep up.

"He's out in front of the saloon," he called.

"Of course." Her skirt flapped against her legs. Her breath echoed harshly in her ears. Ahead she could see a crowd gathered around something in the street. Billy.

"No need to take that tone, Miz Sally. Nothing wrong with a man having a drink."

No indeed. Except that whenever men gathered with just such a purpose, bloodshed ensued. Pushing through the crowd, she pulled up short as she saw Billy. He lay in the dirty street clutching his stomach, his blue shirt—the one his mother had sewn for last month's social when he'd gone sweet on Jennifer Hayes—dark with blood. There was more blood on his lips and a steady trail trickled from his mouth down his neck.

For a second she closed her eyes as horror, fear and a niggle of hope roiled within her.

Dear Lord…

The medical satchel made a rattle as she set it on the ground. Why was it that the only way for a man to prove himself was to go out and kill something? Animal, human—sometimes she wondered if they truly saw a difference. Another glance at Billy's face showed just the bare traces of a beard. Children…

Jed limped up beside her, his breath rasping harshly in his chest. She placed her hand on his arm, steadying him, not liking the paleness of his complexion. "Can you help him, Miz Sally?" he wheezed.

The answer stuck in her throat. She just didn't know.

"We left him just as he was, Mrs. Sally," Peter, the town merchant offered. "Dr. Jonah was always real particular about not moving anyone bad hurt."

The last was said with a bite. Since the day the first resident had come to her door and asked her to take that monumental step into her husband's shoes, these subtle hints that any deviation from the pattern Jonah had lain down would not be tolerated had been constant. As was her annoyance. One complication to being taught all Jonah knew was that she'd developed her own opinions on how some things should be done.

"Thank you, Pete."

She knelt beside the boy, forcing a smile to her lips as his eyes focused. "Hi, Billy."

"I messed up," he whispered. It was an attempt at maturity that did nothing to offset the fear in his eyes. The instinctive knowledge of impending death. The victims always knew. So did she. And after one glance at the blood soaking Billy's clothes, she was afraid the answer to Jed's question was not going to be positive. Keeping her smile firmly in place, she unbuttoned his shirt. "Well, let's see if we can fix it, all right?"

The crowd closed in. "Scandalous," she heard a woman whisper.

It always amazed her that people could assume she experienced lecherous thoughts while attending the wounded. Especially when she wasn't a woman prone to lecherous thoughts. Scenes from the night before flashed through her mind, and she was forced to amend. Unless it came to Tucker McCade. And even if it were Tucker lying here like this, about all she would feel was a sense of horror.

Keeping her impatience in check, she ordered the men nearest, "Push the crowd back, please."

"All right folks. Give Mrs. Sally room to work."

There was a grumble and the shuffling of feet over dirt as she parted the lapel and revealed the small round hole in his torso bubbling blood.

The blood pumping from the wound was black. Not good. That meant the bullet had hit the liver. Billy would bleed out into his abdomen. That would spare him the agony of infection, but it wouldn't spare him death.

Billy grabbed her wrist with bloody fingers. "It's bad, isn't it, Mrs. Sally?"

She wanted to lie, but her God forbade her to lie. Even to save the feelings of a boy who'd tried all the wrong ways to become a man. She couldn't get words to push past her lips, so she just nodded.

From down the street, a woman screamed Billy's name. Only a mother's cry could contain that much anguish. It had to be Hazel.

A peculiar calm came over Billy's face. "I'm dying, aren't I?"

She could only nod again, tears lodging in a choking ball in her throat. Billy's eyes focused for a moment when his mother cried his name again. Sally Mae gave Billy what she hoped was an encouraging smile, and buttoned his shirt back up. He looked at her with understanding in his eyes at what that meant. He blinked back tears. She blinked back hers. He coughed. Blood sprayed and ran down his face. She wiped at the streams with her fingers, a stupid effort. Her touch would do nothing to stop this. A wet handkerchief came into her field of vision, along with a pair of knee-high moccasins. Only one man wore moccasins like that. Tucker. She glanced up and accepted the offer.

Tucker wasn't looking at her. He was looking at Billy and the expression on his face made her want to slap him for not stopping whatever had happened earlier. A foolish notion. Tucker lived by the same code as everyone out here. The one that said a man looking for trouble was probably going to find it. And likely, in his eyes, Billy going into that saloon last night meant he'd been looking for trouble.

As quickly as she could, Sally wiped Billy's face. There was no way she could get all the blood, but she could at least remove it from the places where it would leave the worst memory for Hazel. Nothing was going to lessen the impact of when Hazel saw her son. Nor her reaction when she realized Sally couldn't save him. It always went that way with the survivors. First the optimism of hope and then the anger of helplessness. Reaching deep inside, Sally Mae stretched for the strength that would sustain her through Hazel's grief and her own sense of failure. Her eyes went to Tucker even as her lips formed the prayer.

Please, Lord, give me…

Hazel pushed through the crowd, a plain, thin woman with graying hair, a tanned complexion and soft blue eyes. With an inarticulate cry, she dropped to her knees beside her son. Her work-worn hands pushed through his dark brown hair as she drew him to her bosom, cradling his cheek in her palm, her sobs wrenching her shoulders. Sally Mae sat back on her heels and immediately felt the support of Tucker's strong thighs. She expected him to step away, but he didn't, and she was glad. For too long, she'd been expected to be strong, independent and steadfast. But in this past year, she'd begun to realize that being self-sufficient, dependable and needing no one was not the ideal place she thought it would be. It was stressful and sometimes scary, but mostly it was very lonely. In a silent thank-you, she pressed back against Tucker's knees.

He took the blood-soaked handkerchief from her hand. She gave him a shaky smile, not caring if anyone thought anything of it. He was always there for her and though he insisted on being treated like one shunned, she wasn't doing it anymore. She wouldn't endanger his life by forcing an open friendship, but she wouldn't shun him. Friends didn't do that to friends.

"I thank thee."

With a nod that sent his hair falling about his face, he stepped aside.

"Do something for him."

Hazel's hoarse whisper hammered at her composure. Reluctantly taking her gaze from the calm of Tucker's, Sally Mae met Hazel's anguish with the simple truth that she just couldn't change. "I can't."

"You help criminals. You help bandits. You help dogs, but you won't help my son?"

In the folds of her skirt, she clenched her hand into a fist. "Thee know I would help him if I could."

Sally Mae was too slow to prevent Hazel from lifting Billy's shirt away from his wound. The shirt bunched in Hazel's hands and she held on as if the tightness of her grip could change reality. "There has to be something you can do."

"I can pray."

Hazel didn't move as the import of those three words sank in. Then she gave a nod so brittle it was inevitable that it shattered into a harsh sob.

"Thank you."

Sally knelt in the dirt beside Hazel and placed her hand over one of the other woman's as she reached inside for the serenity that evaded her in moments like this. God's will was God's will.

It was her duty to accept it serenely and to make choices in accordance with his wishes. But looking at a sixteen-year-old boy dying in his mother's arms? It was very hard to feel serene.

Around her, men took off their hats and women folded their hands. Death was so common here. A boy being shot down in the street elicited no more reaction than that. She seemed to be the only one who couldn't get used to it.

Dear Lord, grant me the serenity to accept this.

Looking at Billy propped in his mother's lap, pale and shaking, fresh rivulets of red already flowing over the paths she'd partially wiped away just moments before, she was struck anew by the impossibility of the task she had set for herself. No one should have to accept this. Sally put her hand on Hazel's shoulder, trying to absorb her grief into her palm as Billy coughed up fresh blood, then sucked air back into his lungs in a short, strangled gasp. The end was almost here.

Looking incredibly young and vulnerable, Billy shaped the words *I love you* to his mother.

The pain almost took Sally Mae down. Instinct sent her gaze to Tucker. He was watching her, his dark face impassive, his eyes cold. She'd never felt the differences between them so keenly. The corner of his mouth twitched, and though it was illogical, she knew he wasn't as remote as he would have her believe.

Tucker didn't lower his head and she didn't take her gaze from his as she recited the Lord's Prayer. As the prayer ended, a woman in the back began singing "Amazing Grace." For the purity of the tone, Sally Mae knew it was Alma Hitchell, Dwight Hitchell, the saloon owner's, wife. Sally Mae always wondered how Alma, a deeply religious woman, reconciled her beliefs with her husband's profession. As the notes of the hymn slowed around her, Sally Mae closed her eyes and added a private prayer to the public one.

Please grant us all the serenity to accept this.

"What happened?" Roger, the town's newly-appointed sheriff, came to a stop a few feet away, startling Sally Mae into opening her eyes. Inevitably, he started shifting his weight from foot to foot. Sally Mae knew if she looked up from where she knelt, he'd have his thumbs stuck in his vest pockets, looking down his nose at everyone. As if he had a right. The only reason he'd gotten to be sheriff was because the appointment had occurred over a drinking match. And the only reason the appointment had stood was because everyone thought he would have been shot dead long before now.

"Billy got himself shot," Dwight offered.

The wording grated on Sally Mae's nerves. Billy hadn't wanted to be shot. All he'd wanted to do was walk into that saloon and prove he was a man to the men he admired. And all he'd ended up proving was that he could bleed like the rest of them.

"Kids his age have no judgment," Peter interjected. The fingers of Sally Mae's free hand curled into a fist. The ones with no judgment were the men who'd accepted Billy's challenge when they should have sent him home. They probably even thought it made them big and tough to kill a young boy whose only flaw was wanting to grow up too fast. And looking between Hazel, rocking her dying son in her arms, and the crowd standing witness, she knew something else. Tonight, tomorrow, maybe the next day, there'd be another knock at her door and another call for her to help another person who'd been shot. The cycle would continue round and round, death begetting death, death begetting hate. In the end, only the undertaker would profit, but no one seemed to see how pointless it all was. How much better they would do if they worked together.

Pushing to her feet, Sally Mae brushed at the blood smearing the dark gray material of her dress. Some came off on her fingers, but the stain didn't diminish.

Please, Lord, give me…

The words stuttered to a halt in her mind. The murmur of voices rose to a cacophony in her mind, shattering her concentration. She blinked and looked around. No one seemed bothered by the noise other than her. The noise continued to rise until it became an accusing roar that only she could hear, a roar she couldn't block out. Brushing at her skirt again she took a step back. She couldn't pray here. She couldn't think here. She couldn't be here. Turning on her heel, she headed toward home, ignoring the few who called after her, blinking as tears burned over her stiff skin.

Someone stepped into her path. She shouldered past. The scent of leather, sage and man followed, telling her whose hand grazed hers, whose fingers managed a discreet squeeze. Tucker again. Tucker, who'd showed her such tenderness last night. Tucker, who, if he'd been in town instead of being with her, would have slipped into the violence that had taken Billy as naturally as he took his next breath. She didn't squeeze his fingers back, didn't hold on to his hand—just let it fall behind. She kept walking until she reached the door of her house. Behind her there was a scream of anguish. Her fingers tightened on the handle before she opened the door and slipped into the peace of her home.

The scent of lemon, wax and the faintest hint of carbolic surrounded her in a weak greeting. Lyle called to her from the sickroom. She ignored him as she climbed the stairs. In her bedroom, she knelt down, folded her hands and prayed. For Billy. For his family. For an end to the violence, but mostly she prayed to forget how her husband had looked as she'd last seen him. The hole between his eyes had looked too innocuous to have stolen the intelligence and life that had been there. And then she prayed again, because it was too easy to see Tucker's face superimposed over her husband's, to see him coming to the same violent end.

Please, Lord, give me the strength.

Tucker watched from beneath his hat brim as Sally Mae strode down the street. Those slight shoulders were squared, but he knew she was crying, knew she felt the boy's fate keenly. Hazel's wail announced Billy's last breath as Sally Mae opened the door to her house. The shadows of the porch emphasized the slump in her posture when she thought she was safe from prying eyes. He ached to follow her, to take the burden from her, to hold her. He was her lover. He should be there with her, comforting her, not standing on the fringes of the crowd listening to a lot of people grumbling about a lot of things they'd never work up the courage to do.

Someone brought a sheet and put it over the kid's face. Hazel sobbed and traced the silhouette of his profile through the worn material with hands that shook. *Her oldest boy,* he'd heard someone say.

"They just shot him down," he heard Old Jed tell the sheriff. "The kid came in this morning and bellied up to the bar. Everyone knew it was his first time. No one expected trouble. The loco next to him said something to him. The kid looked surprised and, faster than you could blink, the no-account just shot him."

"Did you see who he was?"

"I think he was one of Tejala's old gang, but I can't be sure."

"Bastard."

"Soon as he fired, he lit out of here."

"No point going after them then," the sheriff huffed.

"He killed my son," Hazel snapped. "It's your job to bring him to justice."

The sheriff straightened to his full height. "It's my job to keep the peace, not to get good men killed chasing shadows, which is all Tejala's men would be."

"Damn you for being a coward!"

"Here now! Watch what you say."

Hazel glanced at the sheriff. "I know exactly what I'm saying and who I'm saying it to."

So did Tucker, and he couldn't blame the woman. He also couldn't blame the sheriff. The man was a coward and his appointment a joke gone bad, but that being the case, a body couldn't do much. Especially against Tejala's gang, which was becoming a bit of a problem. With Tejala now dead, they'd all struck out on their own, but pickings were sparse for so many rival efforts and the fighting over leadership left everyone going no place fast. Dangerous men with no outlet and no money often found negative ways to amuse themselves to the point that Tucker would almost be glad if the gang did get another leader. Then, rather than putting out wildfires in different directions, the law could focus their peacekeeping in one spot.

"What are you going to do about this, Ranger?"

He'd wondered how long it would take for someone to remember he was a Texas Ranger. He pushed his hat back. "I think I'll get a description and maybe do a little hunting."

Hazel looked around, her face ravaged with grief, her voice dripping with sarcasm, and asked, "Are any of you brave men who stood by while my son got shot going with him?"

Tucker couldn't blame the men for hesitating. They had families to worry about. Retribution to fear.

"Your little boy bellied up to the bar like a man and a man takes his chances," one of the newer residents countered.

Maybe he did and maybe he didn't, Tucker thought, but picking on a kid was low in anybody's book.

"I'll go," Old Jed said.

Jed had been a force to reckon with in his day, but his joints were rheumy now and his health fragile. The one thing Tucker didn't need was the old man's death on his conscience.

"No offense, ma'am," he said to Hazel, touching his finger to the brim of his hat, "but I want to catch him before he reaches his friends. A man can sneak up on his quarry a lot easier when he's not dragging a posse along."

Hazel's expression tightened. "But you will catch up with him?"

He looked at Billy, still holding his mother's hand with his death grip, blood staining his cheeks. Hell, the kid hadn't even sprouted whiskers yet. Hunting for Ari was going to have to wait until this debt was settled. "I'll make it a point."

6

Two hours later, Sally Mae opened the back door at Tucker's first knock. Almost as though she'd been expecting him.

The look she gave him was knowing, disapproving. Disappointed. She didn't hesitate to state why.

"Thee are going after him."

It wasn't a question. Sally Mae might not hold his skin color against him, but his profession? That was a horse of a different color.

He didn't know whether he wanted to kiss her or shake her for the irrationality of it. She might think the meek would inherit the earth, but out here the meek got stomped. "If you mean Billy's killer, yeah. Any man who'd shoot a kid for the fun of it can't be left roaming free."

She folded her arms across her chest. "I thank thee for telling me."

Kiss her. He definitely wanted to kiss her until that stubborn conviction in her expression softened to desire. "You're welcome. However, before you go all soft with gratitude—" She huffed, interrupting him. "I didn't just come to tell you. I have a favor to ask."

She eyed him suspiciously. And why not? He'd never asked a favor before.

"What?"

"I need you to take care of something for me."

Before she could work up to a no, he whistled for Crockett, calling him from where he was exploring. The puppy came, all flopping skin and lolling tongue, a big grin on his face. Sally Mac looked at him uncomprehendingly. "A puppy?"

"Yeah."

Crockett came right up to her and jumped. Tucker caught him before he could put his muddy paws on her clean version of her ever-present gray skirt. The puppy wiggled as he held him back. "I haven't gotten a chance to teach him any manners yet."

She folded her arms across her chest. Never a good sign with Sally Mae. "What's his name?"

"Crockett, after Davy Crockett."

She eyed the puppy skeptically. "Thee think he will become a mighty fighter?"

"I don't know about that, but I do know he shows a strong streak of mischief."

Her lips twitched as Crockett moaned and plunked into a sit.

"He needs watching while I'm gone."

"And how long will that be?"

"A week, week and a half on the outside."

Her hands dropped to her side. "Usually thee are gone much longer."

"With a fresh trail I won't have to spend so much time."

Her mouth twisted as she knelt down and rubbed Crockett's ears. "What am I supposed to do with him if thee don't come back?"

"Send a message to Hell's Eight and somebody will come get him."

"Like they'll come to get thee?"

If he didn't come back for the puppy, there really wouldn't be any reason for anyone to come get him. He suspected she knew that from the tight set of her mouth. Sally Mae was a smart woman.

"You can count on Hell's Eight. They'll take care of him. Desi's right fond of the little fool, I'm told."

The stiffening was slight but there. "Desi?"

"Caine Allen's wife."

"I didn't know Hell's Eight were the marrying kind."

But Sally Mae was. And she was also jealous. Tucker settled his weight deeper in his boots, enjoying the knowledge. "We don't like to let the cat out of the bag on some things."

"Afraid the women will be too willing?"

"Them being willing isn't the issue." He said that just to tweak the intriguing flare of jealousy a bit. He watched her reaction from the corner of his eye. Her shoulders set in and her mouth flattened to a thin line. "It's when they start attaching their brand to my saddlebags that I have a problem."

"Thee are such a catch?"

He shook his head and squatted on the other side of the pup. Rubbing Crockett's ears, he hid his smile. He rather liked Sally Mae in a snit at the thought of him with other women. "No, but I'd appreciate your spreading that around anyway."

She frowned. "Do thy own dirty work, McCade."

The pup moaned and leaned into him. "Can't. I'm leaving."

She reached out and touched one of Crockett's overlong ears. Her fingers brushed his. She drew them back, albeit slowly. "Then thee can handle it when thee come back."

He looked up, catching the fear in her eyes that she was trying to hide. "I will come back, you know."

"I'm sure there will be many women glad to hear it."

"Including you?"

"Thee have been gone before. Usually for a month or so."

But that was before they had been lovers. He shook his head, accepting she wasn't going to soften up before he left this time. "You're a hard woman, Sally Mae Schermerhorn."

"I'm a sensible one, and wish to avoid the gossip thee seem to enjoy."

"You think I like being the center of attention?"

"I think thee have become so accustomed to the attention people give thee, that thee no longer notice it."

He cocked his eyebrow at her. "If I settled down with a good woman, that might diminish."

Not even by a bat of an eyelash did the hint give her pause. "A woman would not welcome the violent life thee live."

"Not all women have your peaceful bent."

"All woman want children, peace in which to raise them and a husband's guidance in their lives."

She had a way of making her point effectively. "Rather than a memory?"

She nodded, stood and straightened her skirt. "Loving a man who courts death and revenge is not a wise choice."

He stood also, staring at her lips, her eyes, wanting all of her, frustration at not being able to have anything but that brief time with her eating at him. "And you believe love is a choice?"

"I have no choice where I love." Her eyes deepened with sadness. "But I will choose with whom I make a family."

He remembered how prepared she'd been last night, leaving nothing to chance, using her sponge and vinegar. How she'd looked this morning, cradling Billy, completely without hope. "And you think you'll be happy with a namby-pamby man who doesn't know how to defend you and these kids you want?"

"Strength is not all physical."

"When someone's trying to rape you, a healthy amount of muscle beats the hell out of strong thought."

"God does not smile on violence."

Looking at her standing there, pale and wan, he felt like punching his fist through the wall.

"Well, neither do I, but sometimes there's no choice."

"There is always a choice."

The urge to punch the wall got stronger as he watched her, standing there with the courage of her convictions wrapped around her like a shield. As if they'd do her any good in a tight situation. "Sometimes you terrify me, Sally Mae."

"Because I hold my convictions dear?"

"Because of how vulnerable they leave you."

"I think the flaw in thy thinking is that thee think thee have control of God's will."

Frustration curled his fingers into a fist. "Well, maybe your God put me here to make sure you don't head his way too early."

She tucked her chin, that way she did when she was thinking on something, before touching his fist briefly. The frisson of energy that flared up his arm from the quick contact damn near had him shuddering like a green boy. "He is thy God, too."

"God abandoned whatever interest he had in me the day I was born."

"That's not so!"

Despite the danger of being seen, he cupped her chin in his hand, cradling the delicate point in the center of his palm. So small. So fragile. So easy for a man, even a third his size, to break. His grip tightened. "Believe what you have to."

"I don't have to believe anything. It is always my choice. And I choose to believe that my God would never desert the man thee are."

"I'm a killer, remember?"

"Thee have only lost thy way."

It took him a moment to understand what put that tightness in her voice. He gentled his grip. He'd seen Sally Mae bring a patient back from certain death on nothing more than belief and hope. And now, she'd apparently decided that he, Tucker McCade, should be saved. From the interior of the house, someone called Sally's name. Tucker frowned at her. "Lyle's not still here, is he?"

The pseudo-outlaw wasn't particularly violent, but he was none too long on scruples and Tucker wouldn't trust him as far as he could throw him. And considering Lyle's weight, even with his strength, that wouldn't be too far.

She had the grace to look uncomfortable as she confessed, "Yes, he had a setback."

Tucker just bet he had. A convenient one. Lyle was always on the prowl and his interest in Sally Mae was no secret. Lately, Tucker had noticed more of that impatience in the attitude of the townsmen toward Sally Mae. An implication that maybe the widow's mourning period should be coming to an end. Well, for those who thought it, they needed a rethink. Starting with Lyle.

Disregarding Crockett's muddy paws, Tucker picked him up and shoved him at Sally Mae. She took a step back before reaching out and taking the puppy. She took another as Tucker slipped past her into the house.

His moccasins made no sound on the polished wood floors. Lyle was in the bed, fussing with his hair. Primping for Sally Mae's arrival to his screeching, no doubt. The no-account son of a bitch.

Tucker grabbed him by the shoulder and hauled him up, ignoring the wrench on his muscles. Lyle came around swinging. Tucker blocked a punch with his hand. He held his gaze as the other man realized who he was dealing with and how much trouble he was in. Cursing, Lyle leaned back. Tucker bared his teeth in a smile and let him go to the end of his reach and then squeezed hard in warning.

"It's time for you to go."

"You overstep yourself, injun."

Tucker smiled. "Feel free to teach me my place."

"Sure as shit someone's going to. It ain't right you making yourself so at home on a good woman's property."

The son of a bitching weasel. "If I hear any of that filth spread about Mrs. Schermerhorn, I'll gut you and leave you for coyote bait."

Lyle sneered. "People are already talking. You'd better watch your back."

Shit. Lyle was too confident for that to be a lie.

He could hear Sally Mae coming down the hall. "Shut the fuck up."

"Afraid the widow will kick your ass out?"

He was more afraid she'd hear and decide to make a stand. Lyle opened his mouth. With a pop of his elbow, Tucker shut it for him.

Sally's gasp preceded her into the room. "Tucker, what are thee doing? I just got him healed."

"And you did a darn fine job," Tucker said, baring his teeth in a fair imitation of a smile. "Lyle here was just telling me it was time for him to leave, though, he's feeling so much better." Tucker gave Lyle's hand another warning squeeze. "Weren't you, Lyle?"

"He was running a fever this morning," Sally said, coming around. The only fever Lyle had been running was one of lust. Lust for *his* woman. Tucker blocked her approach with a shoulder. Sometimes being his size came in handy.

"He had a fast recovery. That last dose of medicine you gave him must've been a cure-all." He didn't really know if Sally Mae had given Lyle any medicine, but it was a fair guess that she had. She had all kinds of potions she believed in. Something she'd no doubt picked up from Jonah, who'd decried the practices of bleeding the sickness out of a body. Tucker had to agree it made more sense.

"You're feeling better, aren't you, Lyle?"

Lyle tossed a glance at Sally Mae. Tucker tightened his grip, bringing Lyle's eyes back to him. The scum had no right to even glance at a woman like Sally Mae with any kind of thoughts other than gratitude.

"That's right, Mrs. Sally, I'm feeling right better."

"That's Mrs. Schermerhorn to you," Tucker said, whacking him on the back of the head before handing him the shirt from the pile of clothes that were neatly folded on the chair by the bed.

Sally Mae pushed forward. "I need to check his bandages before he goes."

There was no blood staining the bandage that wrapped the other man's corpulent chest. "His bandage is fine."

"I need to check for infection," Sally Mae insisted. "Knife wounds can turn nasty."

Tucker handed Lyle his pants. "Lyle will come back if he sees a need. Won't you, Lyle?"

Lyle nodded. But they both knew that was a lie. Unless he was at death's door, Lyle wouldn't be coming back to visit Sally Mae. Not unless he wanted to face Tucker. And if he came back for any reason except death and maybe even then, Tucker would gut him. The man was a worm, playing on Sally Mae's sympathy in the hope of getting into her bed. He ought to just gut him now. He sighed and smiled inwardly. No doubt Sally Mae would consider that unnecessary.

Lyle was still fastening his pants when Tucker placed his hand between his shoulder blades and sent him stumbling to the door. "Get going."

"I don't want thee to do too much, Lyle," Sally Mae called, turning her face away from one of Crockett's kisses. "Thee don't want to tear that wound open again."

Lyle grabbed his hat on the way to the back door and all but tripped out. "I won't, Mrs. Schermerhorn."

As soon as the door closed behind his fat ass, Sally turned on Tucker.

"Thee can't just do that, Tucker. Thee can't come into my house and endanger the life of my patients."

Tucker looked at her. He'd made love to every inch of that willowy body, breathed her cries of pleasure, savored her sweetness. His hands clenched into fists. She should be his. "Seems to me I just did."

"That's what I'm telling thee. Thee will not do it again."

His teeth snapped together on the acrid bite of frustration. "I'll do whatever the hell I need to, to keep you safe."

"I slept with thee. I didn't marry thee."

"You gave yourself to me last night."

She held Crockett in front of her like a shield as she snapped, "We had sex."

The hell they had. Tucker grabbed the puppy out of her arms, placing him on the floor before moving in, using his greater size to trap her against the wall. Her hands came up against his chest. Their heat warmed the leather of his vest. This close, he couldn't miss the passion that flared in her gaze, right along with the worry. She should be worried. He was damn pissed.

"Tucker…"

With the press of his thumb, he lifted her chin. The back of his fingers just naturally stroked along the silky underside. Watching her as he was, there was no missing the shiver that went through her. Her tongue smoothed over her lips, leaving them moist. He lowered his mouth to hers, kissing her once, twice… The automatic parting of her lips placated some of the anger inside him. "You gave yourself to me last night, Sally Mae." Frustration, anger and pounding desire hoarsened his drawl to a growl. "Make no mistake about it. Even if nothing comes of it, I've still got rights, which I'm not letting go."

She nipped his lower lip, no doubt under the impression that the sting would make him release her. Fire snaked from his mouth to his groin. A shudder took him. In her he felt an answering response. He let her separate their mouths the slightest bit, taking her words as a caress against his cheek.

"What rights?"

"The kind that say I might not get to share your bed openly, and I might not get to marry you, but I sure as heck get to keep you safe."

She blinked. "Who's going to keep me safe from thee?"

He wanted nothing more than to lift her skirts up and sink his cock into her tight pussy, reestablishing once and for all what was between them, the depth of his claim, but there wasn't time.

"Not a damn soul." One last kiss, one last graze of his hand down her buttocks. The crease between drew him. He pressed his fingers into the tempting groove. She gasped. He brushed his lips over her cheek, gliding along the smooth surface until he reached her ear. He caught the lobe between his teeth, smiled internally at her shudder, bit... He caught her as her knees gave out, taking advantage of the moment to center his touch. She moaned. He didn't back off as she shivered.

"Are you sore?"

A nod and another airy squeak preceded the parting of her legs. She was making it easier for him. *Ah, damn.*

He slid his knee between hers, nudging her legs farther apart.

"Remembering?"

Another nod, and another squeak as he gently massaged the tender spot through the layers of material.

He knew damn well she'd been a virgin there, but she'd taken him. Not all, but most and the taking had stolen his control. Remembering the relentless need to thrust and claim once he'd gotten inside that sweet, dark channel, he felt a twinge of guilt. And another overwhelming surge of lust. His cock hardened.

"Do you regret it?"

This time there was a longer pause. And then a tiny shake of her head that had her cheek pressing into his lips. An accident, or a request? He didn't know and didn't care. That tiny acknowledgment was too potent a lure. He had to see for himself.

"Good. Because you're going to know me a lot like that. And next time, you'll take all of me."

Gathering her skirt, handful by handful, he finally reached the point where all it took was a toss and a tug and then it was draped over his forearm. There was nothing between his hand and the smoothness of her thigh.

Sally Mae gasped. Tucker groaned, his heartbeat pounding in his ears and his blood thundering through veins as memories of the night before poured over him in a wash of flame. The inherent acceptance as she'd taken him, one inch at a time, her heated cries punctuating the moment, his desire feeding off hers until both of them were nearly mindless. He remembered it all and he wanted it again, her mouth, her pussy, her ass. More than anything else, he wanted the pleasure of her acceptance. Damn, he wanted that sweet acceptance.

It was no effort to part her legs farther. All it took was the press of his knee against hers, followed just as quickly by a delicate bite to her lower lip. For such a peace-loving woman, she loved to flirt with danger, and the edge of his teeth on her lips was all it took for her thighs to relax and her lips to part. He took advantage of both, claiming her mouth and her pussy in a single motion. As the heel of his hand came in contact with the pad of her pussy, he found her damp and eager. The nub of her clitoris slid along the rough surface of his palm as he worked his fingers into the well of her vagina and then beyond. She tensed.

"Shh. Just hold still."

"I can't."

She could. Would. "Just a minute."

He touched the tight, swollen ring of her pussy with his thumb as his finger probed her ass. It was still slick.

"Shit." He dropped his forehead to hers. "You're still wet."

"With you."

The confession was seduction itself. Only him. The forbidden thought slipped past his control, settling on his want with the same precision that his finger centered on the tender opening and pressed.

Sally's nails sank into his shoulder as she came up on her toes. "Tucker…"

He could see the tight bead of her nipples against her dress, feel the convulsive flutter of muscles around his finger, see the hunger in her eyes.

"Open for me."

She tightened and froze, her eyes locked to his as the tight ring stretched, as her pussy opened.

"Oh!"

"Does it feel good, moonbeam?"

She nodded and dug her nails into his vest.

The tip of his finger snuggled into the slight well created by the pressure while his thumb slid deeper. "How good?"

He knew the answer, but he wanted to hear her say it as he penetrated her now, the proof of their passion from the night before easing this moment.

"I don't know."

He turned his head and kissed the corner of her mouth. "Yes, you do. I can feel the passion in you, the need… You want to press back, baby. You want my thumb in this sweet pussy, stretching you, reminding you of how good my cock felt. You want my finger in your ass, stretching you there, too. You came so hard on my cock didn't you, baby? You came so sweet and hot, milking me until I came for you, filling you with my seed."

"Yes."

"I wanted you very badly." He pressed and withdrew, pressed and withdrew, timing the pressure to her shivers. "I want you again."

Her head thumped back against the wall. "Oh, heavens."

He had the advantage. She couldn't go any higher. He pressed a little harder, easing his fingers in.

"Show me how much you want me, Sally." The resistance gave on a high cry. "That's it. Just like that."

Hot and tight, the smooth channel of her ass closed around him, caressing his finger in tiny pulses, the way it had caressed his cock last night, holding him just as tightly. She took him to the second knuckle on a soft gasp. He lifted his knee, drawing up her leg, opening her farther to the thrust of his thumb. He rocked the heel of his hand on her clit as he tested her readiness for a deeper possession.

She bucked up. He caught her as she came down and let the momentum facilitate the culmination they both craved. Her high-pitched cry shivered down his cock as she took him in both openings.

"Tucker!"

He dropped his forehead to hers, lust and a more powerful emotion sweeping through him as her climax rolled over her. He eased his fingers out, and then in again, milking the moment, wanting it all—her pleasure, her acceptance. The illusion that she was his. "Who else?"

Her mouth sought his as she opened farther, took him deeper and gave him what he needed. Damn, she always gave him what he needed.

"No one. No one else."

7

S he hadn't anticipated Tucker's possessiveness.

Sally Mae stood in the parlor and watched Tucker stride across the street as if he owned it. It was a lot like the way he'd taken her just minutes before, as if he owned her, but then he'd kissed her as if she'd been his world, let her skirts ride the slow glide of his hand back down her thigh, kissing her one more time before he left her and Crockett to stare after him like lovesick fools. She didn't know what she resented more. The way he could control his feelings or the way she couldn't control hers.

Crockett whined from the kitchen where she'd barricaded him. The frustration in the sound echoed the frustration inside her. She and Tucker were supposed to be having an affair. That was the deal. They'd enjoy the pleasure they could give to each other, one night at a time, and then move on. Nothing deeper between them than the enjoyment of each other's bodies. But he was changing the rules. Or maybe they'd been playing by his rules all along and she'd just been too naive to see it. She leaned back against the doorjamb, her body still pulsing with pleasure, her pussy still aching.

Show me how much you want me.

She shuddered. She didn't know if she could, but she wanted to try. She wanted to please Tucker. To give him the same pleasure he gave her. To hold him with her body and her heart, she admitted to herself. Pushing stray tendrils of hair off her face, she sighed. She'd known that starting something with Tucker was flirting with danger, but she'd just wanted to feel alive. For one night, she had wanted to have the illusion of belonging, but Tucker was a big man whose impact stretched beyond one night. Something she hadn't allowed for when she'd made her decision. She'd wanted to believe he was a shallow womanizer, worked hard to convince herself of that even, only to find out there was more to him than sex and violence. He intrigued her, inspired her, drew her like a moth to the flame. She rubbed her hands up and down her arms. Maybe more than was wise. If she were half the woman Jonah always bragged she was, she would not be here when Tucker came back. She'd walk away, head high, convictions in place.

But she wasn't the woman Jonah had wanted her to be. Because he'd been such a paragon, it had been easy to bask in his virtue. But the success on her part hadn't been real. While Jonah had easily followed the path of acceptance, it had always been a much harder struggle for her. Sometimes to the point that she felt Jonah hadn't understood. But even then he'd hidden his disappointment, attributing the lack to the fifteen-year age difference between them. Sometimes she wondered if she'd just been honest with him would she be more at peace now. But how did she tell someone who'd known her since she was ten that he didn't know her at all?

But Tucker, who'd only known her a year, and not as an intimate, was able to see into those parts of her soul she wanted hidden. He'd poked and prodded every time he came into town, dragging them out one by one for questioning, not letting her be. Pulling the curtains aside, she glanced out the glass inserts, watching her personal temptation walk away, those broad shoulders squared, those long legs eating up the ground, the small puffs of dust punctuating the purpose that colored everything he did. And everything he did touched her by association. She wasn't deaf to the murmurings around town. Prejudice was not a new thing, even among Friends. A prolonged association between Tucker and herself was dangerous for them both. But apparently, neither could walk away. She wasn't sure what held Tucker, but for her, it was the undercurrent of something bigger than them both that surrounded her when she was with him. The feeling of rightness that sank deep. It was good to be with Tucker, but was it really worth everything?

She'd worked a long time to be who she was and the acceptance that came with it. She wasn't in a perfect place, but what she had provided stability. If she lost it, she'd be back to that scared ten-year-old with no home, no family and no purpose who had been brought to the Quakers for healing. She rubbed her hands up and down her arms. She couldn't go back to that dark place. Didn't want to, but if she continued her association, that might be just where she landed.

She watched as he stepped up on the walk on the far side of the street. Her lover. He adjusted the revolver at his hip. It was a painful reminder of what he was going to do. He was going to kill a man. Hunt him down like an animal and kill him. Her stomach twisted as images flashed through her mind. So many men had bled in her care. So many had died because of the belief that might made right and that death was the perfect resolution. She rested her forehead against the glass pane and wrapped her fingers in the lace curtain. And she was so tired of it happening over and over while she just sat there picking up the pieces she could.

Tucker stopped to talk to a tall blond man and short, voluptuous woman. The couple turned and she immediately recognized Isabella Montoya and Sam MacGregor. While Tucker was very fond of both, Sally Mae hadn't made up her mind about Sam. He was a bit of an enigma. He had an easy way of smiling, but it wasn't often that she found the humor reached the stretch of his lips. His fiancée, though, Sally Mae liked very much. Bella was a ball of fire, unconventional and smart as a whip. She kept Sam on his toes.

As Sally Mae watched, Tucker shook his head, and Sam smiled in the startling way he had that transformed him from deadly to charming. Tucker said something that Isabella obviously didn't like. Sally Mae could tell she'd planted her feet, and for anyone else, that would have been the end of the conversation, but Bella's only weakness was Sam, as evidenced by her reaction when Sam reached out and ran the backs of his fingers down her cheek. Even from where she stood, Sally could see the softening in the other woman's stance. And for the first time, Sally Mae recognized that something she often saw in Tucker's expression. Hunger.

Not hunger for Bella. Sally touched her fingers to the window as her heart twisted, the heat of the glass a pale substitute for the heat of Tucker's skin. He would never hunger for his best friend's woman, but hunger for the emotional closeness Bella and Sam shared. She'd never thought of Tucker as a lonely man. That had been selfish. How could he not be lonely? His Indian heritage put him outside most social boundaries. His size earned him some respect, but not enough to truly belong in any world, Indian or white. He didn't have the freedom to love where he wanted. Didn't have the option of just making friends. Didn't have any of the common bonds that allowed people to find common ground.

Like they'll come to get thee?

She realized he'd never answered that question. She wondered if Tucker doubted even the loyalty of Hell's Eight. Her heart twisted again. How awful for a man to have to live that way. How tempting it would be for such a man to feel God had deserted him. How easy it would be to turn to the solution of a quick fix. There would be solace in the immediate balance of power that one could achieve with one's fist. Temporary or not, false or not, she could see its appeal for Tucker.

Outside, the discussion came to an end and, judging from Bella's posture as she headed for Sally Mae's house, it had not ended the way the other woman intended. By her side strode Kells, the big wolf dog that had adopted Bella and almost given his life protecting her. A small, curvaceous woman, Bella drew the attention of every male she passed. And just as quickly as every man noticed her, every man whipped around to look back at Sam. Sam had proved himself to be possessive of his fiancée and no one wanted to be on his bad side.

Only one man didn't look away and didn't look toward Sam. Sally Mae bit her lip. Lyle. He had the potential to be trouble for more than just her. She'd heard rumors that his forward ways with women could be more than just talk, but without proof she was obligated to give him the benefit of the doubt.

But after having him in her house, Sally Mae suspected the rumors could be true. Thank goodness Bella had Sam.

In this land, a woman's only protection was the strength of the man who guarded her. Sam had a deadly reputation. Six months ago when Bella had been kidnapped by Tejala, it had been made clear to all in the territory that nothing came between Sam and his Bella. Plenty of men might have distanced themselves from Bella after her ordeal, but when Sam had brought Bella home, she'd been in his arms and, despite her bruised and battered appearance, she'd been smiling. Sally Mae's respect for Sam had gone up because of it.

Yes, Sam loved his Bella, and if Lyle acted on the thoughts Sally suspected he harbored, he was courting an ugly death. The thought should bother her. It didn't. More proof that she was changing. And not for the better.

Sally Mae wasn't the only one who'd noticed Lyle's focus. Sam pulled his hat down and took two steps toward Lyle. Tucker reached out, his bare biceps rippling in the morning light as he placed his palm in the middle of Sam's chest and stopped him cold. Sam wasn't a small man by any means. Tucker was just that strong as to make the effort of stopping him seem inconsequential. A trill of pride went through Sally, followed just as quickly by a trill of alarm as Tucker strode to where Lyle stood in front of the saloon. For a big man, Tucker could move silently. Lyle, still watching Bella, became aware of his presence too late. He turned just in time to take Tucker's fist in his face.

Sally smothered her cry with a hand over mouth. Though there was no way he could have heard, Tucker looked directly at her. She couldn't see his eyes under the brim of his hat, but his mouth was set to a straight line of disapproval. One of Lyle's friends came up. Tucker had a few words with him. The man looked at her house before nodding, grabbed Lyle by the arm and dragged him back into the saloon.

Obviously, Tucker told the man not to bring Lyle to her. If it had been any potential patient but Lyle, she would have taken Tucker to task, but truth be told, the last couple days of his recovery, Lyle had been making her uncomfortable. No matter what her beliefs preached, she didn't want him back in her house.

Bella might be fortunate to have Sam's reputation to protect her, but Sally's husband was dead. She had only her usefulness to protect her. She was the closest thing the town had to a doctor, and that gave her some value, but apparently not enough to quell prejudice. Right after her husband had died, the townsfolk, men included, seemed to watch out for her, but in the past few months that attitude had been changing. Women had started asking delicately about her "plans" and men had started looking at her with something more than pity. Quaker or not, the message she was getting from the town's citizens was clear. Her time of mourning was over.

It wasn't so different from what would've occurred back in her own community. The difference was there were no Quakers here in Lindos, no one who believed as she did. She and Jonah had expected more Friends to arrive as time went on. Part of Jonah's purpose in coming west was to found a new community for them to expand into, but then he'd died, and everything had changed. Including the way she saw things. Sally bit her lip as Bella reached the gate. She was a woman alone in a barely civilized town whose illusion of protection was slipping. She would have to make a decision soon. She looked at Tucker and her heart wrenched. She released the curtains, letting them fall between them.

Please, Lord, give me the strength.

Bella reached the porch. Motioning for Kells to stay, she climbed the steps with a lively bounce that projected her personality accurately. There was no pretense with Bella. Bella knocked. Crockett barked and the crates she'd put across the kitchen doorway scraped across the floor. Sally Mae opened the door, forcing her bleak thoughts aside.

"Good morning to thee, friend."

Bella smiled and reached down and petted Crockett, who came bounding up. "Would you be willing to offer me sanctuary?"

"From what do thee seek shelter?"

She made a face. "The stupidity of men." Without looking over her shoulder, she asked, "Is Sam still watching?"

Sally Mae glanced over Bella's shoulder. "Yes."

"Rats. Always, he ruins my plans."

"Thee have plans?"

"Yes."

Sally Mae caught Crockett's makeshift collar before he could dart out the door. "Thee had better come in."

"Sí." Bella nodded, sending the feather on her hat bobbing, a wry smile on her lips. "It is probably best." She unfastened her hat and removed it, then announced, "I am displeased with Sam."

Crockett whined, his attention on that tempting feather. "Thee might want to put that up high," Sally suggested.

"Or I could just let one of us have a little fun." Bella tossed the hat to Crockett, who pounced on it immediately. She waved away Sally Mae's dismay. "Sam hates that hat."

Sally let Crockett go. With fierce puppy growls, he shook and tossed the hat. "I thought thee were mad at him?"

"I am, but not to the point I want him blinded."

At Sally's blank stare, she explained, "The feather keeps poking him in the eye."

"Thee could just replace it with something else."

Bella grinned. "Sam will enjoy the telling of this more. He very much hates that hat and has promised it much worse."

Sally Mae envied Bella her confidence when it came to Sam. "So thee are mad at him, but not that mad?"

"I make no sense, do I?"

"Not really."

Bella sighed. "Sam rides out with Tucker."

"Thee don't approve?"

"It is more that I worry. I know Tucker and Sam are skilled, but I fear that this is the time they won't pay the attention they should and…" Her explanation ended on a shrug. "It would be better if I were with him."

"Thee can't go with him. Thee could be hurt."

Bella flipped her braid back over her shoulder and glared across the street. "This was Sam's argument. As if it is better that he is injured than I."

What was she supposed to say to that? "He's a Ranger. He has years of experience."

Bella sighed and shook her head. "This is also his argument, but it is not fair that I must be always the one who waits."

Sally Mae could understand the frustration behind the argument. Every time Tucker left, she lived with her heart in her throat until he returned. "Thee must have faith."

Bella dismissed that with a snort. "Faith I have, but Sam takes risks, believes himself invincible."

"Sam is a smart man."

"Yes, very clever, and sometimes he forgets I am clever, too." She ran her hand over her hair. "You saw how he brushed my cheek with his fingers?"

Sally Mae nodded.

"He promised me that he'd come home." She threw up her hands. "As if that is a promise he can keep."

"He doesn't want thee to worry."

Bella turned to face her, a small frown between her big brown eyes. "Are you not afraid for Tucker?"

As hard as she tried, Sally Mae didn't think she'd success-fully hid her start. "It's not the same."

Bella's frown lifted, to be replaced with speculation. Sally Mae would have preferred the frown. "If not, it will soon be. There is much between you two. I saw it the first time we met, and it has just grown stronger."

Dear God, were they that obvious to everyone? "Thee are imagining things."

"This you would like to think, but I know magic when I see it."

Magic. Yes, it did feel like that when Tucker touched her. "I think I liked it better when thee were mad at Sam."

"Rather than speculating on you and Tucker?"

"Yes."

"Then I will change the topic." Bella sighed and pushed the curtain aside so she could see out. "At least Tracker and Shadow ride with them."

All Sally Mae could see was a rear view of a tall man dressed in black. He had the broad shoulders and lean hips of a man who was used to hard work and long hours on horseback. The long, black hair that fell down his back marked him as likely Indian. "Tracker and Shadow?"

"They are Hell's Eight and, to my eyes, the scariest of the men."

"I've heard Caine Allen is the scariest. A very possessive man and vengeful when what he regards as his is threatened."

"This I will have to see to believe. But I believe it will be hard to find men scarier than Tracker or Shadow. They have much anger inside. Much like my Sam had."

"Had?"

Bella grinned. "I have given him love. It is a better anchor."

It was such a Quaker thing to say. "Are thee sure thee are not a Friend?"

"Of course, I am your friend. I have been since we met those months ago."

"I meant Quaker."

"No, I am not, but maybe you are *Catolica?*"

Bella's grin invited Sally to smile back. She did, but shook her head. "No."

"No matter. My Sam has a saying. It is a good one. There are many roads to the same place. The choice we make depends on how hard we want to work to get there."

"Are thee saying I chose a difficult path?"

"I am saying it does not matter to me which path you take. In the end, I know we will be at the same place. This is all that matters."

Sally Mae looked out the window again. The men were talking. From their stances, the discussion was a serious one. "So they're all going together to hunt Billy's killer?"

"You do not think the men of Hell's Eight would let Tucker go alone, do you?"

She didn't know. She knew Tucker as lover and protector. She didn't know more because she hadn't wanted to know more. She'd wanted there to be a distance between them for the simple reasons she didn't want to care about anything enough to get hurt. The look Bella gave her reflected the disappointment she felt in herself. She had not been fair to Tucker. Or to herself. "No."

"Hell's Eight are as loyal as the *vaqueros de Montoya* are. It is said they came out of hell bonded to each other in a devil's pact."

"Do you believe this?"

Bella shook her head. "I know what happened to their town was terrible. I know they almost died afterward with no adults to provide, and I know they grew strong enough to take vengeance, but not in any of them have I seen evil. Just—" she sighed "—such sadness mixed with incredible strength."

Sally knew about the sadness. She'd seen it in Tucker's face often enough. "They're good men."

"Who have lived a hard life," Bella interjected. "Do not expect from them the placid reactions of other men."

"No. I don't. Not anymore."

The men went into the saloon. Out of sight. Bella let the curtain drop and turned. Sally stepped back.

"You have found this out for yourself, *sí?*"

Sally Mae smiled weakly. It was useless to keep up the pretense. "Yes."

"They are overwhelming, these men, in their determination to get their way."

"Yes."

Bella cocked her head to the side. "And very hard to resist, maybe."

Sally Mae sighed. "Very."

Bella tugged her skirt free of Crockett's teeth. "You do not want Tucker to go, either, do you?"

"No. I don't."

"But for more reason than fear, I think."

Bella was very perceptive. "The only thing killing on top of killing will bring is more killing."

Crockett dove back in with fierce mock growls. "Sometimes killing is necessary."

Sally Mae caught him by the collar. "I believe in peace."

"No matter what?"

Sally nodded. Bella whistled. "You are a stronger woman than I."

"It's a matter of faith."

"God helps those who help themselves."

There were plenty of times she'd helped herself. "Because I don't believe in violence doesn't make me a doormat."

"To most, it would."

"Then most would be wrong."

Bella folded her arms across her ample chest. "I think I like you very much, Sally Mac with the unpronounceable last name."

Sally chuckled and let Crockett go. "Thee have been talking to Tucker."

"He much enjoys teasing you."

"He enjoys a lot of unhealthy things."

Bella nodded. "Yes, he does. You must cure him of this."

"Why is that my job?"

With a suspiciously innocent expression, Bella pointed out, "You are the healer."

So she was. "I think he's incurable."

The other woman's expression lost some of its innocence. "I think you must try."

"Why?"

"Because he has waited all his life for you."

Oh, darn. She was saved from having to answer when Crockett whined and circled at her feet.

"Excuse me, I have to take him outside."

Scooping Crockett up, she hurried to the back door, frowning at him once again as she took in the state of her kitchen and put him down. He immediately squatted, watching them with anticipation in his eyes. Crockett loved to be praised.

As he was finishing, Sally Mae said, "Good boy." He practically vibrated with impatience as he finished up before bounding over to them, all wiggles and joy.

He reached Bella as she stepped off the porch. She knelt down as he leaned against her. Lifting his outrageously long ears, she kissed the end of his nose. "You are very cute."

Crockett took the compliment as his due, leaning harder against her, the skin under his eyes sagging farther as he angled for more attention.

"What is his name?"

"Crockett."

Bella looked over her shoulder at the disaster that used to be Sally's kitchen. "I think it should be *Trouble.*"

"I should've taken Tucker's penchant for directness into consideration when I agreed to watch him, but he looked so cute and innocent—how could I believe he was capable of such mischief?"

"There is much more to Tucker than you see. He has a wicked sense of humor."

Sally was beginning to get that impression. "So I've been learning."

A disturbance around the corner caught her attention. From where she stood, she could see down the alley to the main Street. Sam, Tucker and two men she assumed were

Shadow and Tracker walked down the street. The two strangers had similar muscular builds with dark hair flowing from under their hats. Even from here she could sense the leashed violence they emanated. Trouble. Where those two went, trouble swarmed. Sally knew it in her gut. And they were riding with Tucker and Sam. That couldn't be good.

Her dismay must have shown in her face, because Bella put her hand on her arm. "They will be all right."

Sally had seen too much death to believe such platitudes. "Thee cannot know."

Hooking her arm through Sally's, Bella sighed. "Then we will go talk to someone who will know."

"A fortune-teller?"

Bella rolled her eyes. "Your God."

"What makes thee think He's talking to me right now?"

"I am not sure He is talking to me, either, but it cannot hurt to 'bend his ear' as Sam says."

"I'm not Catholic."

Bella's smile gave her a lush beauty. "That is okay, I do not think the town has either church." She touched Sally's arm. "I wish to pray for Sam. Would you not like to pray for Tucker?"

Sally had missed the moments of communion in church when members gathered to contemplate their path, or pray for those in need. "Yes. I would. What will we do with the puppy?"

Crockett was too busy chasing his tail to be concerned about what they intended to do with him, but Sally Mae couldn't conceive of leaving him alone. Tucker had trusted him to her and she would not fail. In a tangle of paws, Crockett fell on his side, bounced up and looked at her to see if she'd noticed. She tapped her thigh. He came to her side, immediately licking her fingers.

"We will take him with us."

"I don't think Reverend Schuller will approve."

Bella whistled three short notes through her teeth. Kells came trotting around the corner. Crockett snapped to attention. Sally put her hand on his head. Kells was very big.

"Friend, Kells," Bella instructed.

Somehow, Sally didn't see those two words as much of a deterrent if Kells decided to eat Crockett for breakfast. She held her breath as Kells strolled over and touched his nose to the puppy's. Crockett wiggled and licked the bigger dog's lips. She'd take her cue from the puppy if she knew him better. But all she knew about Crockett was that he could be a brainless idiot that might not recognize death when it stared him in the face.

Bella stood to the side, watching. "There is no need to worry. Kells is Hell's Eight. He protects the small ones."

Sally Mae didn't have much choice but to accept Bella's statement as Kells walked around to sniff Crockett from head to tail. Apparently satisfied, he sat down and glanced over at Bella. Bella pointed to Crockett. "Guard."

There was no discernible change in Kells's expression or demeanor, but Bella seemed satisfied. She brushed the puppy prints off her skirt. "Shall we go?"

Sally Mae eyed Crockett. "I still think the Reverend Schuller isn't going to be happy to see Crockett."

"Then he can discuss it with Kells."

Kells chose that moment to yawn, showing his large, white, very sharp teeth.

"That would work."

"*Sí,* I think so." Bella headed down the alley toward the main street.

As she followed, Sally Mae realized it had been a long time since she'd made a friend. She'd learned to put some distance between the people around her because of their lack of understanding how her view of the world differed from theirs. She'd thought she'd been protecting herself, but maybe what she'd been doing was running away. She pondered that.

The church was cool, soothing in its peace, and it suddenly didn't matter that it wasn't a Friends meeting place or a Catholic church. It was the right place to be at that moment.

Bella genuflected as she entered and crossed herself, reaching automatically for the holy water that wasn't there. With a complete lack of self-consciousness that Sally envied, she drew her hand back and shrugged. "Some things are different, are they not?"

"I'm not sure they matter though."

"Neither am I."

Bella led the way down the aisle between the pews, stopping in the middle. Sally followed, letting the peace sink past the turmoil. She missed the gathering of Friends at times like this. The prayer, the quiet reflection had been solace to her young mind when she'd come to the Friends. Moments like this reminded her of everything she'd walked away from, yet she didn't want to go back. Something out here in this wild land called to her, kept her here, gave her a peace she'd never found back in her very quiet, established community. She liked the uniqueness of this land. The violence disturbed her, but worse, she understood it and it felt good on some level to be among people who accepted violence as much a part of themselves as laughter and tears. Even though she didn't believe in giving in to that violence, their acceptance helped her accept the struggle within herself as also natural.

Jonah had been a naturally peaceful man. At peace with himself, his religion. At peace with his ethics. It was a peace she'd never achieved, and one that had often made her feel inferior because she couldn't match it, no matter how many hours she spent in meditation. She always seemed to empathize with the violence better than the ideal. Always had the initial impulse to strike back rather than to turn the other cheek. So while here she was still a misfit because of her beliefs, she didn't feel as inferior here.

She slid into the pew beside Bella. Closing her eyes, she opened her mind to the quiet. Beside her, Bella murmured in her native tongue, her prayer rising and falling in a smooth cadence that made it easy to ride. She wanted to pray for understanding, for strength, for forgiveness. She wanted to pray for so many things, but the only thought that occupied her mind was, *Please, bring him back to me.*

They caught up to Billy's killer three days out. The bandit hadn't even bothered to hide his trail. Tucker glanced over at his companions, seeing the same suspicion on their faces as had to be on his. "What do you think?"

"I think he's either begging for a beating, or laying a trap," Shadow offered from where he knelt studying the tracks.

Tracker pointed to the canyon ahead. "If a man had friends, that'd be a good place to lie in wait to ambush a posse."

"Anyone been in that canyon before?"

"I have," Sam said, leaning on the saddle horn, a smoke between his fingers. "The best place to trap someone is about three-quarters in. The valley narrows and there's plenty of cover up on the ridges." He took a draw on his smoke. "There's a back way in we can use to our advantage. Maybe have a couple of us up on the ridge and get a drop on them while they're focused on ambushing us riding in."

"You think they're really waiting in there, expecting us to follow this trail to our death?" Tucker asked.

Tracker shrugged. "It would make sense. The only law about these parts are you and Sam. They get rid of you both and there's nothing much standing between them and anything they want to do."

Sam tapped the ash off his smoke. "For sure, the townspeople would be easy to cow." Wetting his fingers, he doused the still glowing tip. "They've gotten pretty complacent."

Tracker chewed on a blade of grass. "They have at that. One good ambush could take care of a lot of problems for a lot of bad people."

Tucker glanced over at Sam, knowing the same tension was running under his skin that ran under Sam's despite his nonchalance. Sam had always been good at hiding what he felt. It didn't mean he didn't feel things. "Which is why I didn't want you to come. You've got a fiancée to think about."

Sam tugged his hat lower, the way he did when he didn't want anyone to see his eyes. "Just because I'm engaged doesn't mean I want to miss out on the fun."

Tucker shook his head. He'd give up the old ways in a heartbeat if he could have Sally Mae. "You'll be Hell's Eight until the day you die, Sam, but you've got responsibilities now, maybe a baby down the road, and I, for one, don't want to be the one to tell Bella you're not coming home."

Tracker switched the blade of grass to the other side of his mouth. "That's one woman who'll likely kill the messenger."

Shadow grunted. Tucker took that as agreement. Apparently Sam did, too. "I appreciate the concern, but there are some decisions that are mine to make."

"Fine. But do me a favor and quell that reckless streak of yours."

"I already promised that."

"To Bella?"

"Yeah."

"Was it easy for you to leave the widow, Tucker?" Shadow asked.

Tucker slapped the reins against his thigh. "There's nothing between Sally Mae and me."

Shadow snorted. "That lie would fly better in front of idiots than us. We know you, remember?"

"There can't be anything. If anybody got a whiff of me being around her, they'd string me up, Ranger or not."

Sam spit and took a drag on his cigarette. "They'd have to come through Hell's Eight to do it."

Tucker met his gaze. That was the kind of no-win fight Tucker didn't want anyone engaging in on his behalf. "And they would. You know how white men feel about their women."

"You're half-white," Sam pointed out.

"Only the half no one cares about."

Tracker flicked his piece of grass to the ground. "Damn hard to miss with those eyes of yours."

"My eyes aren't the part people are worried about."

Sam chuckled. "I just bet."

"You're playing a dangerous game with the widow," Tracker opined.

"So you said before, but what I do with her is my business."

"Nobody's arguing that." Tracker looked at him from the shadow of his black hat. The scar on his cheek was vividly white in the bright sun. "Thought I'd mention that we'd be watching your back, just in case you slip a time or two."

He didn't know whether to be insulted or flattered. "I know what I'm doing."

Or at least doing a real good job faking it.

Sam shook his head. "I have a feeling, friend, that you don't have anything you want anymore."

"That's a dangerous place for man to be," Shadow interjected quietly.

The problem with riding with people for so long was that they had a way of knowing things others couldn't see. "I didn't say I had what I wanted. I said I knew what I was doing."

"You want her?" Shadow asked.

Shadow rarely spoke, but when he did it was usually a good idea to listen. Except Tucker couldn't hear this. Not and keep his perspective. "Don't go interfering, Shadow."

"If you want her, you should take her." He shrugged. "She will have no other, anyway."

"It's not that easy."

"It's not that hard. You want her, she wants you, so take her."

Like the savage everyone thought he was. "I'm only *half*-Indian."

"Seems your claim on ancestry gets real convenient," Sam cut in. "First you were all Indian, but now you're claiming to be all white."

Shadow shrugged in that enigmatic way he had. "So pick the side that gets you what you want."

The degree to which he wanted to do that shook Tucker. "She's just amusing herself as she comes out of her mourning."

Shadow grunted. "I always thought it was a good idea to understand the woman you're screwing."

Tucker's hand went to his knife. "Show some respect."

Shadow didn't flinch. "I show more respect than you do. I do not see her through other's eyes. She's not like other whites. And like you, she has no place. Take her, and give her one."

"And how long do you think that would last?"

Tracker scanned the ridge. "I imagine as long as you're strong enough to hold her."

"That would be about five minutes, around here."

Sam pushed his hat back. "Well, maybe around here isn't where you should be with her."

"We have a job to do, remember? We're supposed to be finding Billy's killer and Ari, not courting widows."

Sam smiled. "Courting widows is a lot more fun."

Shadow joined in. "And likely to yield a lot more results."

"I've finally got a good lead to where Ari might be," Tracker said. "Heard about a blonde woman living with Mexicans just below the border."

"Do you really think it's her?" Sam asked.

"The timing fits."

He didn't sound too hopeful. Tucker couldn't blame him. In the eight months they'd been searching, they hadn't found hide nor hair of Desi's sister. Not a surprise since she'd been captured nearly a year before Desi had come to Hell's Eight, but it wasn't Hell's Eight's way to go back on a promise, and they'd promised to come back with the information on her sister, good or bad, that Desi needed to know. "I hope for Desi's sake it is."

"I'll head down and check it out after we finish this. Right now, we've got company." With a jerk of his chin, Tracker indicated the ridge. Tucker had already seen what had drawn Tracker's attention. The reflection of the sun off glass.

"Curious bunch, aren't they?"

Shadow swung back up on his horse, barely seeming to disturb the air around him. There was no better rider anywhere than Shadow. No better hunter, no better killer. No one better to have on your side. No one harder to understand.

"Then I guess we'd best not disappoint them."

The familiar byplay settled like an old friend around Tucker.

"Have I ever told you there's nobody I'd rather die with than you three?"

"Anybody ever told you you've got a damn pessimistic bent?" Sam scoffed, settling his hat on his head. "Besides," he asked, sending his horse in a circle with a touch of the reins, "who the hell says we're going to die today? Sure as hell not me. I've got something good waiting for me back home."

And for the first time, Tucker realized, so did he.

"Let's ride, then."

8

A draw of the cards determined that Tucker would be the decoy to distract the outlaws while Tracker, Shadow and Sam would get in position to pick off the ones who were lying in wait. Being a decoy was dangerous, but that wasn't why it always took a draw of the cards to decide who got the role. The real truth was it was wearing on the nerves to so passively wait to see what would happen. It wasn't Tucker's first time as decoy, not even his fifth. He had notorious bad luck at cards, but experience didn't make it any less nerve-racking to ride between long-ago rock slides, knowing the outlaws could be tucked behind any of the giant boulders, knowing all it would take was one shot and their plan, not to mention his life, would be over. His only protection was the assumption that the outlaws were intelligent and lazy. Lazy, because they'd want to spend the least amount of effort to get the Rangers off their tails, and intelligent, because Tucker needed them to be able to come up with the basic, most obvious plan to accomplish their goal.

The hairs on the back of his neck rose as he passed the rock slide that guarded the entrance to the canyon. Tucker put his hand to his holster and checked his revolver, sliding it up to make sure it was clear. He laid his rifle across his thighs. The barrel was warm from the heat of the sun. The familiar weight settled his impatience. This wasn't the first time outlaws had thought to ambush Hell's Eight. It wasn't the first time Hell's Eight had decided to cut such attempts off at the knees. They knew what they were doing. He'd dawdled a good hour before riding in, pretending to cook dinner, giving the others time to get through the back entrance and into position.

Tucker surveyed the tumble of rocks ahead. As traps went, this was a pretty obvious one, which boded well for Shadow's plan to succeed. His horse, Smoke, stumbled. Tucker couldn't have timed it better if he'd wanted to—just short of halfway in, on the edge of the likely ambush spot, and a deadfall to the side to provide cover for him if necessary. Pulling Smoke up, he swung off, resting his rifle against a rock before running his hand down her front leg to lift her hoof. With any luck, the bandits would assume he'd stopped to check her shoe. Hopefully they'd see it as their chance and have their guns and attention trained. And hopefully, Tracker, Shadow and Sam had had time to work around to the hidden back entrance and had their guns trained also. He was taking the latter on faith.

He patted Smoke's shoulder. "Sally Mae would say that was a step forward, wouldn't she? Me taking something on faith?"

The gelding tossed his head and whickered, his eyes rolling slightly. "Yeah, I can feel them, too. Just relax, boy, and we'll have it all sorted out in a few minutes."

He released his hoof. He stomped it down, shifting restlessly. But he stayed. He'd chosen Smoke from his remuda for this ride precisely for his obedience. The tingling on the back of his neck increased. Picking up his rifle, Tucker swung back up into the saddle, nerves dancing under his skin. He flexed his fingers. When the shots started flying, there'd be no time for mistakes or hesitation.

To the right, birds stopped singing and a jay squawked a warning on the hill to the left. Was it friend or foe hiding there? Another jay took off from a thicket ahead. He kept riding, the steady clop of Smoke's hooves on the hard ground matching his heartbeat as the cold calm of prebattle settled over him. His senses sharpened, picking up the warmth of the sun and the rhythm of the unnaturally quiet land. The muscles in his chest tightened. He hated this. He was much better at creating action than passively waiting for it to happen.

On the ground ahead, a spray of wildflowers made a home between two rocks, splashing the dusty surface with a bright flare of yellow. A surprising moment of beauty thriving in the midst of rubble. He took it as a good omen, touching the bullet around his neck in confirmation. As Smoke carried him forward, the light shifted across the petals until they shone with the same pale gold as the moonlight on Sally Mae's hair. Ah, damn, for sure she was the beauty in the midst of the ugliness of his life, and if he were anyone else, if she were anyone else, he'd have her hog-tied and chained to his side, branded in every way a man could think of as his, wedding ring and all.

He remembered the wild way she'd taken him when he'd plunged deep into her body, the way she'd wrapped her long legs around his hips and pulled him deeper as he'd come, so deep he couldn't think of anything else but giving her his child. That had been a first for him. He'd never thought like that before. He liked children well enough, but he hadn't seen the need to have one of his own. With Sally Mae, he became a different person inside, his thoughts not so clearly on the turmoil around him, but more on the possibility of a future. When he was around her he was not the outlaw Ranger, but someone more…respectable.

Shit. He spit the dust out of his mouth. There wasn't enough respectable in the world to make a relationship between him and Sally Mae possible. That was going to take a miracle.

She has no place. Take her, and give her one.

Damn Shadow for laying that temptation out in front of him. He could imagine it too easily. Wanted it too much. Sally Mae back at Hell's Eight. Safe, protected, *his*. He spit again, this time to get rid of the taste his selfish nature left in his mouth. What was good for him was not good for Sally Mae. She was a woman of principle and strong ideas and, with the right partner, would flourish. He just wasn't that partner. He was so deep in thought he almost missed the alert when it came in the feigned squawk of a jay.

Shit. Inattention like that would get them killed. He waited until the call came again, this time a perfect robin tweet. Not a note off-key to betray the frustration that Sam had to be feeling in trying to get his attention. Hell, next time Tracker accused him of being a lovesick calf, he'd have to hold back on taking a swing, because a clear-thinking man would not be daydreaming when he knew damn well there were more guns trained on him than he could shake a stick at.

Out of the corner of his eye, Tucker scouted the perimeter. There was a flash to his left. The sun off a rifle barrel? Sam's call said he had one man, south wall. They'd been tracking five. From his right came a subtle imitation of a bobwhite. Tucker slowed Smoke and waited. The call came again, this time in rapid succession once, twice, three times. Tracker had three men in sight. That made four accounted for, possibly five with the one he'd located. Behind him, a covey of quail took flight, the pounding of their wings spooking Smoke. The horse bolted. A bullet whined off the wall rock where they'd been seconds before. The gunshot echoed immediately thereafter.

Suddenly, the canyon exploded with gunshots. Tucker recognized the report of Sam's rifle right off. The special powder the other man used lent a distinctive "oomph" to the shot. Hauling Smoke's head around to the right, Tucker hunched down and urged him to the deadfall. The shelter was meager, but it beat standing tall in the opening. Smoke took one look at the tight confines and balked. Tucker didn't have time to argue. He let him go, grabbing his ammo off the saddle horn before he reared, spun and took off. Damn, it was going to be hell catching him again.

"You hit my horse," he called out, offering Smoke the only protection he could, "and I'll skin your worthless asses alive and leave you as ant bait."

A bullet hit the tree by his head, detonating an explosion of splinters that stung his cheek.

"Keep your head down, Tucker," Sam called, almost cheerily. "Still got one lollygagging, who needs to hurry on to meet his maker."

"Shit!" Tucker ducked before Sam could warn him again, eyeing the raw wood just a few inches from where his head had been. Anyone but Sam would have likely blown off his head while trying to deliver that warning. Hell, a shift in the wind and Sam could just as easily have missed.

Tucker palmed his revolver. In rapid succession, he fired at the blur of movement to his right. There was the unmistakable sound of a bullet hitting flesh, a grunt and then the sound of something heavy hitting the ground. "One of these days, Sam, you're going to push me too far."

There came a single rifle shot and Sam's still cheery, "But not today."

Three shots came in rapid succession from above and to the right. They were high and wide, as if the shooter couldn't get a better angle. He followed the trajectory back. That wouldn't last. All the shooter had to do was move over to the right and down to the next patch of rock, and picking off Tucker would be as easy as shooting fish in a barrel. But not if Tucker shifted his position one hundred feet over. He'd be the one with the clear shot as soon as the bandit got into position.

Gambling that the shooter was already on the move, Tucker sprinted up the hill, every nerve ending alive with excitement. Fifty feet up the hill he almost stepped on the outlaw he'd shot first. The wounded man raised his pistol. Tucker dove to the left, rolled to his feet and with a flick of his wrist he buried his knife in the man's throat. The outlaw's gun fell harmlessly to the ground, the shot that would betray Tucker's position still in the barrel.

Tucker retrieved his knife. As he wiped the blade on the dying man's shirt, he recognized the report of Tracker's buffalo gun and, for a moment, as he looked down at the face of the outlaw, who was clearly Mexican, he flashed back twenty years to the time when the Mexican soldiers had raided their small town. He touched the bullet hanging around his neck. For years, all of Hell's Eight had lived on the hatred that night had birthed, vowing never again to be so helpless, never again to lose so much because they were weak. And they hadn't ever lost again. They'd been as cold and as vicious as they needed to be to survive as boys living in a man's world, and by the time they'd become men, they'd made themselves so strong that they could win battles on their reputations alone.

The outlaw stared at him, eyes wide in terror, his last breath cut abruptly short. Tucker blinked, realigning past and present, feeling the oppressive silence rather than the satisfaction of victory. The bullet felt warm against his skin. He sheathed his knife.

From ahead came a high-pitched cry of agony. Shadow's knife had found its mark. The scream raked down Tucker's spine long after it stopped. The scream itself was just another signal. Shadow always let the last man scream. It shouldn't bother Tucker, but lately a lot of things had lost their luster, including, he realized, his job. Hell, when had justice lost its shine?

Might does not make right.

Tucker angled back down in Sam's direction, pushing Sally's belief out of his head. Out here, the *only* thing that made right was might. It was ridiculous to believe otherwise. Halfway down the ridge, he saw a rifle propped on a rock, sighting a target. He followed the trajectory. Twenty feet away, Sam stood, back against a tree. As he reached into his pocket to pull out his makings, Tucker heard the hammer cock back. Shit! Six. There'd been six.

Tucker was too far away to grab the rifle. "Sam, duck!"

A single shot rang out at the same time as he shouted the warning. The rifle barrel jerked upward, discharging harmlessly into the air. Two seconds later, the man stumbled into Tucker's path, clutching his chest, his eyes meeting Tucker's in one moment of silent realization before he fell to the ground, arms akimbo. His open eyes stared at the sun in a last-ditch effort at clinging to life. From habit, Tucker kicked the gun out of his reach and continued onward toward Sam, anger flaring with relief.

"Jealous because you didn't get to play decoy?"

Sam smiled that easy smile of his that meant nothing. "Couldn't resist when Shadow up and gave me the opportunity." He leaned back against a tree. His fingers were steady as he rolled his makings. "Thanks for the warning though."

Apparently not everything about Sam had changed. He still took chances. Even when he had no right to. "You're welcome."

"That's the last of them," Shadow growled as he dropped out of the tree to the ground in front of them before melting into the underbrush and disappearing back up the ridge.

Sam struck a sulfur. "I never get used to seeing him do that."

Tucker blew out a breath, wishing, not for the first time after a battle, that he smoked. "Me, either."

"You hurt?"

"No. You?"

Sam pulled his shirt away from his side, exposing a rip. "No, but Bella is going to have a fit when she sees they put a tear in my new shirt."

"You'll have some sweet-talking to do."

Sam's smile was easy, and…genuine. "I'm getting to like that."

Sam was a man who'd always had women chasing him. He'd never had to resort to sweet talk. All he'd needed to do was smile and they'd tumbled into his arms like ripe fruit. Tucker couldn't suppress the spurt of unwarranted resentment that finding love, for Sam, had been so easy. "Just smile at her."

Sam smiled around the cigarette, his blue eyes slightly

narrowed against the smoke. "You'd think that would be all I'd have to do, but Bella's different. She doesn't find me charming."

Tucker snorted and reloaded his revolver. "The woman is head over heels in love with you."

"Yeah. She might love me, but that doesn't stop her from having expectations."

Sam's attempt to sound disgruntled fell flat.

"You might as well give it up, Sam. A blind man could see you love every expectation that woman throws at you."

Sam's smile broadened and he rubbed his chest. "Yeah, I do. Especially when she emphasizes them with her teeth."

"I think that qualifies as more than I need to know."

Sam laughed. A genuine laugh, and once again Tucker marveled at the change Bella had brought to his best friend's life. She was like Sam's private sun, lighting up every corner of his life, driving away the darkness that Tucker and the rest of Hell's Eight had worried was consuming him.

"You wait until Sally Mae gets more comfortable with you, and you'll see what I mean."

"I told you, there's nothing to get comfortable for."

Sam looked at him from beneath his hat brim. "Just because you say it doesn't mean I believe it."

"Humor me and pretend, okay." He pushed away from the tree. "It'll keep you healthy."

Sam chuckled and jerked his chin in the direction of the hill. "I suppose we have to bury them."

"We could just leave them for the coyotes. By now, Tracker and Shadow have relieved them of anything valuable."

"Hopefully they had a lot. Billy's mother could use every penny."

"Yeah." It was Hell's Eight's policy for the dead to reimburse their victims. Money didn't right a wrong, but it could help the survivors live in the aftermath. He looked at the rocky ground. Digging a grave was going to be almost impossible.

"Too bad I forgot my shovel."

Sam took a last drag on his cigarette. "Bella sent one."

"What the hell for?"

Sam ground out the cigarette under his boot. "She feels strongly about such things."

Tucker smothered a laugh. "I guess that means you're shoveling."

On a shrug, Sam said, "There's a price for my not being able to see her tear up."

Tracker stepped out of the trees beside them. "There's a price for everything."

His hat, as always, was pulled down over his face, hiding his eyes, showcasing the scar. Not for the first time, Tucker wondered if he did it on purpose.

"Everyone all right?" Tracker asked.

"Yup. How about you?"

Tracker looked at the body near them and then down to where Shadow was removing guns and valuables from another. "Shit, the fight this lot gave us hardly makes it worth their burying."

"That is a fact," Sam agreed.

Tracker nudged the dead man with his foot, as if he expected him to get up and redeem himself by putting up a better fight. "Almost made me feel guilty for killing them."

Tucker looked at the dead man, Sam and then Tracker. They'd stood this way too many times to count after a battle, but this time something was missing. Instead of feeling edgy and restless in the aftermath, today he just felt...empty. Had the outlaws been that inept or had they just gotten that good at killing?

He pulled his hat down over his brow, blocking the sun, his thoughts.

"It does at that."

It was midnight before they got back to town. Anyone with any common sense would have stayed overnight at the campsite as Tracker had suggested, but Sam hadn't wanted to be away from Bella and, claiming the quarter moon gave enough light to see, had headed out. Tucker had his own motivations for tagging along. About fifteen minutes later, Tracker and Shadow had ridden up, not even bothering to hide their amusement. Fortunately, they held their tongues. At least until they got to Lindos.

"Hell, even the saloon is shut down." Tracker shook his head at the quiet. "It's a sad day when the drunks have more sense than the law."

"Or it could be that whiskey doesn't have the allure that my Bella does," Sam countered.

"Yeah," Tracker scoffed, with a lift of his brow. "Or it could be, there's just no fool like a fool in love."

"Say what you want. Bella's waiting for me in that hotel yonder, which is a hell of a lot better than anything you three have waiting."

The truth hit like a punch in the gut.

"You talk too much, Sam," Shadow snarled.

Sam swore. "Hell, I didn't mean it like that, and you damn well know it."

Tracker and Shadow just stared at him. There were some things Sam just couldn't understand and one of them was the barrier their skin color put between them and most of the world. As one, the twins turned their horses toward the livery. The hotel didn't allow Indians beneath its roof. It didn't allow Mexicans, either. Tracker and Shadow were out of luck on both sides of their ancestry.

Sam stared after them. "Shit."

"They know you didn't mean it," Tucker said.

"Making it up to them is going to cost me a fortune in pancakes."

Tracker and Shadow were always willing to let Sam pay off his debts in food. Of course, getting a restaurant owner to serve an Indian usually accumulated a few bruised ribs, but Sam always pulled it off and Tracker and Shadow always forgave him. "Beats them taking the insult out of your hide."

"That is the truth." They rode down the street in companionable silence. Sam took a last pull on his smoke and pushed his hat back from his face.

"What I said earlier, it stands, Tucker. If things ever get to a point between you and Sally Mae where you want to move forward, there is a place for you at Rancho Montoya."

Damn, why did everyone keep holding out the impossible, as if it were possible?

"Thanks."

The abrupt response was supposed to dissuade Sam from talking anymore on the subject. Sam never was good at taking hints.

"Sally Mae always impressed me as the kind of woman a man made changes for."

"She scares the hell out of me."

"Bella scared the hell out of me, too."

He cocked his brow at Sam, who smiled wryly. "Doesn't seem like she scares you anymore."

"In different ways on any given day, but on not a one of them do I regret letting her convince me we're worth it."

"That's a strange way of looking at things."

"We didn't grow up like everybody else, Tucker. We grew up desperate, violent and convinced of the right of our view. I've learned, since meeting Bella, that sometimes that view needs changing."

"Uh-huh."

Sam looked down the street toward Sally Mae's house. "Everything is changing, Tucker, including Hell's Eight." He smiled. "And believe it or not, some of the notions we held as golden when we were little more than kids don't hold water nowadays."

"Like what?"

"Like the belief we don't need love. I've got news for you, Tuck. It feels just as good to us to be loved as it does any other human being."

It wasn't like Sam to be so philosophical. "Son of a bitch, have you been nipping at a bottle tucked in your saddlebag?"

"No, I just hate to see a friend run away from a good thing."

"You know what they'll do to her—us—if they even get wind of my interest, let alone trying to take her to a social."

She'd be ridiculed, raped, beaten. And the ones doing it would say she deserved it.

Sam tossed his smoke in the dirt and wheeled his horse around toward the hotel. "So you don't take her to a social. You take her to Hell's Eight."

"And then what?"

Sam was just a shadow in the night by the time Tucker finished asking.

"Love her."

The answer was so faint that Tucker wasn't sure if it was Sam who answered or just his imagination. Either way it didn't matter. The rhythmic sound of Smoke's hooves echoed in the quiet of the night. Sally Mae couldn't live his life. It would kill her.

The barn behind Sally Mae's house looked as it always did. Dark and empty. There was a note nailed to the door. He read it before crumpling it up and stuffing it into his vest pocket to put with the other five that'd been left before. *Leave or die.*

They weren't getting any more clever in their threats, but the directness of this one did signify a bit more determination. It was time to move on. The door swung open soundlessly as he led Smoke in. He stripped her of her saddle and bridle, giving her a brief rubdown before patting her flank. "I'll do it right in the morning."

Tonight he was too tired. He'd thought everything would be all right when he came home, that being in the familiar surroundings would settle the restlessness inside, but it hadn't. Inside, the nameless feeling grew. He opened the narrow door to the room he'd been staying in ever since Jonah had rented it to him a month before he'd been killed. The first thing he noticed was the supper pail on the bed, sitting dead center of the quilt. He walked over, dropping the saddlebags on the floor. The quilt smelled of soap and sunshine. Sally Mae had washed it. He touched the pail's lid, locked down to keep the rodents out. Sally couldn't know when he'd be coming home, which meant she'd been out here every day making sure when he finally did, he'd find food and comfort.

Damn her. He curled his fingers into a fist, wanting to smash the pail. As if destroying a piece of tin would destroy the relentless longing inside.

She has no place. Take her, and give her one.

He spun on his heel. She couldn't keep doing this. He got halfway to the house and remembered the quilt that smelled of soap and fresh air. Cursing under his breath, he angled toward the pump. He was still going to tear a strip off her, but he didn't need to smell of three days of hard riding while he did it. The water was biting cold. It didn't do a thing to cool his temper.

He expected to see Crockett on the back steps. Concern blended with anger when there was no sign of the pup. It only took a minute to jimmy the door lock. Slipping into the house, he took the stairs two at a time. Her door, the second to the right, was ajar. He eased it open. The wind blew the curtains in a gentle billow that directed his attention to the bed. As if he needed direction. His gaze always naturally went to Sally. The faint light flowed over her like a caress, picking up the whiteness of her skin, the pale blond of her hair, the dusky gleam of her lashes. His moonbeam.

A step closer and the mystery of Crockett's disappearance was solved. He lay curled on the bed. His tail thumped as Tucker came over and scooped him up. With a sleepy little yawn, Crockett snuggled into his arms. Tucker sniffed. The puppy smelled of soap. At least Sally wasn't so softhearted that she would invite fleas into her bed.

He took the puppy downstairs and let him out. Crockett immediately went about his business before bounding back in and sitting down in front of Tucker, his eyes drooping pathetically, clearly looking to be picked up again.

Tucker folded his arms across his chest. "Less than a week in her company and already you're spoiled." The pup made a rumbling noise in his throat, thumped his tail, yawned again and started to slump. Tucker swore and picked him up.

"Don't get used to this," he told him as he carried him back into the house. "For one thing, you'll soon be too big to be carried everywhere."

He got a sloppy kiss across his chin in response to his warning.

"Ugh." He wiped his chin on his shoulder. "You're a hunting dog, for crying out loud. The good life isn't for you."

Any more than it was for him, but the knowledge didn't stop him from walking back into the house, didn't stop him from breathing deeply of that subtle, complex scent he associated only with Sally Mae as he closed the door behind him. It always made him think of moonlight and springtime. He climbed the stairs and paused at her bedroom door.

Damn, now she had him waxing poetic. He really was in bad shape.

He pushed the bedroom door open with his foot. Crockett looked toward the bed and whined.

"Oh, no," Tucker whispered.

Crockett looked up at him with liquid brown eyes. Damned if there wasn't quite a bit of his daddy in him. More than once, Boone had wheedled a biscuit from Tia with just such a look.

"Don't even try it. It's the floor or nothing." Crockett moaned and flopped to the floor. Tucker took off his gun belt, folded it and set it out of the pup's reach on the dresser. Next he stripped off his shirt and kicked off his boots. The right one immediately fell under attack by puppy teeth. Tucker sighed. There was a soup bone on the floor, half-under the bed. Apparently Sally Mae had been battling Crockett's teething tendencies also. He took the boot away and nudged the bone over. Crockett accepted the substitution with a ferocious growl.

"Remember. This is just for tonight."

Crockett paid him no mind. Tucker shucked his pants and lifted the covers and slid beneath. Sally Mae stirred, turned as the mattress dipped. He expected her to scream. Instead, she smiled and, as her arms came around his neck, whispered his name. "Tucker."

He curled her tighter against him with a flex of his arm, sliding his hand down her back as the rightness of holding her sank to his bones. Despite telling himself no good could come of these stolen moments, that he was only begging for a world of hurt down the road, he brushed his lips across the top of her head, "Who else?"

Her sleepy chuckle was as soft as the movement of her hand across his chest. "No one else."

Her fingertips found his nipple. Dawdled. "Thee shouldn't be here."

He smiled and breathed in the scent of her shampoo. Damn, it felt good to hold her, smell her, laugh with her. "Gonna kick me out?"

She snuggled in. "I don't have the strength."

Neither did he, which probably explained why he didn't catch her hand when it traveled down his ribs and across his abdomen in a clinical exploration. His cock didn't care how she touched him, just that she did. It jerked up to tap the back of her hand when she probed his pelvis.

"The only part of me that hurts is about six inches lower," he informed her.

"Thee are sure?"

He caught her hand and brought it down, his breath hissing through his teeth as her fingers curled around his cock. She gave a little squeeze. Lightning streaked under his skin. It was hard to find his voice.

"Very sure."

He skimmed his fingertips up the ladder of her spine as she nibbled her way down his body. Her braid trailed over his wrists in a sultry connection. "But you might want to check for yourself."

"Yes, maybe."

"Just remember the windows are open."

Her teeth grazed the layer of muscle slabbing his stomach. "Then thee will have to be very quiet."

It didn't take brains to figure out her meaning. She found a spot just inside his left hipbone that shot all sorts of sensations straight to his cock. His curse skated his control. She laughed and touched her tongue to it again. Wrapping her braid in his hand, he held her to him, sliding his foot up the bed, shivering as the cotton of her nightgown caressed his inner thigh.

Sally looked up at him from beneath her eyelashes. "I did not sleep for worry."

What could he say to that? "I'm sorry."

"When I got tired of worrying, I started to think."

Her grip shifted and moved down to the tight sack of his balls. The heat seared.

"About what?" The question came harder than he wanted, but the delicate way she squeezed his balls made smooth speech impossible.

"About how good a man thee are. About how good I feel when I am with thee, and how very much I missed thee."

He could see the remnants of worry in her eyes. He touched his finger to the faint circles beneath. His skin was very dark against the fairness of hers. "I don't want to hurt you."

She shrugged as if it didn't matter. "My choices are mine."

It mattered. He traced her cheekbone to her jaw, tipping her face to his. "Then make smart ones."

Holding his gaze, she rubbed her cheek against his cock, the inherent submissiveness in the gesture rippling along his desire. He could do anything he wanted to her and she would let him. The knowledge splintered into white-hot desire as she pressed the softest of kisses against the tip of his cock. "I do."

With steady pressure on the back of her head he kept her mouth there, touching but not engulfing, teasing but not delivering. "I should be shot."

"Thee should be loved."

"Not by you."

Pain flickered in her eyes, followed just as quickly by that stubborn look with which he was familiar.

"Tonight I am what thee have."

"I can still leave."

It was a weak retort and her victorious grin said she knew she had him.

"I have been very patiently waiting for thee." Her tongue stroked up the underside of his cock, tickling just beneath the head. "Will thee give me what I want as my reward?"

He'd give her anything she goddamn well wanted. "What do you want?"

Her smile sent his heart racing and his cock jerking against the moist pad of her tongue. "Thee."

Another pass of her sweet tongue. Another tiny kiss to the crest that had his hips arching off the mattress and then she looked up at him, his cock tucked into the hollow of her throat, her breasts snuggled against his balls. Her eyes filled with understanding. "I would take the violence from thee, Tucker, and give thee peace."

His heart twisted. His past was steeped in blood. His future looked no different. He balanced her chin on his fingertips. "You have no idea who I am."

"As thee do not know me, but we are drawn together."

The truth hung between them, strangers yet lovers, separated by differences and yet drawn together by an illusive, magical possibility.

Tucker slid his hands over Sally Mae's shoulders, lingering on the delicacy of the bone.

"We couldn't be more wrong for each other."

"Yet we have been presented with this opening."

He cupped her breasts in his palms. She shivered and the nipples pulled into tight beads. He watched the spread of goose bumps over the creamy white of her skin. "You said that before. What exactly is an opening?"

There was an infinitesimal pause and then the plain truth. "An opportunity to grow."

"If we grow like this, Sally, there'll be no going back."

"I have decided that forward is the way I want to go."

Each word spread over the sensitive tip of his cock. Ah, damn, she was so sexy. A pearly bead of fluid formed on the tip. He waited to see what she would do. Leaning forward, she scooped it up on her tongue, holding it so he could see before swallowing.

Son of a bitch. He held her mouth to him, helpless against the moist temptation as she sucked him deep. "I can't give you what you want."

She let him go with a soft pop and loving squeeze that milked a groan from him. "But thee will give me what thee have, Tucker McCade. I won't settle for less."

She might not settle for it, but she would regret it. He

knew that just as he knew there could be no future for them. But they had right now, and now had the burn of passion sanctioned by the intimacy of the night. The plump nubs of her nipples gave easily when he pressed them into the soft flesh behind. The last of his resistance faded with her soft mewl of pleasure. He could never get enough of the way she filled his hands, as if she'd been made for them. He couldn't get enough of those sexy little sounds she made when he pinched her nipples just so, or of the sheer joy he felt to be with her. "Then take me."

"Yes."

She did. Without hesitation, without fear, without anything between them except the burn of desire. He was supposed to be taking her, but as her lips slid down his shaft, the truth rippled through him—she was taking him. One excruciating inch at a time. He held her, hips lifting off the bed as he struggled to get deeper. He had to get deeper, had to hold on to this moment for the time when there would be just memories.

And she took him, accepting every thrust, every pump of his hips—deeper, harder, faster—making demands of her own, pumping his cock, squeezing his balls, sucking until he had no choice but to give her his seed, his loyalty, his passion. He shuddered and held her, his body aching, her name a chant in his mind. His Sally, his moonbeam. And she held him, too, with gentle kisses along his cock, soft strokes along his abdomen and an even softer chuckle.

"Thy control is not what it should be. I think thee have started a scandal."

Shit. He remembered the note. A hint of unease went up his spine. "Anyone who heard will know enough to keep their mouths shut."

Or he'd shut them up. He tugged her up alongside him, still struggling to catch his breath after that soul-shattering orgasm.

Sally Mae settled into the crook of his shoulder as though she belonged there. Her hand covered his heart. "That is good because thee obviously can't."

He fell asleep laughing.

9

Sally Mae woke to Tucker's lips on the back of her neck and the cool brush of his fingers between her buttocks.

"What are thee doing?"

"I'm getting ready to go."

She pressed back into the dark seduction he wielded so effortlessly. "I might point out that doesn't feel like leaving." His fingers centered on her anus, pressed. His promise of that second night whispered in her ear.

Next time you'll take all of me here.

"This," she whispered, just the thought stealing her breath, "is getting ready for hello."

"You think?" His teeth grazed the tendon along her neck. Goose bumps sprang up along her back. He chuckled as his finger parted the tight muscle the tiniest bit.

"The time for hellos will be tonight. Leave the back door unlocked."

"Why? Locks never seem to slow you."

"True."

She turned her face into his forearm and kissed him gently. A second finger joined the first, bringing on that first erotic bite.

"*Oh.*"

"Like that, did you?"

Saying yes was giving away too much. Saying no was too ridiculous, considering how she was pushing back.

"That's my girl. Push back. Take more."

She'd take everything he had to give. She proved it as his knuckles slipped inside. Her muscles locked down hard. She needed more.

All his delicious muscle against her back went absolutely still. "Shit."

He wanted it, too. "Are thee sure thee can't stay?"

She knew the question was unfair as soon as she asked it. Asking him to stay was asking him to risk his life. It was wrong to invite such trouble into a man's life just because she hungered for the pleasure he could give her.

"Make it worth my while."

The edge of his teeth resettled against the cord of her neck. Memories of their last time together broke over her common sense. It would be so easy to let herself believe that maybe exposure was worth the moments with him, but the reality was, it wasn't. For her, the repercussions would be unpleasant. Men would call her names if they saw her leaving her house. Men even might try to take advantage. Women would certainly scorn her. But Tucker? For Tucker, the repercussions would be far more deadly. Tucker, they would hunt down like a rabid dog. And when they caught him, they'd put a rope around his beautiful neck and hang him. A lot of things were forgiven out here in the territory, but a man with Indian blood touching a white woman?

Even she, with all her Quaker ways, knew they wouldn't tolerate that.

She knew better than to say that to Tucker, though. Tucker had his pride, and a rebellious streak that gave him a tendency to thumb his nose at personal danger. She struggled to contain her instincts, to stop the involuntary flexing of her inner muscles. "I think I would rather savor the anticipation."

The heel of his hand pressed against her buttocks. "You wouldn't be fretting about my health, would you, Sally Mae?"

Reaching back, she curved her fingers over his shoulder, holding him to her as tightly as he was holding her. Maybe even with the same tenderness. This affair was getting out of hand.

"Considering it would be my time that would be spent restoring thy health, I consider it a good investment."

He laughed, a soft sound that was pure seduction. She imagined the glint in his eyes, imagined they would be slightly narrowed in a way that indicated high feeling. Tucker was hard to read unless a person understood his ways, but there were signs if one knew what to look for.

She moaned as his fingers left her. Where before she'd felt unnaturally full, she now felt unnaturally empty. It was always that way with Tucker. At first what she thought was too much ended up being just a teaser. The mattress shifted as he stood. Before she could ask what he was doing, he was back. Something round and hard and slick slid between her cheeks. Shivers of something—dread, anticipation?—tingled up her spine.

"What is that?"

"It's a little something to remember me by."

"Little?" It didn't feel little. "I'm not sure…"

His lips brushed over her nape, his breath fanning the sensitive nerve endings there. He was so good at finding those inconspicuous spots that could leap to such incredible sensitivity. Always knew just how to trigger them.

"But I'm going to be very sure all morning as I think about you wearing this. How open and ready you'll be for my cock when I come back later."

"Thee want me to wear this all morning?"

He pressed harder and delicate muscles separated to embrace the now-familiar burn that should have been pain but was always pleasure. "Yes."

"And what will you do all morning, while I—" she gasped as he gave a little twist, working it deeper "—suffer?"

He nudged aside her braid. "I'll be hard as a rock, imagining finally getting to slip it from you, imagining how easily you'll take me afterward." A hot, biting kiss pressed between her shoulder blades.

Her shudder was part arousal and part fear. But mostly arousal. "What is it called?"

"The woman who gave it to me used a name I couldn't begin to pronounce in a language I don't understand, so how about we just call it a toy?"

She clenched the pillow to her chest as he pressed harder, stretching her just a little farther. Reaching out, she grabbed his arm and tugged. He wrapped it around her chest and pulled her back against him. "Toys are fun."

This wasn't fun. This was too dark, too erotic, too... much...to be fun.

His lips skimmed her neck and his teeth tested her earlobe with the same deliberate delicacy that the toy tested her rear. "Do you want me to stop?"

She should. Oh, heavens, she should. His hair fell over her shoulder. Between her shoulder blades she could feel the weight of the bullet he always wore around his neck. A reminder of who he was. What he was. Violent. Tender. Sexy. "No."

But she wanted to wish ill upon the woman in his past who'd taught him such sexy games.

He kissed her shoulder.

"Good." The pressure increased. "Just a little bit more, moonbeam. Just take a little bit more."

Lowering her head to his forearm, she twisted it from side to side, but not in denial. She wanted this. And as her body opened, so did her heart. "It's too big."

Another of those sexy laughs. "It's supposed to be big. It's supposed to remind you of me."

"Lands."

She opened her mouth against the strong muscles of his forearm as the pressure reached the fine line between pleasure and pain.

"This is the worst. Just take this last little bit."

She shook her head at the impossibility.

"Bite down if you need to."

She did, hearing him swear as the last of her muscles gave up the unequal battle. Shock rippled through her. Her muscles clamped on the narrower section at the end. She couldn't breathe for a heartbeat, couldn't think, couldn't do anything but absorb the intimate reality, while Tucker swore against her shoulder, his hand cupping her rear, his fingertips sliding through the wet folds of her pussy to find her clit to circle the hard nub in sensual reward.

She didn't know whether to moan or beg, so she encased both in the syllables of his name. "Tucker."

His teeth found her shoulder. "Just breathe now, relax around it."

She did, shuddering as the aching sense of fullness centered the heat in her womb, moaning as his cock, thick and hot, brushed the inside of her thigh.

"When I come back, I'm going to make this signal." He touched two fingers to his thigh. "When I do, you're going to pull up your skirt and bend over."

She made the token protest because, as an independent woman, she needed to, but inside she melted at the thought of him being in control of her sexually. Another throbbing bolt of lust rocked her. She whimpered and he chuckled.

"Yes, baby, it's going to be as hot as you're imagining." The mattress rustled as he stood. Experimentally, she moved her legs. The toy shifted within her that tiny bit necessary to cause her muscles to flex deliciously around it. His fingers grazed the hair guarding her pussy. She was so sensitive that she could feel the heat from his skin. Her pussy ached and flowered, straining for deeper contact. Parting her legs wider, she begged silently for something she didn't understand. He chuckled and tapped the base of the toy. The percussions shot straight to her core.

"Scoot over here."

Scooting meant moving. Moving created all kinds of unique sensations that sent all sorts of conflicting messages to her brain. Too much. Too little. More. This time, when his fingers tapped the base of the device, they lingered, took hold, twisted slightly, before pressing up. A high-pitched cry lodged in her throat as his finger swirled over her clit. Every muscle pulled tight. Every sense waited for the next stroke, the next touch... Oh, heavens!

Never could she imagine a lover taking his woman the way Tucker was taking her. Never could she imagine a woman would enjoy such a taking, but she was apparently a woman of varied tastes, because she loved the feeling of fullness, loved the tension spiraling through her as Tucker continued the game.

He turned her over. Her eyes flew wide as the toy made its presence vividly known in this position, the stretching burn blending with the flare of desire. His hands caught hers, pressing them into the mattress by her head. His hair fell about her face. The bullet charm around his neck tickled the hollow of her throat.

"You're mine."

Yes. His.

He stood. She lay as he left her. Dawn crept through the window, caressing his strong body in its pale light, touching with a lover's attention on the cut of the muscle above his hip, the jut of his cock. She ran her tongue over her lips, remembering his taste. He reached out. It never occurred to her not to take his hand, not to accept his lead as he tugged her to the edge of the bed. The toy shifted. It was too much.

"Easy, baby. Just give yourself a minute."

She didn't think she could. The possession was too complete. Too perfect. "I don't like this."

The softest of kisses skimmed her temple. "You're too new to this to know whether you like it or not."

"But thee do?"

"Hell, yes." His hand slid over her hair to the nape of her neck. With a tug, he pulled her forward. The device rocked within her, stretching her in new ways. The nerve endings in her rear quivered with anticipation and need. Her clit ached. Subtle pressure at the back of her neck urged her toward his cock. She knew what he wanted. She wanted it, too. He caught her hair, tilting her head until her mouth was precisely aligned. His actions were rougher than normal, less controlled. The roughness was also in his voice. He was as excited as she was. "You're going to like this better, too."

How could he know that? How could he know that this game he was playing appealed to a side of her that she didn't know existed? How could he know how her body ached so much that all it would take for her to explode was a touch to her clit. Just one more...

He didn't give it. Instead, he pulled her forward to his cock. She held his gaze as she ran her tongue all around the broad head.

"Open for me." She did, but only a little, making him work for it, loving the sensual flare of his nostrils, the dominance in his grip as he pulled her forward. She laughed as his cock slid over her tongue. He growled.

She held his gaze, matching his passion with her own, challenging him even as she submitted. His thick cock filled her mouth. The thick toy filled her ass. And her love for him filled her senses. It was too much, but not enough. His hand in her hair held her for the thrust of his cock. His fingers stroked her cheeks in an intense gentleness that belied the violence of his passion. He came quickly, his thumbs pressing against the corner of her mouth, his gaze holding hers. A man of violence, tenderness. She closed her eyes, unable to bear the bittersweet hope that maybe he was also a man capable of change.

The touch of his finger against the diamond-hard point of her nipple snapped her eyes open. He was staring at her nipples with a strange look in his eyes. "You'd look pretty with these pierced." With a soft pinch, he centered the fire that burned in her blood. Her breath caught in her throat. "Very pretty."

Women pierced their nipples? She blinked up at him,

unable to speak with his cock in her mouth. His finger curled under her nipple, squeezed.

She moaned and shuddered, rubbing her thighs together, needing him so much.

"Come here, moonbeam."

"Here" was up, into his arms, cradled against his chest. The toy shifted and she cried out at the perfection of the sensation that stopped just short of what she needed.

He laid her down. The sheets were cool against her overheated skin. His big hand skimmed over her body. His lips met hers in a sweet kiss, while his hand on her hip steadied her through the worst of the tension. His forehead dropped to hers. This close, the only signs of his smile were the creases by the corners of his eyes, but she could feel it all around her, like the most cherished of hugs.

"Better?"

She nodded. She did love his smile.

"Want more?"

What could she say except the truth? "Please."

"Good. Lean back on your hands and spread your legs."

"Why?"

The sense of amusement increased. He kissed the tip of her nose. "Do it and find out."

She pretended to hesitate, looking up at him from beneath her lashes. "Do thee dare me?"

"Do you want me to?"

"Hmm…" She drew her knee up slowly, letting it fall to the side. "Maybe."

He laughed. His finger teased a path from her neck, down over her collarbone and between her breasts, trailing over her belly, detouring for a trip around her belly button before wandering lower. His dark eyes holding hers, he flicked her clit. "I double-dog dare you."

Oh, heavens! Fire burned through her, arching her back. Once more. She only needed him to do it once more. Her hips found nothing but the kiss of air. She rocked up on the mattress, moving the toy within her. It was almost enough.

Tucker's big hand spread across her stomach, holding her in place. "Moonbeam, I think we talked about you coming without permission that first night."

"Thee talked about it," she gasped.

"Does this mean that you intend to fight me?"

As if she could. "I intend my pleasure."

His drawl rolled over her in a dark promise. "I intend for your pleasure, too, but I want far more than the tiny one you could have right now."

Tiny? She was going to explode!

His fingers slipped between her thighs, sliding through her slick folds, rubbing delicately until she caught his wrist, not sure whether she wanted him to stop or continue. "Tucker…"

Something cool and metallic closed on her clit. The first bite of pain caught her by surprise. The second sent shivers down her spine. Wonderfully erotic shivers. Oh, heavens! How did he do this to her? Her fingernails dug into his shoulder as she looked down between them. He held what looked like a garnet earring. His fingers twisted and the pressure on her clit grew, one tiny bit at a time.

She couldn't look away as he applied the intimate jewelry, couldn't hold still. "What's that?"

He didn't seem to mind, just moved with her, keeping the pleasure growing. "A clamp."

"What for?"

"To help you with control."

"I don't need control. I need to come." The clamp bit that last little amount, sending the searing pleasure outward. Pleasure tightened her breasts and raced up her arms in cold chills. "Tucker…"

His hand came around her shoulder, supporting her while he rubbed her stomach, helping her through the transition.

"I'm right here, sweet. Just relax and give it a minute."

In a minute, she wouldn't be able to bear it. "I can't."

His fingers slipped down to her mound, pressing just above her pussy. "Yes, you can. Just a minute more. Like the toy, it takes a little getting used to, but it's going to feel very good to you shortly."

From the message her pussy was sending her brain, she couldn't imagine this getting any better. She could feel her control slipping away with every beat of her pulse. He was always taking her control.

"Take it off."

"Later."

She dug her nails into his arms as her orgasm built, froze. "Now."

His kiss was lovingly firm. A denial. "Stand up."

She'd fall flat on her face if she did. "I can't."

"Sure you can. All you need to do is put your feet on the floor and stand."

Easy for him to say, but right now she didn't feel as if she had control of anything, let alone her muscles. If the chaos didn't involve so much pleasure, she'd be scared.

His fingers brushed her cheek, curved under her chin and his right hand took hers. "I'll help."

She could see from the expectant gleam in his eyes that he

knew what was going to happen when she stood. And was looking forward to it. She wanted to kiss him. She just wanted…him.

When she was vertical, the toy shifted position and the clamp pulled under the swing of the garnet. She almost went down under the sensation. Tucker caught her other hand, drew both out to the side, until she was suspended on the pleasure again—so much but not enough.

When she looked up, he wasn't looking at her, but down.

"Now that is a pretty sight."

She couldn't breathe from the desire raging inside her. Her nipples were swollen and ripe, her thighs were wet. She needed relief. Tucker did not have the look of a man ready to satisfy her.

You'll come when I want you to.

"Of what?" she managed to groan. "The sight of a woman about to do murder?"

"You're a pacifist, remember?"

Her ass throbbed, her womb ached and her whole body burned with unfulfilled desire.

"I'm thinking I would be forgiven for this transgression."

On a laugh, Tucker pulled her up against his chest. The heat of his skin against hers was pure bliss. "I told you I'd own you for the time you're mine."

This was more than owning. This was a branding. A manipulation of her senses and her mind.

"You did." His cock, thick and hot, pressed into her stomach. Her pussy twitched and swelled in silent invitation.

"No objections?"

She had a lot of objections, but none of them were as strong as the joy of belonging to Tucker. "Not yet."

Hooking his hand around her neck, he pulled her up onto her toes. His hair fell around them in a curtain of darkness as he kissed her. "Good."

She didn't know how good it was, but she was hoping it would be very good. "For this, thee must make it very good."

He let her down easy. She found her balance as he let her go. She watched disbelievingly as he walked across the room and shrugged on his shirt. The smile he tossed over his shoulder was positively wicked. "It will be."

"When?"

"When I come back."

When he came back? "When will that be?"

He made short work of buttoning his shirt before stepping into his pants. As he tucked the shirttails into his pants, he said, "When I get here."

He said that as if the heat of passion weren't in his eyes, as if his cock didn't strain the fly of his brown wool pants. He said that as if he truly was leaving her like this.

"What if someone comes?"

"Smile and say hello."

As if she didn't have a toy up her butt and the beautiful jewel dangling from her aching clit? She imagined the scene, the forbidden meeting, the tradition. Lust whipped through her. She caught the bureau for support. A whimper escaped.

"I think I won't answer the door."

Tucker grabbed his saddlebag and settled it over his shoulder before picking up his rifle. "That might be a good idea."

The nonchalance he managed in the face of the passion arcing between them had her snapping at his back as he reached the bedroom door, "And maybe I'll lock the door against you!"

He paused, his hand on the doorknob, and turned back. With an almost anticipatory smile, he tugged his black hat lower, casting his eyes into shadow. "You can if you want, but I'd just bust it down."

Three hours later, Sally Mae could completely understand the frayed nerves that led people to violence. Her body, which she'd always thought such a wonderful, stable gift from God, had turned traitor. Under Tucker's tutelage, the hum of arousal was her constant companion, egged on by the clamp. It swung with every move, maintaining her desire at a restless pitch with each erotic tug. And, with every shift, the toy reminded her of Tucker's possession. Despite the fact that she could end her torture with the removal of both devices, she didn't, couldn't. She was a wanton and a sinner, but she was also Tucker's. Nothing proved that more than the heightened state of her senses as she awaited his return. She slapped the dust cloth on the parlor table as she watched for him through the window. The man would be lucky if she didn't knock him to the floor and have her way with him as soon as he walked in the door and to heck with whatever plans he had. Lord, why didn't he return? To take her mind off the agonizingly slow progress of time, she started to sing. And then stopped just as abruptly when she realized it was a hymn.

"Don't stop on my account."

She spun around, her body reacting wildly to the sight of Tucker, standing so big and tall in the doorway, his hair loose about his rough-hewn face, his silver eyes studying her with all the heat she could wish. The table rattled as she bumped it.

"I did not hear thee come in."

"Good." He smiled, revealing even, white teeth. She

wanted to run her tongue over each of them. He stepped into the room. Not for the first time, she marveled at how gracefully he moved for a big man. He reached over and tugged the curtains closed. There was power in the line of his torso, the flex of his buttocks. She bit her lip as fresh cream coated her thighs.

"What will the neighbors think?"

It was a pitiful defense and he obliterated it with simple logic, encased in a knowing smile. "That you were up late with a patient and are taking a nap."

Very deliberately, he placed two fingers against his thigh. She dropped her dusting cloth. When she hesitated, his smile faded, and he made the gesture again. Feeling awkward, exposed and vulnerable, she turned and leaned over the padded arm of the dark green couch.

"That's a good start."

The rough edge of his drawl caught on her wild side, bringing it forward. "Now, pull those skirts up and present yourself for my pleasure."

Oh, dear God, he'd meant it. Balancing herself on her hips, breathless with excitement, Sally Mae reached back and started pulling up her skirt. It wasn't easy. Between her skirt and her petticoat there was a lot of material. She expected Tucker to get impatient, but he didn't. For all the minutes it took to gather everything up—first past her calves, the backs of her knees, then her thighs and finally, those last six inches, which exposed her fully—she could feel him watching. And still he didn't move, just let the tension build. When she was almost ready to scream, a floorboard creaked. A small, startled gasp broke past her control. His palm grazed the inside of her thigh just above her knee. "Very pretty."

His hand continued the climb up her thigh, the rough calluses abrading her skin deliciously. A little flick of the charm, a chuckle at her start, and then one hand braced at the small of her back while the fingers of the other hooked around the base of the toy. "Push back."

She did, shuddering in anticipation. This time Tucker didn't tease, just pulled it out with a steady draw that burned perfectly. As her inner muscles stretched over the fullest part, he paused, keeping her stretched to the fullest, holding her on the knife edge of sensation. Her fingers clenched in a pillow as she struggled to sustain the position in the wake of the tiny explosions detonating in her womb.

"Tucker! Hurry," she groaned.

"Hell, yes." The toy came free with a shocking quickness. Before she could catch her breath, something cool and slick was spread inside her and then his thick cock tucked into the swollen entrance.

"Keep pushing out."

The toy had been big, but he was bigger. She took the slow, burning push of his cock through her tight muscles with an exultant cry of his name. His fingers bit into her shoulders as he drove forward again. Too much. Too little. She shook her head. Not enough, but so much.

The weighted clamp swung along with every thrust of his hips, teasing her with the possibility that she could come, even as it denied her. His cock worked her ass deeper than before, harder than before. Every sense rippled with the delight of his possession. Every nerve ending wanted more. So much more. She grunted and pushed back. "Harder."

"Hold still." The hand in the middle of her back kept her put for the steady rhythm he wouldn't alter. She bucked, trying to force the issue. He grunted and his hand came down in a stinging swat to her right buttock. All that did was add more heat to the fire consuming her.

"All you need to do, moonbeam, is push back."

She didn't want to push back, she wanted to come. Another swat, this one harder, and not so teasing. She clenched down instead. It hurt, but in a good way. It was indescribable. It was wonderful. She did it again.

"Goddamn it, Sally Mae." Tucker's hand fastened into her hair as he pulled her head back. The light sting in her scalp was just one more pleasure to a body drowning in it. With a moan, he drove those last few inches in, until he pressed his balls against the wet pad of her pussy. Grinding his cock into her sensitive ass, the hot flood of his seed soothed her raw flesh. Wild with need, she reached back and grabbed his thighs and pulled him closer, trying to get more, wiggling back for more. "Tucker!"

"Oh God...take it then." He pulled all the way out, leaving her empty for a split second. Deft fingers removed the clamp a second before he flipped her over. As she tumbled back, he caught her leg, holding it high. The next spurt landed on her sensitive clit, leaving it awash in pleasure.

"Come for me, moonbeam."

She arched into the sensation, even as his cock claimed her ass again. The burn of possession combined with the return of feeling to her clit was too much. She exploded, screaming into the pillow, bucking back, her body open and vulnerable, her soul open. Tucker rested over her, taking his weight on his elbows, his hips just grinding against hers as if he, too, felt the need to be closer, get closer. To be inside her the way she wanted to be inside him.

After a minute he asked, "You all right?"

She shook her head. She didn't know. Her clit throbbed as if the orgasm he'd just given her was not enough. Her ass clenched around his cock, milking it. One orgasm wasn't enough. She lied to spare herself the embarrassment of being overeager. "Yes."

His chuckle drifted across her cheek. "Liar. This sweet little body isn't near done."

His withdrawal was no easier than his initial entry. Even softening, he was still a very big man. He worked his cock out by degrees, letting her catch her breath when just the head was inside her. His hand tested the point of their joining, slid across and up to her swollen clit. He circled it once, twice. She couldn't bite back her cry. He pressed a kiss to the inside of her calf.

"Goddamn, I'm tempted to keep you always wet with my seed."

Oh, yes! She pressed up as he pulled out, leaving her clenching on air when she wanted to be squeezing him.

"No." He couldn't leave her like this, with the flames licking at her control and her body crying for more of his.

"Easy." His finger slipped inside her, stirring the embers again. Kissing his way down her leg, he didn't stop until he was kneeling in front of her. Looking down her torso, she saw him part the outer lips of her pussy, exposing the pink and swollen inner folds and her clit, sitting hard and hungry above. He leaned in. She grabbed his hair, holding him back. She was too sensitive. His slightest touch would be too much.

"Shh, baby. Let me. It's going to be a good month before I get back here again, and I need this."

A month? That was forever. Forever without his kiss, his

touch, his mouth. Oh lands, she wanted his mouth but... "I'm too—"

"Sensitive," he finished for her, sliding his finger in and out of her ass in an easy rhythm. With a butterfly caress, his tongue curled around her clit, surrounding it tenderly. He waited until the apprehension left her before he started to suck in the same gentle rhythm that he used on her ass.

"Come for me, Sally." The order flowed across her eager nerve endings with the devastating power of a stroke. His thumb tucked against her pussy with a tenderness that was as devastating as his passion of before. He gave her pleasure, keeping her so full she didn't have an empty place inside. There was just him and her and the beauty they created together. And this time, when she came, it was for him. And herself.

10

"Y ou need to be careful."

Sally looked up from her list. Peter Bloom, the shop-keeper, stood in the entrance to the back room, looking at her from beneath his heavy eyebrows. If he was about to warn her about Tucker, it was the fifth warning she'd received this week. Apparently, along with the town's realization that her mourning period should come to an end, came a nervousness about with whom she intended to end it. "Of what?"

"That Indian."

She placed her list on the front counter. "Thee will have to be more specific."

There were plenty of other men in town whose skin betrayed their mixed heritage. Of course, she knew he was talking about Tucker. She just wasn't going to give him the satisfaction of letting on. Bigotry was a way of life. It had been six weeks since Tucker had ridden out of town with Tracker and Shadow to look for Ari, and she'd become very aware of how deeply it was ingrained in this community. She mentally sighed. A relationship with Tucker would never be possible here. It might not be possible anywhere, even if he could not give up the violence she sensed had begun to weary him, but it could not occur here.

"That uppity Ranger."

Uppity? She'd called Tucker plenty of things—arrogant, decisive, intimidating—but uppity? No. She cocked her head to the side. "You mean Mr. McCade?"

"He's a dangerous man."

"In the stories I've heard, he's a hero."

"Huh." He snorted. His beady eyes narrowed. "He spends an awful lot of time over to your place."

Sally Mae had often thought the way Peter's eyebrows nearly met over his muddy-green eyes was indicative of his narrow-mindedness. His accusation was just proof that she was right.

"He sleeps in the barn."

"It ain't right, what with your husband being dead and all."

It wasn't right that her husband was dead. It wasn't right that her parents had been killed. It wasn't right that a good man like Tucker wasn't seen for what he was. "My husband hired him to help around the place and to provide me with protection." The latter was a lie, but it was an excuse Peter would believe. "With Jonah's death, I was afraid to be alone and kept him on."

There was a scuffling sound a few feet from the corner. There was no mistaking the brown-stained, slouchy hat she could just make out over the row of canned goods. "As Lyle pointed out last week, it's not safe for a woman to live alone," Sally Mae added, as if Lyle's threat had actually been an expression of concern.

Peter made a sound between spitting and snorting. Probably choking on his wad of chewing tobacco. It was a disgusting habit.

"It still ain't right."

"I didn't notice thee saying anything when Lyle recuperated in my house."

Peter scoffed and spit tobacco juice at a spittoon in the corner. It hit with a repulsive clang. "Lyle was near death's door. The Indian's healthy."

And more of a man than Peter would ever be, no matter how much he sought the truth that came with the inner light. It was an uncharitable thought. Sally Mae didn't care. "And I, for one, am grateful for that." She included both men in her glance. "There are some elements in this town that make a woman afraid to be alone."

Peter stepped up to the other side of the counter and set the box he was carrying on the polished wood top. The corner covered half of her list. "All the more reason for you to be careful of your reputation. Doctoring the sick is a man's job."

Sally Mae's temper slipped another notch. "If the men of Lindos could take care of the rabid element in this town, we *would* have a man doing the job. Unfortunately, there seems to be a lack of capable men." She tugged her list free, turned it and slid it across the counter. "That being the case, I feel safer knowing there's a Texas Ranger bedding down in my barn."

"I thought you didn't hold with violence?"

"I don't believe in violence, but I believe in preventative measures, and I believe Mr. McCade's reputation is strong enough to dissuade the most persistent of miscreants."

"A husband would be better protection," Lyle said.

Sally Mae barely restrained herself from rolling her eyes as Lyle sauntered closer. Lyle's insistence that she should accept his suit had not diminished with his departure from her house. She had no interest in the man. It wasn't so much the fact that he was overweight, but the fact that he was lazy. Sally Mae had no use for lazy men.

"I'm still in mourning for my husband. Entertaining the suit of another would be sacrilegious and disrespectful."

Lyle leaned his elbow against the counter, standing closer than was decent, his gaze taking a leisurely path from her head to her toes. "You can't be in mourning forever."

She could if she was clever.

"I owe my husband the respect he deserves. He was a good man."

Peter grunted and ripped open the box. "He was that."

He started taking out cans and putting them on the counter. Beets. Can after can of beets. She sighed. She'd been hoping this week's shipment would include peas. She'd woken up this morning with a taste for them. Unfortunately, her garden wouldn't come in for another month.

She gave her list another nudge. Peter took it this time. Unfortunately, Lyle wasn't so good at taking hints.

"Mourning periods aren't that long out here."

She moved a step away as his body odor encompassed her. Her palms grew damp, the way they always did when she was nervous. She didn't know why she was nervous. These two weren't anything to make a woman scared. Maybe it was the way they looked at her. Or maybe it was the bigger truth they represented. She was going to have to do something soon to change her position as she feared tolerance for her mourning period was over. At least in the men's eyes. That was going to be a problem.

Peter started grabbing items off the shelves, putting them in the box he'd just emptied. "You got enough fresh meat?" he asked. "I've got some venison hanging out back I can sell you."

"I thank thee, but Mr. McCade keeps me supplied as part of his payment for the bed in the barn."

"He's been gone for quite a spell."

"He keeps the smokehouse full."

"Any idea when he's coming back?"

She didn't like the look in Peter's eyes or the way Lyle seemed to hang in anticipation on the answer, so she lied. She was doing a lot of that lately. "I imagine any day now, which reminds me, could thee add a pound of coffee beans to the list?"

"No wonder he's getting uppity. The man's living pretty high off the hog for an Injun." Lyle sneered.

Sally bit her tongue. One whiff of how uppity Tucker was being and there would be no safe place for him in the state, but it did gall her, having to bite her tongue when such a small man said such small things.

"An awful lot of sugar in this order," Peter commented.

She forced a smile. "It's my birthday this week. I'm going to indulge in a cake, to celebrate."

"I'm all for indulging," Lyle hinted.

Peter smiled. It seemed genuine. "Well, happy birthday then."

She ignored Lyle. "Thank you."

"How old will you be?" Lyle asked.

She didn't turn to look at him. Everything about the man made her skin crawl. She'd treated him because that was the way—do no harm, help when thee can. But it was harder with some people than it was with others.

"That's not a question a man asks a lady," Peter snapped.

"It ain't as if she's fresh off the vine," Lyle retorted.

No, she wasn't, which meant she wasn't fooled by pretty

compliments or cowed by veiled innuendo and implied intimidation.

"It's fine, Mr. Bloom." She met Lyle's gaze directly. "I'm
twenty-six."

Peter tallied the order and told her the price. Reaching into
her reticule, Sally Mae pulled out the last of her precious
coins. Jonah's savings had been slight. He'd always said God
would provide, and she'd expected him to provide through
Jonah because Jonah had been a very good man and God had
rewarded him constantly. But Jonah had died and everything
had changed, and she wasn't as good at commanding a steady
income as Jonah had from his doctoring skills. Placing the
coins on the counter, she pulled the box toward her. "Thank
thee very much."

"There's a social this Saturday," Peter mentioned. "Are
you going?"

"I don't think so." She'd only attended one social since
Jonah's passing. And look what had come of that.

"There'd be plenty of men there willing to dance with you,"
Peter said, something in his gaze making her uneasy again.

"I'm not interested in dancing." She picked up the box and
turned. Lyle blocked her way.

"I'd be first in line."

The same look was in his eyes as Peter's. She flinched as
realization dawned. Lust. They lusted after her. And Peter was
a married man!

"It wouldn't be right." She could tell from the flash of
anger in Lyle's eyes that her mourning excuse was wearing
thin. She was going to have to make some decisions sooner
than she had expected. "But I thank thee."

Lyle didn't move. The rank aroma of body odor swept over

her. Practically ripping the box from her arms, he said, "I'll carry that for you."

She had no choice but to say, "I thank thee," and follow. Feeling very conspicuous, she walked down the street in Lyle's wake. Lyle didn't slow when the wood walk ended, just kept on as if the mud from last night's rain wasn't a deterrent. And maybe for him it wasn't, but she wasn't used to wearing grime like new shoes. She stopped at the edge. Someone had placed a board over a muddy rut. The hard soles of her shoes clicked across the rough surface, making hollow sounds that were so conspicuous she felt like everyone was watching and speculating why Lyle Hartsmith was carrying her purchases.

She took a breath to stabilize the frustration roiling inside. She hated being manipulated. And that was exactly what Lyle was doing. Manipulating her in such a way as to give the impression that she favored his suit. Hazel stepped out of her house and stood in the doorway. Her only reaction to the sight was the slow twist of her hands in her apron. A woman had to be practical out here. No doubt she'd decided Sally Mae had reached the end of her resources and no doubt the gossip would start as soon as she turned the corner. Why did everything have to be so complicated lately?

"So, what you think?"

Sally Mae blinked. How long had Lyle been talking to her? "About what?"

"Going for a picnic with me this Sunday."

She looked at the girth of his belly. Preparing a picnic for Lyle would take her all morning. And no doubt add another layer of fat to the layer he already had. She couldn't help but compare him to Tucker. It would probably take her a day and a half to cook enough food to fill Tucker's big frame, but it would all probably go to muscle. She remembered how defined the muscle was. Sharp cuts stretching over the bone without an ounce of softness anywhere. Tucker needed to eat more. She smiled, imagining his reaction if she told him he needed softening. Lyle mistook her smile for agreement.

"Good, then we're settled on Sunday."

Oh, heck. "I'm afraid I'm not free Sunday."

"Your religious teachings forbid you to socialize on Sunday?" He didn't give her a chance to reply. "Because I've heard some newfangled religions have lots of strict rules about things like that."

She didn't waste her breath telling him there was nothing newfangled about her beliefs. She could, however, use his misconceptions. "They do have that."

He gave her a strange look, but didn't say anything.

Two men leaning against the side of the saloon straightened and touched their hat brims as she passed. The speculation in their eyes did nothing to take the edge off her anger. It was a shame she was against violence, because she would love to hit Lyle on the back of his arrogant head. Or kick him in his broad posterior. With one miserable move he'd shattered the illusion that had worked to protect her for a year. She fumed the rest of the way to her home.

At last they reached her house. With a complete disregard for the flowerpot hanging from the gate, Lyle kicked it open. She'd just painted that gate last week. His boot left a black smudge. He stood to the side. "After you."

To squeeze through, she'd have to brush against his belly. That was not an option. She gave Lyle her most congenial smile. "Thee first. The box must be heavy."

She could tell from the way he was breathing, and the sweat on his florid face, that carrying the package had taken its toll. He puffed out his chest as if she couldn't see the redness of his face or the sweat on his brow. "Doesn't weigh a thing."

Riding on his lie and his delusion that he was impressing her, he headed up the path. Taking another breath, holding on to her patience with an effort, she wrinkled her nose at the stench of sweat. New mixed with old. Lyle was not fastidious about his personal hygiene.

When he got to the porch, he looked expectant. She gritted her teeth. From the way he planted his feet and shifted his weight he wasn't a budging off her porch easily. Holding out her hands, she reached the box. "Thank thee very much."

"I'll take it in for you."

There was no way she was letting him into her house again. "That's not necessary. I thank thee."

The coldness and her voice had no effect on his determination. If anything, his tone just got more insinuating.

"On a morning like this, a glass of lemonade wouldn't go amiss."

She ignored the hint and practically wrestled the box out of his arms. "Do they serve it at the saloon?"

His eyes narrowed. She wished she hadn't made that a question.

"I don't know." He reached for the doorknob. As quickly as she could, she stepped between him and the door, using the wooden box as leverage. Still, his fingers managed to brush her hip. Another mistake. His eyes narrowed more and a small smile curved his mouth. Oh, no.

"I can always do without the lemonade."

"I wouldn't want thee to." Hitching the box on her hip, she fumbled behind her for the knob.

His hand settled against the doorjamb beside her head. His belly pressed the box into her side. The bag of sugar wobbled on the top. "There are other things that could be more refreshing."

A tingle of warning went down her spine. She was now effectively trapped between the door and him. He was watching her mouth as though he wanted a kiss. A shiver of distaste went through her. Her fingers closed around the knob. "I thank thee very much for thy help."

He leaned in. "You'll find I can be a very helpful man to know."

With a bump of her hip, she dislodged the sugar. When Lyle bent down to retrieve it, she slipped inside and turned the lock. She took another step back, tripped on the braided throw rug and tumbled backward. A hand closed over her upper arm. Another slid across her mouth. Oh, dear God! She was being accosted in her own home and she couldn't even scream.

"How long has this been going on?" a deep voice rumbled in her ear.

Tucker. Relief surged through Sally Mae in a debilitating rush. Her knees gave out. Tucker's hand left her mouth and took the groceries from her hands. The other pulled her into his embrace. For a moment, just a moment, she leaned her cheek against his chest and breathed the scent of horse and man. He must have just arrived, otherwise he would have bathed. Unlike Lyle, Tucker was fastidious about his personal appearance. She pressed closer, listening to the steady beat of his heart, her fingers twisting his shirt. She'd always thought of Lyle as harmless. Too lazy to be a threat. It was disconcerting to realize she'd read him wrong.

A knock came at the door. "You all right in there, Mrs. Schermerhorn?"

Tucker set the box on the floor and reached for the handle. The harsh planes of his face were set in lines of granite. There was no doubt what he would do if he opened that door. She pushed his hand away and shook her head. He narrowed his gaze.

"Ma'am? I heard something."

She smoothed her hair and straightened her spine, shaking her head at Tucker once more, for good measure. "I tripped on the rug. I'm fine."

There was a pause and then, "I've got your sugar."

Was it her imagination or was there some sort of tacky innuendo in that statement? She wrinkled her nose and tucked a loose strand of hair behind her ear. "That's nice of thee, but—" But what? Tucker folded his bare arms across his massive chest and cocked his eyebrow at her. She frowned at him as she called out, "I don't want it now."

"The package didn't split open. It's fine."

"It touched the ground. Just throw it away."

"You throw things away just because they touch the ground?"

Good, let him think she was a spendthrift. A man as lazy as Lyle had to worry about things like that. "Yes. Goodbye, Lyle."

With a sigh of relief she heard his heavy tread on the steps. He was leaving. She didn't immediately turn around. She needed a moment to gather her composure. Tucker's hand on her arm didn't give her a choice. Neither did the finger he tucked under her chin. His beautiful eyes narrowed.

"Lyle scares you."

Darn, the man was discerning.

"It's more like he makes me nervous. The only man who's ever courted me was Jonah and it's different among Friends. Men aren't so…blatant."

His pinky stroked down her throat. "You think he's courting you?"

No. "Yes."

"You can do a lot better than him."

She jerked her chin to the side. "Really?"

He forestalled the attempt by simply catching her chin between his fingers, holding her face up to his. This close, she could see the flare of his nostrils. Anger or frustration?

"If you are not encouraging his suit, why the hell let him carry your purchases home?"

Angry. He was angry, but not nearly as much as she. The effects of the past hour were just beginning to hit her. "There wasn't any way not to let him. In case thee haven't noticed, Lyle can be very obtuse when it suits him."

Tucker frowned. "Obtuse?"

She made a motion with her hand, reaching for the groceries. "Dense."

Tucker glared at the door. "I'll give him that."

Holding the box to her, hiding behind the fragile protection of having something to do, she headed for the kitchen. "When did thee get back?"

"Just in time to see Lyle declare his intentions."

She placed the box on the table. Crockett scratched at the back door. "Stop it, Tucker."

He came into the kitchen and leaned against the doorjamb. "Stop what?"

"Stop pretending to be jealous of a man who'd be lucky to stand in thy shadow."

He watched unnervingly as she unloaded the box. "I've got news for you, moonbeam. I'm plenty jealous."

She paused, a can in her hand. "Of what?"

"His right to state his intentions."

The can fell from her hand and rolled across the table. She just stared at him as he caught it. Him with his size, his confidence, his always-bare arms that showcased his strength. "Nothing to say?"

"We are having an affair."

"So you keep saying."

"It was only supposed to be for one night."

He placed the can on the table. "That's stretched into two months."

He was right. "I cannot marry a man of violence."

"Honey, what you can't marry is an Indian."

"Thee are a good man, Tucker McCade."

He shook his head. "You refuse to understand."

"I refuse to live the lie that others believe."

"Which leaves us where?"

She took the sack of coffee out of the box. "I don't know. My life is not thine."

There was silence as he watched her unpack. Silence laden with sadness, hope. Silence that draped around her like a wail. "I've got to leave again."

No doubt the reason involved killing. The silent wail grew louder in her mind. How could a man so tender with her be so ruthless with others? She picked up the now-empty box. "When will thee be back?"

"I don't know." He came up behind her and took the box

out of her hand and set it on the table, effectively trapping her between a chair and the edge. His lips brushed her hair. An apology?

"Did you get everything you wanted?"

She shook her head.

"What did you want, baby?"

"Peas."

"You like canned peas?"

She could tell from his tone that he didn't get the attraction.

She shrugged, trying not to let on how much she wanted them. "I've had a powerful hankering for them lately."

His fingers brushed her throat. "If I pass by a mercantile, I'll check to see if they have any."

Saliva flooded her mouth. "That's not necessary."

He smiled. "But I'll check anyway."

His fingers traveled downward over the collar of her dress to the placard of buttons running down the front, continuing their journey until they rested just below her breasts. His touch was so light that it was impossible to feel through the heavy cotton, but it didn't matter. Her imagination could easily fill in the blanks. Nerve endings stirred and came to life. Her nipples hardened. She watched as he skimmed the backs of his fingers up and out. Her next breath wouldn't come as he slowly brushed the small peaks. He did it again. Tears burned her eyes.

"I'll miss you."

Surprise jerked her eyes up. They never talked about the feelings between them. Her vision blurred. She couldn't cry. "I would think thee would have had thy fill."

His fingers tucked under her braids with incredible ease and he pulled her forward. "I think we've got a bit to go before we reach that state."

His pinky pressed in at the vulnerable point that always seemed to command her obedience. Her lips parted beneath his, demanding his passion, and when he withheld it, she bit at his. If this was a goodbye, she wanted a kiss to remember. Just in case. She closed her eyes on the possibility he wouldn't acknowledge. He would come back to her.

Tucker didn't disappoint. He never did. His hard lips moved over hers, his teeth nipping, until her mouth opened farther and her breath left in a gasp. When the kiss ended, she clung to him with her hands, her mouth, her heart. When he pulled back, she opened her eyes to find him staring down at her, a strange expression in his gaze.

"Stay the hell away from Lyle."

She would have bristled at the order, except she could tell he was concerned. "I'll do my best."

He kissed her hard and fast. "Succeed."

11

Avoiding Lyle was not as easy as it should be. Over the next two weeks, he seemed to be everywhere. And every time he got near, it was another innuendo, another furtive touch. And every time Sally Mae rebuffed his advances his hostility increased. To the point that, when the knock came at the back door that morning, her heart jumped into her throat. "Who's there?"

"Hazel."

Hazel? Carefully placing the instrument she was sterilizing back into the carbolic from which she'd just removed it, Sally Mae wiped her hands on her apron. They were shaking. She was going to have to do something about Lyle. She stood. The room spun. She steadied herself with a hand on the table before taking a deep breath. "Just a minute."

"Hurry. It's Davey. He cut his hand badly."

The room came back into focus. Sally Mae rushed to the door, opened it, and there was Hazel, holding little Davey on her hip. The boy had his father's height, and his legs tangled halfway to Hazel's calves while his face was buried in her neck. His injured hand was tucked out of sight between their two bodies.

Sally Mae stepped back, blocking Crockett's attempt to come in with a raise of her hand. "Come on in."

Crockett whined. She shook her head. He flopped back down to the porch with a huff that had her smiling. He was a character.

Hazel hurried in. "I just took my eyes off him for a second." She stopped a few feet into the kitchen and looked around, half-dazed. "Where do you want us?"

"The kitchen table will be fine."

She'd meant the chair before it, but Hazel plunked Davey on the sturdy table and gave him a stern look even as she held him close. Looking over his shoulder, she explained, "In that time, he decided to cut his own bread." Another breath and then a very controlled, "With a butcher knife."

Oh. Sally Mae's stomach dropped. Had he cut the tendons? She couldn't do anything about cut tendons. For six years she'd assisted Jonah in surgeries, absorbed every nuance she could of every procedure she'd seen, but she didn't have his education and she dreaded the day she would be called on to do more than dig out bullets and sew up cuts. Dreaded the day her lack of formal schooling would cost a patient an arm, a leg, their life. And that dread was so much worse with a child. Worse than a child's lack of understanding of why she sometimes had to hurt them more to make them better was their absolute certainty that she *could* make them better.

"Is that what happened?" she asked Davey, taking his bandaged hand in hers.

He nodded, peeking at her from the corner of his eye.

"Well, let me take a look then."

He shook his head, keeping his arm locked so she couldn't turn his hand over.

"Please?"

All her "please" got was a jutting out of his lower lip.

"You do as you're told, Davey!"

Sally smiled to counter Hazel's sharpness. "I'll be very careful."

The muscles in his wrist relaxed. She turned his hand over and mentally grimaced. There were just some wound locations that bled a lot. Hand wounds were one of them. The knowledge didn't help her keep her smile solid as she turned his hand over and saw the amount of blood, old and new on the white cotton. Likely it was going to need stitches. She pulled out the chair at the end of the table.

"Could thee sit him here?"

Hazel nodded. Davey clung and shook his head.

"He's a little frightened."

"I can understand that." Placing her hand on Davey's back, Sally Mae tried a different approach. "Would thee like to sit in thy mother's lap?"

That got her a nod and another cautious glance.

"Then that's what we'll do, honey."

Hazel gave her a weak smile. Sally Mae couldn't imagine what she was going through. Losing her husband eight months ago had been devastating enough, but then to lose Billy… Though little more than a boy, Billy had been able to do a man's work. Sally didn't know how Hazel was managing economically or emotionally, but Davey was all she had left. Hazel stood.

Sally Mae's palm retained the sensation of the boy's sturdy back. She closed her fingers around the sensation, longing striking her hard as Hazel murmured softly to Davey and turned. Sally had wanted a child for years, but Jonah had wanted to wait, so they had practiced restraint and contraception. While the methods hadn't worked for many couples, they'd been all too effective for her. To the point she'd wondered if she were infertile… And now Jonah was gone and she had nothing. Water under the bridge.

Please, Lord, give me the strength. Not to resent. Not to long for what could have been. She thought of Tucker and the impossibility of loving him. *Not to be bitter.*

Sally Mae waved Hazel to the chair, and Davey settled into her lap. Before reaching for his hand, Sally carefully slid surgical instruments out of sight behind a tin of cooled bread. No sense scaring him. "Now, let's see what this looks like."

Davey wrinkled his nose. "It stinks in here."

"Davey!"

She smiled at his mother's reproach. "I wasn't expecting thee." She unwound the layers of cloth. "Thee caught me in the middle of cleaning my tools."

Davey's little body tensed as she got down to the last wrapping. He wasn't dreading this any more than she was. Hopefully, he hadn't cut any tendons. Hopefully, the knife had been clean. Hopefully, two weeks from now she wouldn't have to perform a first amputation because infection had set in. She looked up into Davey's face, his puffy cheeks and red eyes. "I promise I'll be very careful with this last one."

His lip quivered. "I made a big hole."

More to distract him from the unwrapping than to get a description of the wound she asked, "A straight line or a curvy one?"

Hazel answered. "A straight line."

Sally caught Davey's gaze and held it. She didn't want him to see the cut and get scared again. "Is that right, Davey?"

After a little hiccup, Davey nodded. "Straight."

Ignoring the evidence on his face, Sally asked, "And thee didn't cry?"

He pulled his little shoulders square. "Only a little."

"Your father would have been so proud of thee." She couldn't imagine any father not proud of the sturdy little boy. It was so hard to understand God's will sometimes, and the Lord taking Davey's father in a flash flood was one of those times. Every time she looked at Hazel, saw the toll the tragedy in her life had taken on her once sunny nature, she struggled to accept all over again. Her faith wasn't what it should be. Sometimes she thought Tucker had it easier with his lack of faith. Things just happened. Life turned to manure, and he didn't question why, because there were some things over which he easily accepted that he didn't have control.

The last of the bandage came off. The wound was a large slice. Not as deep as she'd feared. "Thee were indeed very brave."

"Is it bad?" Hazel asked.

Sally Mae cut a warning glance at Hazel before softening her smile for Davey. "I just need thee to wiggle thy fingers."

"You talk funny."

"I do. Wiggle please?"

Very carefully, obviously fearing pain, Davey gave them a brief clench. Not a full wiggle, but he could move them and that was the important thing.

His lip quivered and he looked up at his mom, obviously wanting to cry, but being brave like she'd asked. Sally Mae wished she'd kept her mouth shut about his dad being proud of him. This young boy shouldn't be worried about being a man.

A knock came at the door. Sally Mae's heart leaped into her throat, but this time with excitement. There was only one man who knocked like that. Tucker was back. Her pulse beat in her ears and the breathless excitement that always ensnared her in his presence flared. "Come in."

The door opened and Tucker stepped into the room, dominating it with his broad shoulders and the force of his personality. Davey's eyes went wide. Hazel tensed. Sally Mae held on to her smile.

"Hello, Mr. McCade."

He tipped his hat. "Ma'am." His gaze fell to Davey. "Everything all right?"

"Davey had a run-in with a kitchen knife."

It only took two long strides for Tucker to reach her side. The scent of leather and man came with him, embracing her in a familiar hug as he eyed Davey's hand. It took everything she had to control the urge to turn her head and kiss his bare arm. Why did the man never wear a shirt with sleeves under his vest?

"Looks like the knife won."

"Davey's been very brave."

Tucker took the boy's hand in his. It was like the hand of a giant comparatively, but Davey didn't even wince. Tucker could be as gentle as he could be violent. "That's going to leave a scar."

Davey's eyes grew bigger.

Tucker smiled one of his rare smiles. Sally Mae couldn't help but stare. It seemed like forever since she'd seen him. And standing this close, all her senses were making her aware of him.

"A couple weeks and you'll be able to show it off."

Clearly, that thought hadn't occurred to Davey.

The last of his tears dried as realization dawned. "Yeah."

Sally Mae shared an amused glance with Hazel. The other woman shook her head and mouthed, *Boys.*

Tucker flexed the boy's fingers. "Good thing you didn't cut the tendons though. A thing like that can cripple a man."

Davey nodded, staring at Tucker with rapt attention, absorbing every word as if it were gospel. Clearly the boy had a case of hero worship.

Tucker tested Davey's pinky. "Bet your mom told you not to touch the knives."

A little nod of his head.

"You listen to your mother about such things."

Davey's expression was stuck somewhere between terror and awe. He was at the age where any man's attention mattered to him. Tucker was a big man, both in size and reputation.

"Until you're big enough, you do what your ma says. A man's got no right worrying his mother."

Davey pouted. "She treats me like a baby."

Sally Mae hid a smile at Tucker's blink. He slowly took off his hat. Sunlight streamed through the window, glinting off the blue-black of his hair as he set his battered hat carefully on the table. "There's a proper way to do things, son, and an improper way. And as you found out, the wrong way isn't the best."

Davey's lip stuck out mutinously. Tucker nodded to Hazel, his silver eyes striking in the bright light. "If you don't mind, ma'am, when Davey's done here, I'll teach him the proper technique with a knife."

Davey bounced on Hazel's lap. "Please, Ma!"

"I'm not sure..." Hazel's protest trailed off.

Sally got out her needle and thread. She wouldn't have thought Tucker would know what to do with a six-year-old boy. Then again, she hadn't thought he'd know what to do with a puppy, but he was comfortable with both. As Tucker released Davey's hand, she had the thought that he'd be a wonderful father. But—she glanced at Davey's excited expression—maybe a little too eager to pass on his wisdom.

"He's so little."

That got Hazel a glare from Davey, and a cock of an eyebrow from Tucker.

"Little or not, it seems to me he's pretty determined. A little education could save his hide."

Hazel bit her lip.

"Mr. McCade has a point," Sally Mae added.

"Yeah, Ma, he's got a point. You know I can be stubborn."

The corner of Tucker's lips twitched. "I won't take it far, ma'am. I'll just make sure he learns what's proper."

Sally had trouble suppressing her own smile at the excitement on the boy's face. She had no doubt that what Tucker thought was proper was a far cry from the murder and mayhem the boy was imagining.

With a sigh, Hazel gave up the battle. "I guess it'll be all right."

"You can't stop the boy from growing up, ma'am. The only thing you can do is try to see that he grows up sensible."

Hazel nodded. "Thank you, then."

"You're welcome."

Davey whooped, then saw the needle and thread and froze. His little face went white. She felt like a monster. Tucker's hand brushed hers as he reached for his hat. Hazel's eyes narrowed at the familiarity. The reaction, so typical of townsfolk, irritated Sally Mae. Tucker had done nothing to deserve such suspicion. Quite the opposite. He risked his life for the people of the territory, constantly fighting battles they couldn't or wouldn't. Like hunting Billy's killer. He should be seen as an equal. Yet he wasn't.

Though he couldn't have missed Hazel's reaction, Tucker's tone was as level and as calm as always. "Mrs. Schermerhorn is a good nurse. As good at medicine as any doctor. She'll stitch you up right."

"It'll hurt," Davey said.

"Yeah, it will."

Tucker caught Sally Mae's eye. Davey stared as she reached for the needle. Swallowed.

Tucker pulled out a braided strip of leather. "I could teach you a Ranger trick to deal with the pain." He held the strip up. "You bite on this real hard and you won't feel a thing."

Still in the grip of hero worship, Davey opened his mouth. Tucker slid the leather between his lips, his expression church-serious, if she discounted the slight crinkling at the corners of his eyes. He cocked his eyebrow at the boy. "Are you ready?"

Davey nodded. Tucker patted his back and nodded at Sally Mae. "Go ahead."

"I'm going to have to clean the wound."

"Davey's ready for it, aren't you, Davey?"

Sally Mae hesitated after picking up a small metal bowl of water. Hazel rubbed her hands soothingly up and down her son's arms. Davey swallowed and nodded his head.

Tucker met Sally's gaze. "The sooner you get started the sooner Davey and I can get on with our lessons."

He was right—putting off the inevitable accomplished nothing. "Let's get started."

Sally Mae picked up the last of the rags and looked out the window. Tucker was sitting on the edge of the back porch with Davey. He was showing Davey the proper way to hold a knife. At least that's what she thought he was doing. Both were bent over the leather sheath lying across Tucker's thigh. Crockett chewed a stick at their feet.

Hazel came up beside her with a bowl of dirty water. "I'd dump this out, but I hate to disturb them."

"It'll keep."

Hazel put the bowl down on the cabinet shelf, watching the two through the window. "I'd forgotten how much difference a man makes in a little boy's life."

A pang of jealousy stabbed deep. Had Hazel set her cap for Tucker? A second later she felt small for the uncharitable thought.

"Tucker won't let him do anything dangerous." Sally watched as Tucker put his hand over Davey's and adjusted his grip, helping him in deference to his bandaged hand. "He knows he's just a little boy."

"At his age, Billy had his own knife for cutting bait." Hazel's breath caught. "His father gave it to him."

"It's been hard for thee since thy husband passed."

Hazel nodded. "Too hard." She wrapped her hands in her skirt. "I'm taking Davey back East."

"Back to your family?"

"Yes. There's nothing for me here anymore."

Involuntarily, Sally Mae's gaze went to Tucker. She'd thought going back home was her answer, but she wasn't sure anymore. "I'm going to miss thee."

"Thank you." Hazel wiped at the tears on her cheeks. "Maybe going home will…" She shrugged. "I don't know. Make everything stop hurting so much."

Sally didn't know what to say. "I hope so."

In companionable silence, they cleaned the small mess in

the kitchen. Hazel looked out the window again. "He's good with children."

"He's a good man."

Hazel slid her a look from the corner of her eye. "A woman could do worse."

"Yes." Much worse.

"Too bad he's Indian."

Her hands clenched on the cloth. "In God's eyes all men are equal."

"But not in all men's eyes." Hazel turned to face her. "There's been talk, Sally Mae. And some of the men have been making threats."

Oh, heavens. "Against Tucker?"

"And you."

The shock of that took the strength from her knees. "Why?"

"Because you didn't look at them."

"But most of them are married."

"You'll find most men aren't too particular about that."

"They should be."

Hazel stared at her, sighed and shook her head. "I can't say I approve of such relationships—"

"I don't remember asking for thy approval."

Hazel shook her head and wiped down the counter. "It's a hard row going against the tide, but I've heard the Europeans are more open to more...difficult relationships."

Difficult. That was one way to put it. "The color of Tucker's skin is not my concern."

"It's not?"

She needn't sound like there couldn't be another issue. "Tucker's ways are not mine."

Hazel didn't pretend to misunderstand. And why should

she? Jonah's and her beliefs had been the grist for gossip for years. "Every marriage requires compromise."

She knew that. Tucker ruffled the boy's hair and smiled. In moments like this, it was easy to believe that he could give up the violence. He turned and the sun highlighted the battered bullet he wore around his neck. Always, there was a reminder of what he was. A man born to this land. Comfortable with its violence. Capable of surviving whatever came his way. A man who thrived on the challenge of it.

"Sometimes compromise isn't enough."

Hazel sighed. "You really feel that strongly about his job?"

"Violence is abhorrent to me."

"Well, you wouldn't be doing the hitting."

"But I couldn't sanction it for my children."

"The only law here is the law a man can make for himself, and if a man can't defend himself, all he's doing is setting him and his loved ones up to be victims."

And the cycle continued. "I know that's the belief."

Hazel let the curtain drop back. "So maybe I'm not the only one who would be better off going back home."

She'd had that thought herself. "Maybe."

But every time she did, she got a sense of panic in her gut. The feeling that going backward was wrong. That her future was here. And every time she thought of here, she thought of the longing she saw in Tucker's eyes every now and then. For a man who courted violence, how could she so often see in him such a need for peace? "I haven't decided."

The kitchen curtains fluttered as they were once again dropped back into place. Tucker resisted the urge to shake his head. If the women were so worried as to what he was going to teach the little boy, why had they let him take him outside? The curtain pulled aside again. He could make out the blond of Sally Mae's hair. He could understand Hazel's concern. Davey was all she had left, and his reputation wasn't the cleanest, but Sally Mae? He held the sheath while Davey carefully extracted the knife with his good hand, blade pointed away as he'd been instructed. It bothered him soul deep that Sally Mae checked up on him. He'd thought she knew him better, that maybe they'd reached an understanding these past couple months. It wasn't the first time he'd been wrong. Likely wouldn't be the last. But he'd be lying to say it didn't hurt.

"Did I do it right, Mr. McCade?"

"You did it just fine."

Davey looked up and smiled at him, showing the gap between his front teeth. "Thanks."

It was such a small thing, showing a boy how to safely handle a knife, but it was a good thing. He wondered if Caine's wife would have a little boy or little girl. He hoped to hell Desi had a boy. He didn't think any of Hell's Eight were ready for a little girl in their midst. Davey's smile faded. Tucker mentally cursed. Hell, he'd forgotten to smile back.

"You're doing fine, son. Just remember—a knife can be a very good friend to a man, but you always have to show it the proper respect or it will turn on you."

Davey nodded. "And I always have to use the proper knife for the proper job."

"And what do you do if you don't know?"

"I don't touch until I ask."

Tucker smiled and ruffled Davey's too-long, shaggy brown hair. "You're a smart kid."

Again Tucker was amazed at how that small bit of attention

puffed the boy up. He thought of his childhood. He couldn't recall any soft moments with his dad. If he screwed up, he got beaten. If he didn't, maybe he wouldn't get beaten, but there was never a time when the touch of his father's hand had filled him with confidence. And his mother? He remembered the downtrodden woman who walked with her head down and seemed to haunt the shadows. By the time he'd been born she was so fear ridden that she wouldn't stand up for herself, let alone him. He brought his hand back to his side and curled his fingers into a fist as the desperation from the past came calling. There'd been plenty of times when he was little that he'd silently pleaded for her to help him, show him she cared, maybe by sneaking to his bed and treating his wounds the way he'd sneaked over to treat hers after his father left the house. But she never had. As he'd gotten older, he'd just settled for praying she'd get a backbone, though what the hell he'd expected her to do against his father's muscle, he didn't know. He'd just wished that once, just once, she'd make the effort.

The window curtains fluttered again. Sally Mae, checking on them. He smiled ruefully, picturing Sally in the place of his mother. For all that Sally held to her pacifist beliefs, he was willing to bet no man, husband or not, would lay a hand on her child. He wasn't sure how she'd arrange it, but he knew in his gut that she would. She was a woman whose ability to love ran as deep as her convictions. She would protect their children. The pronoun stopped him dead in his mental tracks. *Their* children. Shit.

Take her…

Like a tease, Shadow's suggestion sidled up to his scruples, tempting him with the possibility. Damn Shadow. He had no right to place such ideas in Tucker's head. Not a man like him.

A wife, kids, a family—they weren't for him. His taint would haunt them. And even if he could have that dream, the only woman with whom he wanted to have them was out of reach.

He took the knife from Davey and slid it back into the sheath. It was a small knife, but it still had a sharp edge. "You hold it this time, but be careful," Tucker said as he handed the sheath to Davey.

Tongue stuck in his cheek, Davey placed the sheath awkwardly in his lap. The curtains fell closed, leaving a blank window upon which his memories could paint their vivid images.

You're always dreaming big, boy. That's a bad habit.

The memory of his father's accusation slammed out of the past, punching into his gut with the same force that his father used to make his point with his fist. His existence was a mistake. His father had tried to beat him out of his mother and then he tried to beat the life out of him. The only justice Tucker had ever seen for his mother was when someone had beaten the life out of his father. But it was only after his father died that he realized that others were standing in line to pick up where his father had left off. A man who wasn't strong went down fast under the strength of others. He'd made damn sure he was strong. He flexed his fingers, shaking off the memory. He'd gotten to the point now where the past didn't matter. He was big enough and mean enough that he did the ass kicking if there was a call for it, but that didn't mean he didn't see the ideal of Sally Mae's beliefs. They were just impractical.

Crockett growled. That in itself was enough to snap Tucker's head up. He'd yet to meet anybody the pup didn't love. Lyle stepped around the corner. As soon as he saw Tucker, he drew up short. The shift in his expression brought

Tucker slowly to his feet. Crockett stood, too, all of his baby teeth set in a snarl. Inside Tucker, a snarl also grew. Lyle was up to no good.

"Davey, go inside."

"What'll I do with the knife?"

Tucker kept his eyes on Lyle. From the set of Lyle's chin and shoulders, he could see the man's bluster was on the rise. "It's yours, but I want you to give it to your mother for safekeeping."

"Really?" Davey carefully slid the small knife back into the sheath, his eyes big.

You'd think Tucker had just given the kid diamonds. "Really. But your mom holds it, understood?"

Davey whooped, nodded and raced to the back door. "Mom! Look what Mr. McCade gave me!"

Lyle walked toward the back door. "Right generous of you, injun."

Tucker stood. "You always were a fool, Lyle."

Lyle's courage ran out fifteen feet from the back door. "And you've always been too damn uppity."

Crockett advanced on Lyle. It wasn't like the dog to take an instant dislike to somebody to that level. Tucker's suspicions rose right along with Crockett's hackles. "I thought I told you to stay away?"

"I got a right to come calling on my intended."

Everything inside Tucker went still. "Your intended?"

"That's right."

"You been hitting the bottle harder than usual, Lyle?"

"I've done given up the drink, not that it's any of your business."

There were two constants in Lyle's life. He always flapped

his lips when he should keep them still, and he could always be found at the saloon with a bottle by his side. "Why?"

"Mrs. Schermerhorn does not approve of strong drink."

"Mrs. Schermerhorn doesn't have a problem with drink. It's drunks she doesn't approve of."

That wasn't strictly true. Sally Mae didn't approve of showing disrespect for what God created by poisoning it with drink, but she allowed for personal choice.

"Nevertheless, she's accepting my suit."

The thread of Tucker's patience snapped. "The hell she is."

He took a step toward Lyle, not sure what he intended to do, but for sure he was doing something to wipe the confidence off the bastard's face.

"Tucker!"

Only Sally Mae dared to snap his name out in that particular tone. And only Sally Mae could draw his temper up short with just a word.

"I'll be with you in a minute, Sally."

"Now, Tucker."

Damned if it didn't make him smile, the way she wasn't cowed by the thought of his temper.

"That's Mrs. Schermerhorn, to you," Lyle scornfully injected.

"The day the likes of you will be giving me orders is the day they'll be making snowballs in hell."

Lyle drew himself up to his full height. Word was, before he'd found the bottom of a liquor bottle, Lyle had been the big bull in these parts. But a love of alcohol and a lazy nature had turned muscle to fat and fear of him to contempt. "As Mrs. Schermerhorn's affianced—"

"My what?"

Lyle continued, as if Sally Mae hadn't interrupted. "It's my place to insure she doesn't have to suffer an uppity injun who can't remember his place."

Tucker pulled his hat low over his brow. "Go back inside, Sally Mae."

"He's not my affianced."

"Didn't think he was. Now go inside."

"Why?"

"Because I'm about to commit a violence that will upset your peaceable nature."

Sally Mae hopped off the porch and grabbed his arm. "Thee will not hit him because of me."

Her hands were cool on his skin, yet they might as well have been hot embers, the way his nerve endings caught fire. He kept walking. "Wasn't planning on doing it for you."

She planted her feet. "For me, because of me—there is no difference in my eyes, Tucker."

He had two choices. Drag her with him or stop. He stopped. It wasn't as easy as it should be to ignore the pleading in her big gray eyes. He held his arm out. She ignored his hint, clinging. He kind of liked it. "Then go inside."

"There is no doubt Lyle is a fool, but he's...harmless."

The pause before harmless got Lyle's complete attention.

"I don't need a woman to take up for me," Lyle spit. "I'm not afraid of him."

"Then thee should be," Sally Mae snapped. "Have thee not seen the muscle on the man? He could snap thee like a twig."

Nothing like a woman being honest to crush a man better than any amount of pounding. This time, Tucker only pretended to take a step forward. Lyle stepped back, his mouth working. Sally didn't give him a chance to get a word out.

"Now get thee back to the saloon."

"I don't drink no more. You cured me of that."

"Do not credit me with God's light."

"God didn't have nothing to do with it." His expression took on a fervency that was disturbing. "It was all you."

Tucker removed Sally's grip from his arm. "Go inside, Sally Mae."

"No."

He looked down. "Now."

She blinked at his tone. "Promise me first that thee will not commit unnecessary violence."

"I promise."

She hesitated at the easiness of his reply.

"Go."

She did, checking over her shoulder, three or four times. He waited until he heard the door squeak shut behind her before closing the distance between him and Lyle. There was a sheen of sweat on the other man's brow.

"I don't know what crazy thought is twisting in that brain of yours, Lyle, but stay the hell away from Sally Mae."

"She's not yours."

"No, she's not, but she's never going to be yours."

"She's a saint."

Again, that fervency. "Whatever you think she is to you, get it out of your head."

"Oh, and you're going to do what? You promised Sally Mae no violence."

"I promised her no unnecessary violence." He bared his teeth in a smile and grabbed Lyle by the shirtfront. "There's a possibility that we differ in opinion as to what's necessary."

12

"What the hell did you say to give Lyle Hartsmith the impression that you're hitching your wagon to his?"

Sally Mae carefully placed the dish towel on the cabinet. She'd known Tucker would come in angry, demanding explanations. That's why she had quickly ushered Hazel and Davey out via the front door. She'd also thought he'd come in bloody. She glanced at his fist.

His gaze avoided hers. "I didn't hit him."

She knew he wouldn't lie to her, so that only left one reason. He'd honored her wishes. She touched his hand. "I thank thee."

"For what?"

"For not hurting Lyle."

Tucker hooked a hand behind her neck. That moment of unease was gone. "It was either him or you."

"And thee opted for me."

His beautiful eyes crinkled at the corners and his lips twitched. "Yup."

He pulled her in one step…two.

She braced her palms against his chest. "Should I be afraid?"

The twitch grew to a soft grin. "Very."

"All right."

He laughed. "All right what?"

"I'll be afraid."

"Ah, moonbeam, you're never afraid of me."

That was true. She placed her palms over the bulge of his biceps and squeezed. There was no give. She could understand why he was always showing them off, but still it bothered her that other women could see the perfection of his arms. "Why do thee never wear sleeves?"

"They don't fit."

She blinked. "They don't?" She'd imagined many things— a need to show off to women, warn men, but that ready-made shirts didn't fit him? She'd never thought of that.

"Store-bought clothes don't fit over my arms. So either I have to take up a wife, sewing or I cut them off. It's easier to cut."

"Oh." She hadn't considered anything so practical. Instead, she'd attached motives.

He tilted his head to the side. "What did you think?"

"I think I'm no better than anyone else."

His eyebrow cocked up. The familiar, endearing habit had its predictable effect on her heartbeat.

"Oh, you're better than anyone."

"Thee are still angry."

"Pissed as hell."

"Why?"

"Because I didn't punch the SOB in the mouth, like he deserved."

She slid her hands up his arms to his neck.

"I'm glad thee did not commit violence in my name."

"Don't be." His hand slipped to the hollow of her spine, tucking her against him. "I'm going to take the payment out of your hide."

"All right."

He snorted. "Any other woman would be shaking in her boots."

"Then any other woman would be a fool."

"Any other woman might realize I have ulterior motives for my restraint."

"Thee do?"

His fingers traced the curve of her jaw. Hers slid up his cheek. "Uh-huh. It's entirely possible, Sally Mae, that I want you all soft and complacent."

"Why?"

"So, when I ask you how much trouble Lyle has been, you'll answer me honestly."

Oh, shoot. How could she not have seen that coming? Tucker had as much brain as brawn. She never should have hesitated before she called Lyle harmless, but in that split second she'd remembered the way he'd followed her, the look in his eyes, the size of him and how she hadn't been able to break his grip.

She tried to believe there was good in everyone, a part of God that had to be respected, but there was something in Lyle's eyes when he looked at her that made her nervous. She didn't know how to answer. Telling Tucker the truth would send him after Lyle. She rubbed her left forearm, the faint bruises from Lyle's grip still there. She'd considered going to the sheriff, but he was rather ineffective. There was also the reality that he would accuse her of inciting Lyle's lust by virtue of her profession. A nurse didn't have much moral ground to stand on.

"That's an awfully long silence, moonbeam."

It was going to get longer, because she didn't know what to tell him. A lie stuck on her tongue, but the truth was too fraught with danger—to Tucker, Lyle, herself.

Tucker's fingertips brushed her forehead. The stray hairs tickled as they dragged across her flesh.

"Has he been pestering you?"

Thank God. A way out. "Just a little."

His fingertips skimmed her temple, lingered on her too-fast pulse. "A man who's only pestering a little doesn't declare himself affianced."

"Why couldn't thee be all brawn and no brain?"

He smiled. "You wouldn't like me then."

The smile didn't reach his eyes. "No, but I could've fooled thee a lot easier."

His fingers tucked under her chin, tilted her gaze to his. "Spit it out, Sally Mae."

"Apparently, while Lyle was staying with me, he discovered his sense of…" She let the explanation trail off. Some things a woman just wasn't comfortable mentioning.

"Sense of what?"

He just couldn't let it go. She glared at him. "Being a man."

"What?"

"Apparently before his injury, he'd been having difficulties expressing himself to women."

"Lyle's a clod. He wouldn't know how to talk to a woman if she came up and handed him a book."

"He wasn't concerned with speech."

"Ah." His thumb settled over her pulse and pressed, connecting them heartbeat to heartbeat. "What was he concerned about?"

"Thee just want to hear me say it."

"Yup."

He could be so aggravating. "As best I can figure out, sometime during the time he was here he regained his virility. Something he feels is due to my presence."

"He thinks you cured him of a limp willy?"

"Yes."

"No wonder he looks at you like you're the Second Coming."

"Don't blaspheme."

"I'm not blaspheming, honey, I'm just talking the truth."

She rested her cheek against his chest, listening to his heartbeat as he tracked hers through her pulse. "His renewed abilities are more likely due to a lack of whiskey."

"I'll set him straight."

There was too much satisfaction in the statement to suit her. "No, thee won't."

"Giving me orders?"

"Yes. Thee will cause a ruckus that will have people talking more than they already do."

"I'll be discreet."

Tucker didn't know the meaning of the word when his emotions were aroused. He went in seeing nothing but his goal, risking everything to attain it. And his emotions were definitely involved now. She could feel the tension humming through him. He couldn't wait to get to Lyle and set him straight. She stroked his chest gently in the way that soothed him after they made love.

"Setting him straight will start talk," she added, thinking about the latest instance in the store and Hazel's warning.

"People are not going to believe that thee are innocently staying in the barn."

"I'm not."

He could be so impossible. "Lyle will get over it. Find some other woman who appeals to him and then he'll move on. Thee just need to wait until then."

He caught her hand. "Petting me isn't going to get you your way."

He made it sound as though she thought of him as a pet tabby cat when in reality he was wild, unpredictable. She frowned. That wasn't right, either. She'd always been able to count on him. "I was soothing thee."

He smiled down at her, his fingers in her hair tugging her head back. For all the tension in him, his mouth, when it met hers, was incredibly gentle. "I don't need soothing."

"Thee are upset."

"I don't trust Lyle."

"I will be fine. He's not all that brave."

He kissed her cheek and her mouth again. "You have a way of inspiring men, Sally mine."

She shivered at the possessive term. "Not on purpose."

"That's the problem. It doesn't sit well with me, leaving you here with a man wanting you."

Her heart dropped. He'd just gotten back. "Thee are leaving again?"

"That's why I'm back early. I've got to send a wire."

"Thee found Ari?"

"No, we didn't find Ari, but we've got a good lead. Which is why I need to wire Desi. We need some more information."

"This is good, though."

He nodded. "It's more hope than we've had in a bit."

"Why do thee not sound happy?"

"The woman we found is dead. We're trying to establish whether the body could be Ari's or not."

Body? Dear heavens. She slid her arms around Tucker's waist and hugged him tightly. "How will thee do that?"

"It looks like the woman had a broken leg that had healed at some point in the past."

For that he had to have seen the bone. "She's been dead a long time?"

His chin rested on her head. "Yes."

He sounded so weary. And no wonder—he'd had to dig up a grave, examine a body, and now he faced sending the bad news home. "I'm sorry. Thy friend Desi will be devastated."

"What's devastating her is the not knowing." His jaw slid along her hair with each word, tugging at her scalp the way the reality of what he was doing for his friend tugged at her heart. He was such a good man.

"I hope it's not her."

"Whether Ari is alive or dead, Desi will feel better if she knows."

She could understand that. Every time he left, she worried that something would happen to him and she'd never know, just be condemned to wonder forever.

He brushed her forehead again. He still had tension in his muscle. "I don't need thee to fight for me. Give my way a chance."

"My way is faster."

"Thee just start swinging."

"It's the most effective means for getting what I want."

A moment of boldness seized her. "I ask this of thee because I don't want to see thee hurt." Opening her palm over his heart, she confessed. "Not inside or outside." She didn't flinch away when he frowned. "I care about thee."

That tension snapped to rigidity. "Don't."

"I dream sometimes of a future with thee."

His jaw muscles bunched. "That's never going to happen."

"I know."

"It can't happen."

"I know that, too."

"Your idealism aside, it's a hard life for a mixed child, Sally Mae."

"Thee would love thy children, Tucker."

"I would, but the world wouldn't."

She didn't want to hear it. At the moment, she wanted the illusion that she and Tucker could have this gift given to them. That it could grow as they grew for the rest of their lives, so she didn't answer. Just hugged him again.

He didn't let the subject go. "It wouldn't be just the adults. Kids would find every reason to mock a boy or else find reasons to beat on him."

"Not all."

He didn't allow her to turn her face away. "Yes, all. A little girl wouldn't be invited to parties. She'd be slighted. And when she got old enough, not viewed with respect."

Even though she'd seen for herself that he was right, Sally couldn't imagine anyone slighting her child. "We could move back East."

"Prejudice doesn't stop at the state line, Sally mine. It's the same in the East. Maybe a little more refined, but the same."

Their relationship, its potential, where would they live, those were issues they'd always danced around. A dream too fragile to stand up to scrutiny. His fingers grazed her lower lip, drifted to her cheek and then down to the middle of her jaw, as if he was memorizing her. Was he thinking of leaving? If so, she had nothing more to lose. She took a breath, held it for a heartbeat and then asked, "Would thee be willing to try peace, Tucker?"

He went as still as she felt inside. "To what end?"

"Sometimes, when I look in thy eyes, I see how weary thee are."

"Some days are more trying than others."

"That's not what I see."

"It doesn't matter what I wish for, Sally."

"It's thy choice, Tucker. To live in peace or war." His silver eyes sought hers. In them she saw the glint of the sun. Of hope.

"What are you saying?"

"I'm saying, if thee would try peace, then I would be willing to try compromise." For the first time ever, she saw him flabbergasted. Oh, it wasn't anything obvious. The man's jaw didn't drop. He didn't gasp. There was just a slightly stunned look in his eyes.

"Thee cannot be surprised that I am thinking this way. There has always been attraction between us, always a feeling that we can't resist."

"I resist just fine."

She smiled and put her hand over his where it rested on her buttock.

"Yes, I see how well thee resist."

He laughed, but didn't give her the obvious answer. Maybe he was thinking about it. Oh, please, let him be thinking.

She asked, "Do thee intend to pretend thee won't mind if I become interested in other men?"

"No. I won't pretend that."

"Then thee need to decide, Tucker, what thee are willing to sacrifice when thee come back to me this time."

"Just like that?"

She sighed, her heart racing, beating in her throat, her fingertips dampening where they touched his cheek. Oh, she loved this man so. Maybe in another time, when skin color didn't matter, in another place, where people were just allowed to be, this would be an easy move forward. But it wasn't. This was now. And now was precarious and scary, but very worth the risk. Of that she was certain.

"Yes. There is a time limit on this choice, Tucker. A future for us together will not be easy. I need a man who has the courage to fight for it. Not with his fists." She brought his hand to her lips and kissed the palm. "But with his heart."

"Are you calling me a coward?"

For all the heat in his snarl, he didn't pull his hand away. She folded his fingers over her kiss. "Yes."

"Son of a bitch."

Silence stretched between them. Fear at the enormity of what she was doing stretched right along with it. Memories flashed in Sally's mind—of Tucker holding her hand in the blackest hours of the night, and cooking her breakfast when she was too devastated by Jonah's death to take care of herself. Tucker mopping her floors after the wave of mourners who'd come in the rain to pay their respects. Tucker standing guard at the cemetery as she'd cried her heart out. Tucker always there. Tucker, who had so much strength. Tucker, who would fight for so many things. Tucker, who'd never offered to fight for them. He'd probably tell her it was because he wasn't a fool, but she knew the real reason. Because this was a fight he wanted to win too much. A fight he couldn't bear to lose.

"I want an answer." It just popped from her mouth.

His eyes narrowed. "You're backing me into a corner."

"I know."

"Why?"

"Because…"

Because if she didn't, he'd end it. For all the right reasons. To protect her. To protect himself. To protect their futures. She could see the resolve in his eyes. The problem was, she didn't want a future without him.

"Because the time has come for me to make a decision about my future."

"There's no rush."

They both knew that was a lie. "I know what I want, but if I can't have it, then I need to do what I must."

"That's a strange way of putting things."

"It's been a strange year."

"You been reading fairy tales while I was gone?"

She puffed and stepped out of his embrace. "I've never in my life believed in fairy tales, but I do believe in thee."

"That's a sucker's bet."

She held her ground, sticking to her point, because she couldn't escape the feeling that, if she let it go, it'd slip away forever to be lost in the morass of social stigma.

He glared at her. She folded her arms across her chest. "And when you come back, I'll know if that faith is justified."

With a curse he turned and headed to the door. At the threshold he stopped, jammed his hat on his head and turned back. "Goddamn it, Sally Mae."

She waited until he was on the back step before launching her parting shot, "God doesn't damn anything. That's a choice we make."

* * *

For the third morning in a row, Sally Mae leaned over the chamber pot in her bedroom, panting through the latest wave of nausea, torn between elation and terror. Tucker wasn't the only one who was late. Her menses were, too, and if she hadn't been so distracted by Tucker's courting and then Lyle's stalking her every move, she would have realized it a lot sooner. She pushed the thick braid of her hair back over her shoulder. She was pregnant.

Leaning on the washstand, she rocked back and forth. What was she going to do? A baby. She'd prayed to the Lord for strength and He'd given her a baby. The miracle of that was enough to start the nausea all over again.

She knew what she wanted to do. She wanted to tell Tucker he was going to be a father. Wanted to spend a lifetime proving to him that the doubts he harbored about himself were nonsense. Wanted to be there when he realized, as a husband and a father, that he was every woman's dream. The strength he so valued in battle was just as important at home. She wanted to see him smile in the morning, laugh in the evening. She wanted to love him, cherish him until death parted them.

She took a breath as nausea surged anew. Oh God, she wanted to marry him. Tucker, with the Quaker philosophy and the violent heart.

The silly man worried about the past as if it was the sole determinant of his future. As if his preferences were just flotsam in the stream of life. Her stomach roiled again. She pushed the chamber pot away. Looking at this morning's revolt was not helping her stomach settle. Breathing in through her mouth, she exhaled through her nose, trying to get her midsection to relax. She wished the same technique worked for her mind.

Tucker never talked about his past, but she could imagine how awful it must have been to engrave on him that he didn't bring good to this world, because more and more she could see that's what he thought. That anything he desired was temporary, so rather than make an honest play for it, he was satisfied with stealing an illusion. For however long it lasted. Like their affair. He'd agreed so easily to just one night when he'd clearly wanted more. And when the opportunity happened, he'd taken more, giving her everything she wanted except the promise of a future. She put her hand over her stomach. But they had made a baby. Both of them were going to have to start thinking in terms of compromise and forever.

She poured water from the pitcher into the bowl. Grabbing a cloth off the washstand rod, she dipped it in the water and rubbed it over her face. The cool cloth felt wonderful against her skin. Holding it over her eyes, she took another deep breath before setting it on the edge of the basin and pouring water into a glass and rinsing her mouth. What she needed was a plan.

Grabbing her bathrobe, she shrugged into it as she headed downstairs, easily navigating the near dark. She peeked out the back door when she got to the kitchen. Dawn was just breaking through the darkness.

Automatically she reached for the coffeepot, filled it with water and slid kindling under the stove burner before setting the pot on top. She reached for the jar of coffee and popped the lid. Her stomach rolled a warning. She put it down and poured herself a glass of water instead, before taking up her pencil and a piece of scrap paper. Sitting at the table, her back to the door, she created two columns—"Yes" and "No"—

and started writing. Ten minutes later, she had a long list as to why she should head back East. There was only one reason in the No column. She placed her fingertip over the six letters that made up Tucker's name. Just as in real life, being outnumbered on paper didn't lessen the man's odds of winning.

A shadow fell over the table and the scent of stale sweat rode the humid air of the morning. Fresh mixed with foul. Fear chased goose bumps over her skin. Only one man thought he had a right to invade her home on his whim. Lyle. She tucked the pencil stub into her palm. As a weapon, it wasn't much. She ran her thumb over the dulled point. Especially after she'd wasted time on a pointless list. There was no right and wrong for her. Only Tucker.

She turned around. Lyle looked as if he'd been drinking all night. "How did thee get in?"

"I jimmied the lock."

"What are thee doing here?"

"I've come to talk to you."

The stench of whiskey blended with the stench of stale sweat and drove her back into the table.

"About what?"

"Our future. You're a woman alone."

The table was between her and the entry to the parlor. Lyle stood between her and the back door. "I'm a widow, yes."

The door closed under the kick of his foot. "It's not natural that a woman lives alone."

She tightened her grip on the pencil. "I'm doing fine, but I thank thee for thy concern."

"You need a man."

A man taking off his hat shouldn't be a threat. Yet, somehow, when Lyle did, it was. Maybe it was because of the way

220

his greasy hair slicked across his broad forehead, emphasizing the smallness of his eyes, his florid complexion. Or maybe it was just the way he stared at her, as if he knew something she didn't. Something dangerous.

"I'm still in mourning."

"No one mourns a man that long."

She rubbed her thumb over the point of the pencil again. "I loved my husband."

"Then you'll find it easy to love me." He took a step toward her. "I need you, Sally Mae."

"For what?"

It was a stupid question, but it just popped out. His hands closed over her shoulders.

"You fire my blood."

The stench of his breath blew coherent thought from her mind. Her stomach roiled. It would serve him right if she vomited. Then again, he likely wouldn't care.

"Take thy hands off me."

"No."

The only response to that was her equally forceful "Yes."

He didn't let go. "I'm staking my claim, Sally Mae."

He was too late. "I am not a cow to be branded and owned."

The pencil was just long enough to serve as a weapon if she aimed for his eye. She stared, narrowing her vision to that one point. She'd have to move very fast after she struck. The one thing she'd learned over the years was that severe wounds didn't always incapacitate a man. An ornery man could still stand, still fight. She bet Lyle could be very ornery.

You must always respect that which is God in all men.

The teachings of her adoptive parents sank deep. She owed them so much. They'd taken her in when she remembered nothing, given her peace, a path to follow out of the terror that had seized her mind. Terror of things she couldn't remember. Things that, to this day, she didn't want to remember. She released her grip on the pencil. Terror rose as the small cylinder rolled out of reach. Confidence followed immediately afterward. God was here with her, within her. Within Lyle. Her path was clear. And it was not one of victim or of violence.

She stood at her full height. "Let me go, Lyle." He hesitated. She pressed her advantage. "A gentleman does not lay hands upon a lady."

"I ain't no gentleman."

"Then thee have exerted thyself for nothing."

His grip tightened. "Like hell."

Her resolve hardened. "Thee will not swear in my home."

"You're awful bossy."

"This is my home."

Lyle looked around. "I'm hungry."

She stumbled backward as he abruptly let her go. He set his hat on the table. The brim was stained with grease and sweat. She didn't know if she could scrub the image of the hat from her mind.

"Make me some breakfast." Paper crinkled as her palm pushed it across the table.

Lyle leaped on it like a rat on a june bug. "What's that?"

She scooped it up and shoved it into her pocket. "My...my shopping list."

His eyes narrowed. "No shopping list ever made a woman red cheeked and stutter."

Why was she so fair complected? "I'm uncomfortable with thee being here and what people will say. Thee need to leave."

"You weren't worried none about how it looked when you were here with that injun." He held out his hand. "Give me the paper."

"No!"

She might as well have been shouting in the wind. He grabbed her arm, yanked her around and reached into her pocket. She grabbed the list with her free hand. The paper tore. Lyle lifted up his half. Through the paper she could see the black lead forming one word. Only one word. So could Lyle.

"You bitch!"

The slap came fast and hard. Stars shattered behind her lids. Water hissed as it boiled over on the stove. Pain exploded in her face. She ducked and threw up her hand, blinded by the surge of tears.

"Stop it!"

"Tucker McCade is your reason to stay?" Lyle raged. "You laid down with that stinking Indian when there were plenty of white men around ready to scratch your itch?"

He raised his hand again. She spun. The next blow glanced off her shoulder, but it was still strong enough to knock her off balance. She went down on her knee.

"Stop!"

"Goddamn you." Lyle snarled, "I was going to make you my wife."

He drew his foot back. She tucked her arms around her ribs, thought of the pencil just two feet over her head, lying on the table where she'd left it.

Please, Lord, give me the strength. To hold to her beliefs, to honor her family. She braced for the pain.

"You son of a bitch!" The curse was blessedly familiar.

Tucker. Oh God, Tucker was here. Lyle was suddenly gone,

the threat of his kick vanishing as sunlight replaced the darkness of his shadow. It wasn't enough. "Tucker."

It was a raw whisper. She wanted to run into his arms, have him carry her away from the fear and the horrible helplessness.

"Come kick on me, you worthless piece of shit." Fists met flesh in sickening thuds.

"Fucking injun. You had no right to touch her."

The door rattled as something slammed against it. Shadows spun past her gaze. Dishes rattled. Something crashed. Water sizzled in an angry hiss on the stovetop.

"You'll never touch her. You're a dead man."

Dead man. Oh, no. "No!"

It was a faint whisper, nowhere near loud enough to be heard over the crash of plates.

"You kill me, they'll hunt you down, injun."

"Let them hunt."

Wiping the tears from her eyes, she stood, swaying as the room spun. A dull throb started in her head, taking up the throb in her rapidly swelling cheek. She blinked. Tucker was down on one knee, his arm around Lyle's neck. His hand on one side of his head. Lyle's face was blood streaked and a ghastly purple and his feet kicked.

"Tucker." She managed more sound this time.

"Turn around, moonbeam. You don't want to see this."

No. She didn't. Her stomach roiled. "Thee can't kill him."

His biceps flexed as he applied more pressure. "No one here to stop me."

"I am."

Tucker's lip lifted in a snarl. She'd never seen him like that, every muscle rigid with tension, his face drawn tight with lust.

Not the softer lust she associated with their lovemaking, but a cold lust. A killer's lust.

Lyle made an awful gurgling sound. She had to hurry. She licked her lips, tasting blood. Taking a step forward, she reached out to Tucker with her voice and her hand. "Killing him only kills the good in thee."

His gaze skimmed her face. "Not much of an argument when I'm looking at your cheek all bruised and your hands shaking."

She tucked her hands into her skirt. "The bruise on thy soul won't heal as fast as the bruise on my cheek."

"By your standards, my soul was lost long ago."

"A soul can't be lost."

"I'd be happy to chat religion another time."

There was no softening of his tone and Lyle wasn't kicking nearly as hard. "Don't do this, Tucker."

"Don't…" Lyle grated out, his nails clawing at Tucker's forearms like a wild animal. She wanted to vomit, to look away. Instead, she took another step forward.

Tucker's biceps bulged as he applied more pressure to Lyle's throat, shutting off the plea she could see lingering desperately in Lyle's eyes.

"I can't let thee do this."

"Go upstairs."

"He was upset."

"Wrong tack if you're thinking on soothing me. I'm a touch upset myself."

"He found out…" She didn't know how to put it into words.

"Whore."

Lyle managed to find a breath and that's what he'd wasted it on? "Shut up, Lyle!"

"You—" Lyle sputtered. A flex of Tucker's forearm cut off whatever Lyle was going to say.

"He won't let this go, Sally Mae."

"Being a fool is not a reason to kill him." She tried another step forward, another tack. "I can't let thee do this, Tucker."

"You can't stop me."

"I'm not that hurt."

"That's debatable."

Her next step brought her within reach.

"Get back."

She touched his arm. "For me. Please. Don't."

The rage was so strong in him. When she looked into his eyes he was her Tucker, yet…not. She didn't know what to do. For the first time, she didn't know how to touch him to make this right. She slid her hand up his arm, feeling the rock-hard muscle, the tension, the anger. "Please."

"Sally."

Was he weakening? "For us."

"Son of a bitch. I'm going to regret this." He jerked his head. "Stand back."

She did, taking those two steps with a sense of elation. Tucker would make a choice. There was hope. Her bare foot came down on something sharp just as Tucker released Lyle. She cried out. Tucker reached for her. Lyle was closer, more desperate. He grabbed her ankle and yanked. She went down hard on her hip. Lyle grabbed her throat, pulling her in front of him. Using her as a shield, he stood.

"Stand back, injun."

"No."

"You don't, and I'm going to snap her neck. She's a frail-built woman. Won't even tax me."

"I don't imagine it will."

"See how much he thinks of you, Sally Mae? First chance he gets he's throwing you to the dogs."

Was Lyle blind? Couldn't he see the coiled tension beneath Tucker's facade of calm?

"No." She wasn't talking to Lyle.

"Yes. No injun is going to risk his life for a bit of pussy." Lyle grabbed a knife off the counter, held it to her throat. "But he might if he thought he could take me."

The steel pressed into her throat. Thank goodness, she was lax about sharpening her knives.

Lyle took a step backward. Tucker took one forward. His eyes never left Lyle. His hand didn't leave his side.

"I'm going to do more than take you. I'm going to kill you," Tucker threatened quietly.

Sally shook her head.

"I'll cut her throat," Lyle barked.

Too fast to see, Tucker's hand whipped forward. Almost in the same moment, something sped past her face.

Lyle jerked back. The knife slipped against her throat. Something wet and hot coated her face. And then Tucker was in front of her. Lyle jerked and wheezed. She'd heard it enough times to know it was a death rattle.

Tucker lifted her up, wiping at her cheek with his arm. "I told you I was going to regret letting him go."

She turned. Tucker caught her shoulders.

"No. Don't look."

She couldn't help it. She leaned back. Lyle was sprawled against the kitchen cabinet, a knife protruding from his eye, blood dripping down his face. She touched her fingers to the wetness on her cheek. More blood. The horror sank into her.

She rubbed her fingers together and then wiped them on her robe. The stain didn't leave.

She looked back at Tucker. There was no gentleness in him now. There was only a seething rage that hadn't abated. He'd killed Lyle. Would kill him again if he could.

"He would have let me go."

His lip lifted in a snarl. "No, he wouldn't have."

She shook her head, stepping away from him, stumbling slightly before catching her balance on a chair. "Thee didn't give him a chance."

He stood to his full height, chin up, shoulders squared, as if ready to take a blow. "No, I didn't."

She'd asked him to make a choice. Glancing at Lyle, she shook her head and stepped back from the realization. "How could thee do this and say it's for me?"

13

He'd known it would come to this. A clash between beliefs. "I did it because it needed doing."

Sally Mae stood before him, her eyes big and accusing in her bleached white face. Christ, Lyle would never have come sniffing around her if he hadn't had his suspicions that Sally Mae was sweet on Tucker. A man with Lyle's hate couldn't stand losing out to an Indian.

Tucker had stayed too long. Brought this on her. The brilliant spatter of Lyle's blood on her face was stronger than any accusation. He gritted his teeth. "You've always known who I am. You just never wanted to acknowledge it. It didn't suit the nice little future you dreamed up for us."

"No."

Was she denying him or the reality? Blood dripped down the cabinet onto her freshly scrubbed floors. He was losing her just as surely as Lyle had lost. Tucker stepped over Lyle's legs and cupped her shoulder. Her flinch, when she'd never flinched away from him before, lashed his soul.

"You don't need to be looking at that."

She leaned back, staring at Lyle's corpse as if it held all the answers she'd always been missing. "There's a dead body in my kitchen, where would thee have me look?"

Anywhere but there. Grabbing a towel, he took the coffeepot off the burner. "Go in the parlor."

Even as Tucker gave the order, she swayed. It only took one step to scoop her up in his arms. A second step to feel the rejection. She turned her head, leaving him staring at her bloodstained cheek. The cheek he'd caressed so many times before. The cheek that was now sporting a bruise. The cheek he loved to kiss after they made love, when she was flushed and panting from pleasure. He set her on her feet in the parlor. "It wasn't your fault, Sally Mae."

"Yes, it was."

She was beginning to look a little green around the gills. "I'll get you a glass of water."

She vehemently shook her head, her gaze locked on the kitchen door. He brushed the back of his fingers down her cheek. She leaned away. He curled his fingers around the pain, absorbing it, accepting it. "I'll get it from the well."

"We can't just leave Lyle there."

"He'll keep."

"The blood…"

"I'll put a towel under—" She probably didn't need to hear the graphic details. "I'll take care of it."

"Thee always take care of things." Her hand waved vaguely between them before settling over her stomach. "I just never understood…"

"What was involved," he finished for her. The time for illusions was past.

She shook her head. "Thee are right. I didn't want to know."

Her fingers dug into her stomach. He caught her arm. "Sit down before you fall down." He practically forced her to the settee.

Fine tremors radiated down her arms. If possible her skin was even paler. "Tucker?"

He stepped back and braced himself for the coming tirade. "What?"

She flinched from his tone, or maybe just looking at him now made her sick. Hell, he'd shattered her world, her illusions. There was no maybe about it.

"I think I'm going to faint."

She didn't faint like the young ladies at a social. There was no graceful crumple. She simply toppled over. He had to dive to save her head from the floor. He glared at the kitchen door. If Lyle wasn't already dead, he'd kill him all over again. She was so light in his arms. So frail. He couldn't even feel the steel he knew lurked beneath the outward appearance of fragility. He glanced at the settee and then the stairs. The least he could do was make her comfortable.

He carried her to her bedroom. Sunshine blazed bright and cheery into the small space that smelled of lilac and…illness? Laying Sally Mae on the bed, Tucker loosened her blouse before unhooking the corset beneath. Her breathing was shallow and she was so very pale that the tracery of veins beneath her skin seemed more pronounced. He touched the start of one violet line just below her shoulder, followed it over the slope of her breast to the valley between. Fragile. Everything about the woman was delicate except for the way she loved him. That was rock solid.

He didn't know if she knew that he knew she loved him,

but Sally wasn't a woman of easy virtue. She could tell herself anything she wanted, but he'd always known she wouldn't lie down with a man unless he held her heart. And he, true to form, had selfishly taken advantage of that love, stealing for himself a bit of a dream that could never be. Deluding himself that he could protect her from the reality of what he was for the duration of their affair. It *had* been a delusion, and she was lying here now, shattered because of his arrogance. Wiping the blood from her cheek with his thumb, feeling weary to his bones, he whispered, "I'm sorry, moonbeam." He kissed her cheek. "You can wake up, now. It's safe."

She moaned and stirred. He could see her pulse beating steadily in the hollow of her throat. She was fine. The only thing wrong in her life was him. He stood and angled the sheet over her torso. "I'll send Hazel over."

She would want someone she trusted if she were sick.

Hazel marched up to Sally's house ahead of Tucker, back straight, skirts swaying with the force of her steps. He stood back, holding the front door open as she passed through. "I'm sure if Sally Mae fainted there had to be some other reason than seeing a man wounded."

"He was dead."

"She's seen plenty of dead men."

"I killed him."

She looked at him.

"In front of her," he added.

"Oh."

Hazel stopped in the doorway to the kitchen. He expected more of a reaction than the glance she sent Lyle. "Can't say that anyone will miss him."

It was a harsh statement for a woman. "You knew him?"

"A lot of men think a widow is lonely."

He frowned. "You should have told me he was bothering you."

Hazel huffed. "He was hardheaded, but his head wasn't harder than my frying pan."

The sharp retort spurred a smile. Hazel was a fine-looking woman, capable. She wouldn't be alone long if she didn't want to be. "Glad to hear it, but if you have any problems in the future, come to me or any of Hell's Eight."

"Thank you, but I'm going home."

He followed her to the foot of the stairs. "Back East? Why?"

She paused on the landing and shrugged. Her mouth quivered and firmed. "My Ben and I came here for a new start, but all that happened to our dreams was that they came to an end."

"You've still got Davey."

She wiped tears on her sleeve. "Yes, and I don't want to lose him. He'll be safer back East."

It was expensive to travel that far. He wasn't above assuring Hazel's loyalty with cash. "I'll pay you to take care of her."

Hazel's chin snapped up. "Sally Mae was there for my Billy and my Davey. You won't insult me again by offering money to take care of her."

Living on the outskirts of society for so long, he'd forgotten the odd feeling of helplessness that settled on a man after being reprimanded by a woman. "Thank you."

She jerked her chin in the direction of the kitchen. "You can thank me by cleaning up that mess. If Sally Mae's stomach is feeling sensitive, she won't want to look at that again."

"Consider it done."

"Just be sure it's done right."

Up until recently, no woman other than Tia, the Eight's adoptive mother, had given him orders. Most feared his size, combined with his reputation. Oh, women might be fascinated enough to sleep with him and might nourish a secret hope that he'd turn savage in bed, but they usually didn't go toe to toe with his will. Yet in the past year, four women had—Caine's wife, Desi, Sam's wife, Isabella, Sally Mae and now Hazel.

"Yes, ma'am." He headed into the kitchen. Hell, maybe Sally Mae was right. Maybe he *was* getting tired.

He was scrubbing the floor when Hazel came down. He tracked her footsteps across the parlor, knowing she stood in the doorway when they stopped.

"Is she all right?" he asked, scrubbing at the last of the blood. He didn't know how women stood cleaning. The stench of lye soap from this alone had about burned his nose hairs off.

She didn't answer. He looked up. She stood in the doorway, face white, arms folded across her chest. He stood, a cold, sick feeling settling in his stomach.

"What the hell is it?"

She came toward him. His world narrowed to the rhythm of her approach, the swish of her skirts, the staccato rasp of her breath, the click of her soles across the wood floor. She stopped just in front of him. Her mouth worked. The cold feeling in the pit of his stomach opened to a yawning void. "What's wrong?"

Hazel made a fist, relaxed it, and then made it again.

"She's pregnant." She slapped him across his face. The sound echoed in the room, in his head, the reverberations building on one another, amplifying the incomprehensible reality.

Shit. Pregnant?

Hazel slapped him again, before hauling back for a third. "What are you going to do about it?"

He caught her hand this time. "Pregnant?"

She yanked her hand. "Don't try pretending it's not yours."

Letting her go, he shook his head. No. He wouldn't be doing that.

He handed Hazel the scrub brush before heading up the stairs, taking them two at a time.

He found Sally Mae in the bedroom, buttoning her top. Her hair hung in a wet tangle about her freshly scrubbed face. She appeared calm. He hated her ability to surround herself with calm when he wanted to rage. "When were you going to tell me?"

Sally Mae didn't prevaricate. "I don't know."

He leaned his shoulder against the door. "You *were* going to tell me?"

Buttoning the last button at her throat and smoothing her fingers over the touch of lace, she picked her brush up off the vanity and sat down. "I don't know."

"What the hell were you planning on doing? Pass an Indian baby off as white?"

She pulled the heavy swath of her hair over her shoulder and began to brush the ends. Her hands weren't even shaking while he felt he was breaking up inside, his longtime certainties detonating under the latest turn of events.

"That would be dishonest."

"So was telling me you knew a way to prevent pregnancy."

That got a disruption in the rhythm. "It worked before."

She watched the brush glide through her hair as though it were a savior. Because she was guilty or ashamed? Guilty would have worked better for his anger, but this was Sally Mae. Peaceable, honest Sally Mae. He reached up to run his fingers through his hair and bumped his hat brim. Shit, he hadn't even taken off his hat. He caught a glimpse of his expression in the mirror. Hell, if he was Sally Mae, he'd be running for cover. He considered using intimidation to get the answers he wanted and then immediately changed his mind. There were a lot of memories he wanted to take away from his time with Sally Mae, but the memory of her cowering from him wasn't one of them. He took off his hat and slapped it against his thigh.

"I thought, you being a healer, that you knew special ways."

"Apparently not."

The brush kept moving up then down, over and over. Seconds stretched to minutes. He had a choice. He could believe she'd tricked him and be angry, or he could accept that it'd shocked her as much as him and empathize. He was better with angry. He tossed his hat on the vanity to the right of the door. She jumped at the soft plop.

"Hazel wants my hide staked to the barn door."

The brush strokes faltered. "She accused thee?"

"Yeah."

"I'm sorry."

Ah, hell, when it came to Sally Mae, he wasn't good at anger. He took the two steps that eradicated the distance between them. Tucking his finger under her chin, he lifted her face to his. She flinched.

"Stop that."

"What?"

"Flinching when I touch you."

"I'm sorry."

"Stop saying that, too."

She settled the brush in her lap and stared at him with those big gray eyes. "What do thee want?"

It came to him then, exactly what he wanted. He rubbed his thumb along her bottom lip. "I want you to tell me we made a baby together. I want you to demand I do the honorable thing. I want you to—"

"Why?"

The question caught on the edge of the void inside him, hauling him closer to the place that made him nervous.

"Because a woman has a right to have expectations of her lover."

"No, she does not. By virtue of the relationship—"

It was his turn to interrupt her. "I *want* you to have expectations of me."

Her lips parted. He placed his thumb over the center bow, cutting off the "why" he could see forming.

"Don't ask, just have them, all right?"

For a second she studied him and then she nodded. He took the brush from her lap and clasped her hand in his, raising it slightly. He turned her toward the mirror.

She brushed her hair back over her shoulder, settling a little deeper into the seat, watching him in the mirror.

He started brushing. "I'm waiting."

"Like this?"

"Yes. Like this." With some distance so he had a little better control over the emotions she brought out so easily.

She licked her lips. He expected her to blurt it out. She didn't. Instead she reached back and placed her hand over his, where it rested against the nape of her neck. Her palm was soft, her voice softer still, as if she understood the emotions that he didn't. Her gaze met his in the mirror. "I'm going to have thy baby, Tucker McCade."

Ah, hell. Emotions churned inside him. Terror and joy whipped through him so rapidly that he had trouble even absorbing them. The last emotion, however, that one lingered. The one that scared him most. Joy. Sally Mae was going to have his baby.

Her fingers squeezed his. "Thee look scared."

He was. He'd never had happiness that hadn't been taken away. He'd gotten accustomed to its absence. "I'm sorry."

Her hand dropped away. He caught it before it could reach her side. He felt awkward and unsure. Two emotions he hadn't experienced since he'd worn knee pants.

His voice was harsher than he intended. "A baby should be wanted."

The words just came from nowhere.

Sally Mae nodded. "And thee don't want this one."

Yes, he did. And every impossible thing that came with it. He tightened his grip on the brush. "What kind of father would I be?"

Her gaze held his in the mirror. "Whatever kind thee choose to be."

Choice. She was always throwing that word in his face. As if everything that happened in life was at his discretion. If he'd had a choice, his father wouldn't have been a son of a bitch, his mother would have loved him enough to protect him, the *soldados* wouldn't have come and wiped out his town, and Desi and her sister wouldn't have been sold to Comancheros. If he'd had a choice, he would have been able to court Sally openly.

"What do you choose?" he asked.

She brought his hand down to her stomach. "I would choose to love this child."

"Goddamn—"

"Thee will not blaspheme."

How the hell did she expect him to resist when she so calmly and matter-of-factly taunted him with everything he wanted? He spread his fingers over the flatness of her abdomen. His child lay beneath. A son or daughter who would have his skin color, her stubbornness and hopefully her endless idealism. "We'll get married, of course."

She got that stubborn look on her face that he'd seen too many times to mistake for anything else. "There's no 'of course' about it."

The hell there wasn't. He knelt, but not before tipping her face up to his. Nothing had changed in the past three hours. She felt as fragile as always. Too fragile to hold his hopes and his dreams. But she did. Whether she wanted to or not, she did. "You have no choice but to marry me, Sally Mae."

"There's always a choice."

"Like?"

"Like going back East. Having my baby among Friends."

"*Our baby.* And that's not a solution."

"Thee are worried because his skin might be as thine?"

He ran his fingers down her spine. "Aren't you?"

"Friends don't judge."

"If that were true, they'd be called Saints."

The twist of her lips was wry. "Maybe it would be better to say they don't judge so much."

Picking her up, he carried her toward the bed. The trust with which her arms came around his neck soothed the raw spot from those times she'd flinched. "You're not going back East."

"That is not thy choice."

"The hell it's not. You gave it to me the day you lay down with me."

"I only made the deal for one night."

He laid her on the bed. "Well, now you can add a lot more nights to the count."

"No."

Anger ripped through him. She wouldn't take herself away from him like this. "Yes."

"When thee left, Tucker McCade, I gave you a choice."

"And I'm making it."

"Not because of the baby."

"There's no undoing what's been done."

"There's no forcing me to do what I won't."

He knelt above her, straddling her hips, pinning her hands to the mattress with his. "Are you going to fight me?"

"Not like thee are accustomed."

"Then how do you intend to win?"

"By virtue of what's right."

She should be cowed by his size, her position. "What the hell does that mean?"

"I will not marry a man committed to violence. I will not raise my children in a home where there is no other choice."

"Damn it, woman, some of the worst scum in the West have tried to out-stubborn me."

"I am not being stubborn." She closed those gorgeous eyes. Her fingers flexed. Was he hurting her? He loosened his grip. She smiled and opened her eyes. "Tell me what thee decided while thee were away chasing hope."

Chasing hope. "Interesting way to describe my job."

The sheets rustled as she shrugged. The scent of lemon rose

around them in a familiar hug. "Thee always leave with the hope that thee can save a killer's next victim, bring a woman home to her family, stop a robbery. Thee are a very giving man, Tucker. I just wish for thee to give something to me."

"What?"

"First, tell me what thee decided."

"What makes you think I made a decision?"

"Thee are not a man who lingers in doubt."

"I decided to try."

But that was before he'd walked in and found Lyle beating her. Tears welled in her eyes.

"I know." He stroked the back of his fingers lightly over the bruise darkening her cheek. "That didn't last long."

She shook her head. "Are thee still willing to try?"

Shit, was he? He was tired, but not stupid. "Are you ever going to forget how I killed Lyle?"

She shook her head again. "But we have many years ahead of us in which to make new memories."

"None are going to top that."

She took his hand and put it over her belly before coming up onto her elbows. "Not even our child?"

He memorized the shape of her, thinking how the soft, warm flesh would burgeon with his child. He wanted his child. He wanted Sally Mae. Damn, he wanted the future she held out like a lure. At least a piece of it. "I can't promise not to fight back."

She lay back down and placed her hand over his, connecting the three of them in one moment. "Will thee promise not to fight first? To try everything else?"

"What good will that do?"

"It would be enough."

"For what?"

She brought his hand to her lips and kissed the back. "A start."

She didn't hide the fear in her eyes, the doubt, but she didn't hide the hope, either. What the hell was he supposed to do with that much hope? Her answer gave him his. He was going to try.

14

Tucker crested the hill above the prosperous Montoya Ranch. Situated eight hours south of Lindos, the ranch was well-tended and—Tucker glanced up—well-guarded. Sunlight glinted off the rifle of the guard standing at the top of the ledge to the right, one foot propped up on a rock, his rifle resting across his thigh. The man was too far away to identify, but from his broad build and the stance that suggested a bone-deep arrogance, topped by a touch of I-dare-you insolence, Tucker was willing to bet it was one of the Lopez brothers. Tough men, bred to the land, they were completely loyal to Isabella Montoya. And deadly in their dedication. If the guard hadn't recognized Tucker, he'd have been stopped. By a bullet most likely. The brothers had been a bit touchy ever since Tejala's gang had overrun the ranch and kidnapped Bella. Tucker lifted his rifle in a salute before surveying the ranch below for signs of Sam.

In one of the corrals, a couple cowboys were working with a green-broke horse, taking it through the initial steps to do the short turns necessary for cutting cattle. He made a note. The horse showed promise. His gaze moved to the house. On the sprawling porch, he could see Señora Montoya dressed in her customary black, tatting. No doubt she was creating something for the grandchildren she hoped to have. The one Sam seemed amazingly willing to give her "in time," as he put it to soften the blow for Bella, who wanted children now but couldn't seem to conceive.

Tucker shook his head. Life was strange. Never would he have expected Sam "Wild Card" MacGregor to be longing for a wife and family. Never would he have expected to be facing marriage and family himself. Yet here he was, about to ask Sam to stand with him as his best man when he married Sally Mae. No doubt, Sally would say the Lord works in mysterious ways. He shook his head. Sally said a lot of things, believed in things with a purity that amazed him. The courage with which she backed those beliefs scared him, because it made no allowances for the foulness of human nature. They offered her no "real world" protection. But then again, that's why she had him.

Tucker urged Smoke down the hill. The horse responded with his usual lazy walk. Tucker always found it funny that people thought Smoke couldn't even get out of his own way, but people liked to judge by appearances, and with Smoke, the appearance of laziness was all they saw, missing the depth of the horse's chest and the muscle development in his legs that told the real story. They missed that, the same way they missed how Sally's gentleness masked a fighting spirit and a will of iron. Both of which constantly put her in danger, with no way to protect herself.

He sighed and rubbed his hand across his face. It hadn't been easy leaving her. Outside of Hell's Eight, there wasn't a white man in the territory who would be all right with her marrying Tucker. And once they knew she was pregnant by him, they'd come calling to vent their lust and anger. Damn, she was crazy to be hitching up with him. What could she possibly expect?

A start.

Soft and sweet, her answer came again. And just as before, it tore at his insides, spilling hope into the emotionless void he'd thrived in, making him vulnerable. Making him want.

God— He cut off the curse. *Son of bitch.* He wanted her. Sally Mae might be crazy, but she was his crazy lady and he needed to get back to her. He'd left her with a gun, but he knew damn well she wouldn't use it except to maybe pray that it would shoot automatically. Heck, she probably wouldn't even do that. Praying for a weapon to go off likely violated her pacifist beliefs. He thought of the big windows in her house, the token locks on the doors. It would be very easy for someone to get to her. Not that there was any reason to believe anyone was going to try. He'd taken care of Lyle's body. No one would ever find it and since the man was known for just upping and moving on, his disappearance wouldn't raise any eyebrows. Hazel would certainly keep the secret, but Tucker couldn't settle his nerves. Sally was too vulnerable here.

He rode toward the house, nodding to the heavily armed *vaqueros* who were busy with assorted jobs. He might have promised Sally Mae that he wouldn't raise his hands in violence, but he hadn't promised not to hire somebody who would. No doubt Sally Mae would call that splitting hairs, but he didn't care. He wasn't heading across the country defenseless, with the most precious things in his world dangling like free pickings for any jackass who wanted a shot.

There was a shout from the house, a flash of red skirts, and a woman came flying across the lawn. Isabella shouted his name again, waving her hand in greeting, calling something over her shoulder to her mother before lifting her skirts and running toward him. Despite his worry, Tucker couldn't help smiling. No one could resist Bella's smile. Bella was all open affection, irrepressible spirit and unshakable loyalty. And for some reason, she had a soft spot for him.

"What brings you here?" she asked, coming to a stop so hard, right in front of him, that she stumbled. Smoke tossed his head and snorted. Tucker calmed him with a pat.

"You need to be more careful, Bella. Don't want you rattling the brains of the newest MacGregor before he gets here."

She waved away his reprimand. "This joke you make, it grows old. Especially as I am not with child."

"Just watching out for my future nephew."

"Ha! You just want me wrapped in wool blankets away from the world."

"That would be cotton wool and what would be the harm in that?"

Her smile brightened her face. "I would be bored."

And a bored Bella, according to Sam, got into trouble. With her beauty, fiery temper and persistent sense of humor, Bella had been giving Sam a run for his money since the day they'd met. But she'd also given Sam back his smile, and as far as Tucker was concerned that earned her his friendship for life.

"Did you come to see Sam?" Bella asked, placing her hand on his boot, where it rested in the stirrup.

He shook his head at the familiarity. There was no sense telling her again that she shouldn't be doing such things, that others might interpret her natural friendliness incorrectly.

Isabella saw the world as it truly was, when she chose to, but she wasn't one to bow to any convention that didn't suit her.

She smiled up at him, letting him know she understood his thoughts. "You do not lecture me. You are learning."

Again, he couldn't help but smile back. This time, not because her smile was so infectious, but because of what she represented. A future that he never thought he'd have. A wife to come home to. Children to tuck into bed. It didn't matter that it had started as a mistake. It didn't matter that others would object. Sally Mae was his now. He'd hold her close.

"Maybe I am."

"And maybe you can learn in other areas, too?"

"Such as?"

"What a beautiful woman Sally Mae is?"

"That's none of your business."

She shrugged. "That does not mean it shouldn't be yours."

He tipped his hat back. "What would you say if I told you it already is?"

She blinked in shock and then her smile softened. "I would say I am very happy for you both."

"The rest of the world won't think so."

She shrugged. "You will have your friends and each other. The rest of the world does not have to matter."

It did, but he didn't have it in him to burst Bella's bubble. "So, is Sam around?"

She motioned to the barn. "He is not happy with the grain we were sold. He discusses it with the merchant."

When Sam discussed things, they usually went his way, or went violent. He cocked an eyebrow at Bella. "How are things going?"

She shrugged. "There is much yelling."

"On Sam's part?"

"No. My Sammy never yells. He has other ways of delivering his point."

Tucker knew exactly what prompted that grin. Sam could be the most aggravating man in the world, but he was definitely the one you wanted backing you in a fight, and he was definitely not the one you wanted to catch you if you were cheating.

Just then, there was a crash in the barn and a man in a blue shirt and black pants came flying out the door. And not of his own volition. Tucker laughed.

"Looks like Sam just settled things."

Bella frowned and placed her hands on her full hips. "I told him not to get violent."

"Seems to me if there ever was a time to get violent, it would be when you're being cheated." He held out his hand. Bella took it. He pulled her up behind him. As she settled, she fussed.

"We are trying to make a success of the ranch." She tugged at her skirt. "We are trying to be leaders. To do this, we must be seen as strong, yet friendly."

He watched as Sam kicked the man in the ass, sending him forward onto his hands and knees. "You might need to refresh Sam's memory on that."

"One can be firm without being aggressive."

"You've been talking to Sally Mae."

"She is an intelligent woman."

Yeah. She was. Tucker reined Smoke around. "You've got your work cut out for you, teaching Sam moderation."

"Sam can learn."

The merchant scrambled to his feet. Sam pulled his hat down over his brow.

"You keep believing that, honey," Tucker said.

"I will."

Bella's arms came around his waist. It was a friendly hug, nothing sexual about it, but when Sam looked over for a split second, Tucker saw his smile slip.

He nudged Smoke in Sam's direction. "Is he still jealous of you?"

"He will go to his grave that way."

"And you don't mind?"

She shook her head and waved at Sam. "No. He would not be my Sam if he did not love with all his heart."

Sam met them in the middle of the yard. Behind them, the merchant scrambled to his rig.

"Howdy, Tucker."

"Howdy, Sam." He jerked his chin toward his shoulder. "I found something of yours in the yard."

"So I see." Sam held up his arms to Bella. "Come here."

She went, in a rustle of cotton and a happy sigh. "You have settled things with the merchant?"

Sam glanced over. "Looks like."

She hugged him hard, burying her face in his chest. Her voice was muffled. "We must work on your ways of persuasion."

Sam laughed and ran his hand over her hair, kissing the top of her head. "All right."

He met Tucker's gaze, a question in his. Long association made words unnecessary. Tucker nodded.

"Let me go, *pequeña*. I think Tucker needs to talk to me."

She leaned back. "Man talk, yes?"

Sam smiled down at her. A body couldn't help but smile at Isabella. "Yes."

"Then I will go do women things, like make coffee."

"Now that, Bella, would be appreciated."

She laughed and tossed her head, causing the thick braid of her hair to swing against her back. "But then you will owe me."

Sam laughed, curved his hand behind her neck and kissed her harder, then shook his head. "Well, for sure I'll be paying up." He turned her toward the house and patted her butt through her thick skirts. "Go tend to your work, and I'll tend to mine."

Her laugh trailed behind her as she obeyed.

Sam didn't take his gaze from her until she went into the house. As if she knew he watched, she gave him a twitch of her hips. Sam's smile grew.

"Good to see you doing that again," Tucker said as he dismounted.

Sam turned and slapped his glove against his hand. "Kind of hard not to, around Bella."

"Yep, that woman has a way about her."

"So what brings you out here?"

"I'm looking for my best man."

Sam paused. "As in 'best man at a gun fight' or 'best man at a wedding'?"

"A wedding."

"Dare I ask who the lucky lady is?"

"You may."

"Sally Mae?"

"Yes."

"Dare I ask how you pulled that off?"

"No."

"I didn't think you'd ever get her to the altar."

"Some things can't be avoided."

Sam narrowed his gaze and pulled a smoke out of his pocket. "She's pregnant?"

"Yeah."

"How do you feel about it?"

He should be upset. He should be horrified. He should be a lot of things, but what he was was the most shocking of all. "I do believe I'm happy."

Sam's expression didn't change. "Good." He lit a sulfur, and put it to the end of his smoke. Tucker had to wait for Sam to take a draw before he got to his point. "You're going to be a good father."

"Going to have to be. Have to be a damn good husband, too. Being married to me is not going to be easy for Sally Mae."

"What was there in the choices the woman's made to date that makes you think she likes easy?"

He didn't have a ready answer.

"She comes, as a pacifist, to the most violent place in the country, works as a nurse, despite folks' opinions of nurses, takes up being a doctor when her husband dies, and for a lover, she takes a man everyone else sees as Indian."

"I am Indian."

"You're no more Indian than you are white."

"The half that doesn't show, doesn't matter to most."

"True enough." He took another draw on his smoke. "But I imagine, to Sally Mae, you're the same as you are to Bella and me. You're just Tucker."

"The woman has no common sense."

"On that we're not going to agree," Sam said, walking back toward the barn. Tucker followed. "Any woman who can see past that mask of belligerence you wear, has a lot of common sense. She's also got a lot of grit mixed with her softness." Sam stopped and ground his smoke out under his heel. "Don't you go underestimating her. And don't go short-changing yourself. You deserve her."

The barn door squealed as he opened it. Tucker caught the door as Sam walked through. "I'm not so sure about that."

"Well, what you think doesn't really matter anymore, does it?"

"I like to think so." The coolness of the barn wrapped around Tucker as he stepped inside. Rays of sunlight filtered through the slats. The familiar scent of horses and hay greeted his next breath. Familiar, peaceful scents.

"Seems to me what matters was sealed up nice and tight for you, by fate."

A sorrel stuck its head out over the door of its stall and whickered a greeting.

Tucker patted the horse's neck before scratching behind its ears.

Sam bent and picked a saddle up off the floor. "Should have kicked that merchant again for making me treat good tack with such disrespect. So when's the wedding?"

"Three days from now."

He cast Tucker a glance as he carried the saddle to the side. "Not wasting time, are you?"

"No."

The horse bumped his head against Tucker's chest in a demand he scratch again.

Sam chuckled. "Red will keep you all day doing that."

"He knows what he wants."

Sam threw the saddle over an empty stall door. "Do you?"

"What?"

"Know what you want?"

"Meaning?"

"Is this marriage what you want?" He turned to face Tucker. "Isabella and I will take the baby, if that's a concern."

It was a viable solution. Nobody would question the baby's

parentage if it lived with Sam and Isabella as Bella had darker skin and eyes and Sam was blond. It would grow up accepted and protected. But without Sally Mae. Tucker straightened. "What the hell are you getting at, Sam?"

"That you don't have to marry the woman."

The hell he didn't. "She's pregnant. The child's mine."

"Never thought it wasn't. Just wanted you to know you have an alternative, if you want it."

"I don't."

"Then act like it."

"Shut up, Sam." Tucker cut Sam off, saving him the trouble of stating the obvious. Tucker had heard it all in his youth. How he was just a darker version of his father. A keg of dynamite waiting to explode, his future as clear as his father's present.

Sam waved his hands. "Before you take a swing at me, hear me out."

Tucker looked down. His fists were clenched.

"You've always kept to yourself, not had a lot to do with women, children—"

"You know why."

We're the ones who make that choice.

Sally Mae wasn't his father. Sally Mae wasn't his mother. She believed in him, them. He didn't need anything else.

Sam took off his hat and ran his hand through his hair. "Shit, Tucker, don't be so damn touchy."

"Hard not to be when you start in with your doubts."

"Son of a bitch, it's not you I'm doubting!"

That drew Tucker up short. Red bumped his shoulder with his nose. He ignored the invitation. "Who the hell are you doubting then?"

"Sally Mae is in a vulnerable position…"

This time when Red bumped him, he took a step forward. "You think Sally Mae's that desperate?"

Sam patted his pocket for his cigarettes. "I think you have no idea how appealing you could be to a widow with no prospects."

"Son of a bitch." Tucker leaned against the stall door and rubbed Red's nose, anger fizzling out as he realized Sam was protecting him, as surely as if an outlaw had the draw on him. No wonder Sam was reaching for his cigarettes. It wasn't often they interfered in each other's personal lives.

"I think I remember asking you the same thing when you got your heart set on Isabella."

"Yeah, well, turnabout is fair play."

"Sally Mae isn't using me."

"How do you know?"

"Because she turned me down."

Sam blinked and then rallied. "She didn't hold out too long. You're getting married in three days."

"I'm working on it. I had to make concessions."

Sam straightened. "What kind of concessions?"

It was Tucker's turn to shift uncomfortably. "I can't hit first."

"Well, shit. I can think of a lot of men who'll be lining up for a chat with you, once that gets out."

Tucker eyed Sam warningly. Sam's sense of humor could take strange turns. "I wasn't planning on that getting out."

"What else?"

"What makes you think there's more?"

"I've seen Sally Mae barter."

The woman could make a penny scream for mercy. "She can be merciless in her own way."

"Care to share the details?"

"No." Some things were too intimate to share. Like Sally

Mae's belief in him and what it did to him deep inside. "I've got a favor to ask."

"Shoot."

"I'm taking Sally Mae back to Hell's Eight after the wedding."

"Taking Shadow's advice?"

"Yes. She'll be safer there. We'll need an escort."

"Done."

"Thank you."

"Hell, Tuck." Sam slapped him on the shoulder. "There's no need to thank me. You'd do the same for me. Hell, you've done more."

"In that case, you got a bottle stashed out here in the barn?"

Sam smiled in the carefree way that Tucker and the Eight had thought he'd lost. "Sally Mae not approve of spirits?"

"Not taking a chance on asking."

Sam chuckled. "I've got one up at the house."

"Then, why are we standing here?"

"Because you're an ornery son of a bitch."

"Not anymore."

"Nope." Sam grinned. "Going to be a real advantage, knowing you can't hit first."

Tucker followed, a smile tugging at his lips.

Shit.

15

Sally Mae was waiting for him just inside the door when he knocked the next morning, palms flat against her thighs, the way she held them when she was nervous. Her lower lip was caught between her teeth. The pale gray dress she was wearing brought out the silver in her eyes and the dark circles beneath.

"What did he say?"

Tucker took off his hat and hung it on the peg by the door. She eyed it cautiously. Did she think he was going to leave her again? When she carried his child? "What did you think he was going to say?"

"I don't know. I imagined he'd just say congratulations. That's what most people do."

"Then why did you ask?"

"For something to say."

"Hello would have done just fine."

She glanced at his hat again.

"What?"

"You're staying here?"

"Yes."

"But people will…"

"Talk." He finished for her. "We're leaving in two days. It'll take them longer than that to work up to action and I'm not leaving you alone again."

Her tongue wet her lower lip, leaving it a shiny pink. It probably marked him as a heel, but he really wanted to kiss it, run his tongue over it, leave it shinier, plumper, ready for him.

"About that…"

"What?"

He went to the stove and grabbed the coffeepot. Liquid sloshed. He checked inside. Water. It was prepped. The burner was hot. The fire beneath freshly stoked. Thank God. The mother of all headaches pounded away behind his eyes. Damn Sam and his challenges. He set the pot on the burner and dumped in a couple handful of the ground beans in the stoneware jar. When he turned around, Sally was waiting. This time her hands were clenched in front of her.

"I'm not sure leaving is the best idea."

She was scared. He could understand that. "Staying is not an option."

"But do we have to go to the Hell's Eight?"

"Yes."

Another pass of her tongue over her lips. "Why there?"

It seemed a silly question. "Because you'll be safe there. Our children will be safe there."

"Will thee be there?"

Hell. She'd asked him how he thought their marriage would go, but he'd never asked her the same. He took a step forward, bridging the tension with touch, feeling the right-

SARAH McCARTY

ness settle inside him as her body came to rest against him. The willowy perfection that made up his world. Damn, it felt good to hold her. "Always."

"It's just that thee are never here much and I won't know anyone there."

"I'm not going to haul you across the state just to dump you, Sally Mae."

Her arms came around him slowly. He waited. Time stood still for the second of indecision before she wrapped them around his waist and hugged him. "I thank thee."

He kissed the top of her head. "Things have been moving pretty fast for you, huh?"

"Yes."

"You're scared."

She shook her head. "Nervous."

He knew scared when he saw it, but he wouldn't bludgeon her pride into the dust by pointing it out. "I'll take care of you, Sally Mae."

"I know."

Did she? He wasn't so sure. Her body tightened against his. He tipped her head back.

"What is it?"

Her complexion was pasty. Circles beneath standing out in sharp relief. "The coffee."

He could just begin to smell it himself. "It'll be ready in a few."

She shook her head and her hand went to her stomach. "The smell…"

Was making her sick. He quickly removed the pot from the stove.

When he turned back, she was staring at him again and the tension was back between them like a wall. "Guess that'll teach me to try and drink Sam under the table. Not even the day-after cure."

"You got drunk?"

"It's something men do to celebrate."

That clearly went beyond her comprehension. "He was happy for thee?"

"He was happy for us." Because she didn't look as if she believed him, he added, "Truth is, moonbeam, Sam, Shadow and Tracker have been pushing me to toss you over my saddle for a while now."

Her lips twitched. "They have?"

"Yup, it's only my sense of fair play that's saved you so far."

Another twitch of her lips, weak but there. He took the two steps to bring him in front of her. She didn't step back and when he put his arms around her, she leaned into him. And that fast the tension disappeared.

"You're tired."

She nodded. "I was worried."

"About what?"

Her answer was a shake of her head and a press of her forehead against his sternum.

"Sally?"

"It was foolishness."

He tipped her chin up. "Spit it out."

"I thought thee might not come back."

He remembered Bella's fears, Sam's promise. What it had meant when the chips were down and Bella had believed that promise. How she'd held on to it through Tejala's attack. How she'd held on to Sam when he'd gone over that cliff. How she refused to let go. He remembered how Caine gentled Desi, took her from terrified to confident by never failing her. A couple should believe in each other.

He bent his head, braced for Sally's withdrawal. She just stood there, a certain desperate quality to her stillness. She wanted to believe. He kissed her once, twice. On the third he lingered, waiting for the flutter of her lips that signaled her surrender. When it came, he whispered, "I'll always come back to you."

Her hands gripped the front of his shirt. She rose up on tiptoe as the passion grew, fueled by fear, caring, love. "I have asked so much of thee."

"Nothing I haven't wanted to give."

"Thee so fear being cared for."

She still shied from the words. "I think I'll learn to like it."

He wanted the words. Cupping the back of her head in his palm, he held her stretched up, poised on the edge of passion. She stiffened and moaned. And even as hungry as he was, he didn't mistake it for pleasure.

As soon as he released her, she clutched her stomach.

"You feeling poorly still?" She nodded and bit her lip. He grabbed a pot and shoved it in front of her. She looked at him, horrified.

"What? Better than heaving up on your toes."

"I've been making tea."

"That help?"

"Sometimes."

Then he'd make her tea. "Hold on."

He grabbed up the offending coffeepot. Throwing open the door, he tossed the water and grounds out the door, barely missing Crockett, who ducked. "Sorry."

The apology was wasted on the mutt, who galloped after the

debris in case there was something to eat or chase. Shaking his head, he closed the door. "That pup doesn't have a lick of sense."

Sally Mae rose immediately to Crockett's defense. "He enjoys himself."

"That he does." Once again there was that tension between them. "You still want tea?"

She nodded.

"Why don't you go sit in the parlor then and I'll make it for you."

She blinked at him. "It has to be made just so."

"Is the making any different from any other kind of tea?"

She shook her head.

"Then you tell me where the tea is and you tell me how long to steep it for and I'll prepare it while you take a load off."

As usual she didn't seem to know what to do with any kindness from him. Which irritated the shit out of him—he'd never been anything but kind to her. But now that she was pregnant, at a time when he should be the most kind to her, she expected him to turn into some kind of devil.

"I'd rather go lie down upstairs."

"Fair enough. I'll bring your tea upstairs."

"It's in the small blue tin beside the stove."

"All right then, you go on upstairs."

She put her hand on the wall and turned.

He studied her closely. "Are you feeling dizzy?"

"I'm all right."

All right wasn't an answer. *All right* was an evasion. He was learning with Sally Mae an evasion meant she didn't want to give him the answer she thought would upset him. The hell with that.

He picked her up easily. He was a big man and she was a slender woman. It wasn't that much work, but she acted as if he had just hefted an elephant. "You're not walking up those stairs so stop your struggling."

She huffed as he carried her through the parlor.

"You wouldn't want me to drop you, would you?"

She clutched at his neck. "I'll never forgive thee if thee drop me."

As if anything in the world could make him drop the mother of his child. "Then stop struggling," he said as he started up the stairs.

"Thee always have an answer for everything."

He smiled. Truth was, it wasn't easy carrying anybody upstairs. He did feel a bit of strain, but at least if he was carrying her he knew she wasn't going to fall down those stairs, so any amount of effort was worth it.

"Yup. Have to among Hell's Eight, otherwise they'll chew you up and spit you out before breakfast."

He set her on the floor in her bedroom. That ever so prim and proper space in which she became a wildcat in his arms. The room in which they'd created their child. His smile stuck as he shook his head. Hard to believe the woman he'd tumbled in that freshly made bed was the same woman who stared at him so starchly right now. He turned her.

"What are thee doing?"

"Unbuttoning your dress. You can't lay down in that."

"I'll take care of it."

"It's easier for me to."

She swatted at his hands over her shoulder. "I'd rather do it myself."

He walked around the front of her and tipped her chin up. "Sally Mae, I've seen everything of you there is to see, every pretty little inch. What are you afraid of?"

"It's indecent."

"How?"

"I don't know, it just is."

"You have some strange ideas, woman. Some very strange ideas."

"Fine." She stood still. "But just the dress. I can do the rest myself."

He wasn't stopping at the dress. She needed her rest and a corset was not conducive to peaceful sleeping. He didn't make his point then, though. He made it later as she was slipping her arms from the sleeves. As she held the front of the dress to her pretty breasts, he went to work on her stays, untying them in the back.

"What are thee doing?"

"I'm untying them."

"I'll never get them back that way again. I have hooks in front that I undo."

"I don't want my son squashed through his growing years."

"It's perfectly proper to wear a corset during pregnancy."

"Not in my book." He untied the last of the strings, slipped his hand beneath the loosened corset. Beneath his fingers he imagined he could feel the curve of her stomach as it would be when she was heavy with his child. He flattened his palm, felt the warmth of her skin, let the heat of her body join with his.

He was going to be a father. She was going to be a mother. Between them they'd created something special.

He nuzzled her hair away from her ear, took the lobe between his teeth and bit it gently. "I'll take good care of you, Sally Mae."

"By killing everything that thee think will harm me?" Despite the snap in her tone, she tilted her head to the side, facilitating the caress.

"I already made a promise there."

"So thee did. I'm just not sure thee can keep it."

"Neither am I."

He turned her again, pulling the dress from her hands, letting it fall to the floor, leaving her in her pantaloons and camisole. He could see the pale pink of her nipples through the almost sheer material. His mouth watered. His tongue itched to sample.

"But we're going to give it a try anyway, aren't we?"

"Yes. For our child."

"Fuck that."

She gasped. He didn't care. They could have a lot of illusions between them, but he wasn't having that one added to the pile. "Maybe you're just trying because of the baby, but I'm here because of you and what I feel when we're together."

She blinked and tears welled in her eyes, washing them from pale to dark. Her hand opened over his chest, pressing over his heart. "Yes."

Before he could say more, she tore out his arms and lurched for the chamber pot. He swore and followed, cupping her forehead in his hands, supporting her through the violent spasms. Wincing when a couple seemed to come from her toes. So much for hearing her say "I love you."

She was weak when the final spasm died off. He lifted her away from the chamber pot, alarmed when she turned lifelessly in his arms. "I'm sorry."

"For what."

"Thee can't have enjoyed that."

"Neither could you."

She shook her head. Her braid tumbled down, taking her lace cap with it. He caught the cap before it could hit the floor.

"I didn't want thee to see me like this."

He shoved the cap in his pocket. "Why?"

"Because…" She waved her hand in the empty space left by silence. "Thee are so strong."

"And you think you're not?"

Her forehead rocked against his chest. "I never have been."

"That's garbage."

"It's true. Thee should know. I tried for my parents, for Jonah and for myself, but I never have been. I'm always afraid. Always doubting."

He slid his arm behind her knees and lifted her into his arms. "Tried what?"

"To believe as they did. They were so good to me, taking me in, giving me acceptance and the room to find my way back."

He laid her on the bed. She sounded very unlike Sally Mae. So defeated. Taking the washcloth from the bedstand, he dipped it in the basin.

"From where?"

"From the silence."

He wiped her face. She stared at him the whole time. "I don't know who I am, Tucker, who I'm supposed to be."

"I don't believe that."

"Yesterday when thee killed Lyle, I was horrified."

"I know."

"Not for the reason thee think. That I should." She grabbed his wrist hard enough that her short nails dug in. "God forgive me, Tucker, I was glad thee killed him."

He didn't know what to say. "Maybe you ought to back up a bit so I can understand."

Her hand didn't let go of his wrist any more than her gaze released his. "It was so long ago."

"I can see how ancient you are."

"Some days I feel ancient."

He'd never seen her like this, full of doubt. "Got to say I like this side of you."

She just blinked. He ran the cloth over her face, pressing it gently against her temples. "I like knowing you're not perfect."

"That doesn't even make sense."

"It does if you think about how imperfect I am."

"Thee are the most beautiful man, inside and out."

"Now I know you've gone and puked up your common sense." He poured and handed her a glass of water. "I'm big, ugly and hot-tempered."

She drank thirstily and, when she was done, leaned back against the pillows. A bit of spirit returned. "I didn't say thee weren't misguided at times."

"That's my moonbeam."

He tugged off his boots.

"What are you doing?"

He hung his gun belt on the chair. "Joining you. All that puking took a lot out of me."

He stood and shucked his pants and his socks. He started to unbutton his belt.

"I did all the puking."

He was down to his long johns. "It still took a lot out of me." He lifted the covers. "Scoot over."

"The morning's half-over."

He slid under the covers, pulling her into his arms. She turned on her side and her cheek settled into the hollow of his shoulder. "This is decadent."

She didn't have the slightest clue as to what was really decadent. "So enjoy it. Are you comfortable?"

"Yes."

He stroked his hand over her shoulder, feeling the tension in her muscles. She was still all wound up. "Tell me about how you came to be with the Quakers."

"There's not much to tell."

"Sure sounded like a lot."

"I was upset."

"And now you're not." He tipped her chin up with his finger. "I'm not going away, Sally Mae, no matter what you tell me."

"I thank thee."

"I don't want thanks, I want explanations."

Her fingers curled into his chest. Her thumb flicked over his nipple. His body's response was instantaneous. Her thigh slid up his. He cupped it in his palm, sliding it a bit higher. "You can't distract me, either."

"I don't remember what happened to me before I came to the Griers."

"The Griers were your family among the Quakers?"

She nodded. "I remember being afraid to go to bed because of the nightmares."

"How old were you?"

"Around ten. I was found hiding in a wagon after an attack. I couldn't talk to give anyone even my name. I was brought to the Friends. The Griers took me in. They figured that when I needed to remember, God would lift the barrier. So in between, they gave me a new name, a new life, and all the love a child could want, but even my birthday isn't real."

Goddamn. "Then we'll try out new ones until we find one that you like."

"I don't want a new one. I was happy until I met thee."

"Bull."

Her hand clenched to a fist on his chest. "The Griers taught me to find God's light inside me. Thee can't understand the peace that comes with that. How grateful I was to have the terror stop and laughter return."

"I've got an inkling." It'd taken him years to stop lashing out and realize he didn't have to react as people expected. That he could control people in a large part through his response to them.

"But following God's way was always a struggle for me. It came so easy for them, for Jonah, but always so hard for me."

"How do you know it came easily for them? Did you ask?"

She shook her head. "Thee could just see it."

"Is that why you married Jonah? Because it came easy with him?"

It didn't make him proud to hate such a good man, but he did. Because Jonah had had Sally Mae's respect, had held her heart, had earned her trust where he was still struggling with her accepting him.

"I don't know. Maybe." She traced a figure eight over his chest. "His parents were friends with mine. He was always around, always there when I needed him. It just seemed natural that he ask me to marry and that I say yes."

As if she felt the jealousy raging within him, her hand opened over his heart soothingly. "It wasn't a grand passion that brought us together, but it was a good marriage."

"Ours will be good, too."

"Thee say that as if it's all under thy control."

"It is." He just had to figure out what she needed and give it to her.

Her lips burned soft and sweet on his chest. "Ours is a

grand passion, Tucker. It's not something that can be managed. It demands to be experienced. That scares me."

"I'd never hurt you."

She waved her hand. "I know that. Thee are the gentlest man I know."

No one had ever called him gentle before. "You sure you're looking at the right man?"

"Yes. Very sure. I sometimes think it would be easier to not see thee as I do. To pretend thee are like Jonah, who was content to have me in the periphery of his life."

Jonah the saint. He wanted to punch the man in the face. He wanted to run. How the hell could he compete with a ghost? "I'm nothing like Jonah."

"No. Thee are not."

He tossed the sheet back. "You should have thought of that before you lay down with me."

There was no way her hand on his chest could have kept him on that bed, but the words she said chained him as thoroughly as steel. "I did."

He turned on his side, looming over her on purpose, needing the truth. "Explain."

"There is a wild side to me, Tucker. My whole life I've tried to hide it, successfully hid it, because my family and Jonah just wouldn't understand it." Her hand left his chest and rose to feather across his cheek to play with his lower lip the way he did with hers. The reciprocity soothed the emotion seething inside. "I couldn't hide it from thee."

"No." He kissed her fingertips. "You couldn't."

"Thee threaten every ideal I value, but thee are the only one who sees me as me and is comfortable with it."

"There's nothing wrong with you."

"To me there is, but one thing that has been revealed to me in this opening is that I can't run from thee or myself any longer. I have to find a way to walk between thy world and mine."

He didn't know what to say to that, so he leaned down and kissed her.

"I'm going to try very hard," she whispered against his lips.

"Does this mean you're marrying me?"

"Yes."

"Good, then there's something we need to get straight."

"What?"

"You don't have to change a damn thing for me."

"Yes, I do. I already am, but—" her hand curled around his neck "—thee will need to be patient."

Patience was not his long suit. "Maybe we should just tackle these fears one by one. What's your biggest?"

She didn't even hesitate. "That I won't have a place at Hell's Eight."

"Honey, everyone's going to love you."

"I need to feel I belong, Tucker. I'm afraid I won't there. That I'll spend my days on the outside looking in."

The way he'd felt until the day he'd met her. "God—" He cut off the curse. "That's a hell of a fear."

"Yes, and one that only time, not thee, can fix."

"You'll find your place."

"Not just as thy wife and the mother of thy children?"

Goddamn, he hoped so. "Yes."

"I hope so."

Hearing her words so immediately echo his thoughts sent a shift of unease through his conviction. He pushed it away. Whatever Sally Mae needed, he'd give it to her.

Her hand behind his neck pulled him down, not for passion

he discovered as her eyes drifted closed, but for the return of her pillow.

As he resettled her against his shoulder, he asked, "Tired?"

She nodded and yawned. "Very. Already thy son makes demands on me."

"Thanks for going along with my decision that it be a boy."

"Thee seem to need it."

And she was always giving him what he needed. "The thought of a little girl scares me witless. I think we should let Desi and Caine break the ice with that one. Caine owes me anyway."

Her smile spread against his chest. "There is such love in thy voice when thee speak of thy friends."

"We've been to hell and back together. That tends to either breed friends or enemies."

"Thee have been together long?"

"Fifteen years."

"Thee were just boys." She yawned again. "What happened?"

He kept it short and to the point. "We got caught in the border wars. The Mexican army swooped in one day and wiped out our town. The members of Hell's Eight were the only ones who survived."

"Thee escaped."

"Yeah, but it was close."

Her hand covered his. He hadn't realized he was holding the bullet. "Thee were injured?"

"Yes."

"This bullet is very old?"

There wasn't any reason not to tell her, but he still hesitated. "Yes."

"Thee got it that day, didn't thee?"

"Yeah. There was a girl in town I was sweet on. Not that she would look at me—"

"She looked."

He shook his head. "I'd be dead if she had. My father was a mean drunk and my mother a squaw he rented out when we ran short on whiskey funds. They'd have fed me my balls for breakfast if they'd had an inkling I was looking at one of their precious girls."

"I'm sorry."

"It was a long time ago."

"Who was she?"

"Caine's sister, Mary." She'd been beautiful with hair that shone in the sun with all the brown of autumn. She'd look at him sideways and his heart would explode with puppy love. Christ, they'd been so young. "I tried to save her."

"Thee were just a boy."

"I was near as big as I am now."

"They were soldiers armed and trained. Thy best would still not have been enough."

"It wasn't. I stopped the first bullet, but I couldn't stop the second."

Her arms came around him, holding him close as if she could shelter him from the memory. The bullet, trapped between them, pressed into both their chests, a physical pain to join the mental.

"At least they didn't rape her."

"And she didn't die alone."

"No, she didn't die alone." He'd managed to crawl to her, the wound in his chest burning like fire, every breath agony, but he'd covered her slight body with his much bigger one as the battle raged around them. She'd been crying, he remembered that clearly. Tears slipping from her eyes as she'd stared at him in bewilderment.

"I'm sorry, Tucker, so very sorry."

So was he, but he'd learned it didn't change anything. "Anyway, when the smoke cleared, only the eight of us survived. Caine dug the bullet from my chest and we headed out."

Her fingers feathered over the ugly scar. "And to think I cursed thy surgeon for doing such a poor job."

"I'd be dead if he hadn't done something."

"I understand."

This yawn was bigger, more pronounced. "Enough about the past or you'll be back to having nightmares."

"I'm sorry, I seem to fall asleep at the oddest times lately."

He pulled the covers over her shoulders. "Go to sleep, Sally Mae."

He thought she had until she whispered his name sleepily. "What?"

"Is there a man of God at Hell's Eight?"

"Father Gerard is close enough."

"Is he a nice man?"

"Nice enough, why?"

"I have changed my mind about the wedding."

His chest tightened.

"I would like thy family to stand witness to our vows."

It wasn't enough. He needed more. "Why?"

"Because a marriage that is blessed in love is always blessed."

"Do you love me, Sally Mae?"

A delicate snore was his answer.

16

Despite her decision, Tucker insisted they be married before they left. Isabella provided a dress. Bright blue with yards of lace, it was a far cry from the plain clothes Sally Mae preferred, but Bella was so excited and the mantilla she carefully drew out of a box so beautiful, Sally Mae had run out of protests. And now she was standing in the middle of her bedroom, staring at her reflection in the freestanding oval mirror, feeling she was looking at a stranger.

"You look beautiful," Bella said, adjusting the mantilla about her face. "Do you like it?"

She touched the rich lace. She wondered what Tucker would think seeing her in this. "I feel so exotic."

Bella laughed and fluffed the ornate lace. "This is not such a bad feeling to have on one's wedding day."

"I wanted to get married at Hell's Eight."

"There is no reason you cannot have two weddings."

"I suppose not."

"As long as you're marrying the right man."

And she was doing that. She touched the blue silk dress draped carefully over the back of the upholstered chair. She had yet to try it on, but she knew it would fit. "Where did thee get all this on such short notice?"

"Señora Lopez sends her wishes for your happiness and that the joy of her marriage blesses yours."

"Señora Lopez?"

"Zacharias's mother."

She let go of the dress. "This was her wedding dress?"

"Yes."

"Why would she lend it to me?"

Bella carefully removed the mantilla before lifting the dress. "Because Tucker is important to all at Rancho de Montoya and all wish him happiness."

Sally Mae had heard the story of how Tucker and Sam had ridden with Zacharias and the Montoya vaqueros to get Bella back after she'd been kidnapped. She slipped her arms under the volumes of skirt. "They feel in his debt?"

Bella tugged the dress gently down before taking Sally Mae's shoulders and turning her around. The smile was gone from her face. "Tucker is a good man. Make no mistake, he is loved."

Sally Mae thought of how isolated he always kept himself. "Does he know that?"

Bella waved her hand. "He is stubborn that way."

Sally Mae ran her fingers over the cool silk. "I've noticed the tendency."

"But now that he has you," Bella said as she buttoned the myriad of buttons running up the back of the dress, "that should change."

"I don't want to change him."

"But you will. As you will change for him. It is the way of things when people love."

Was it? She hadn't necessarily changed for Jonah. Because of the age difference, it had been more that she'd grown into his expectations. Her marriage to Tucker was going to be very different. "Did you change for Sam?"

Bella smiled softly at her reflection in the big mirror. Her eyes shadowed with memories. "Oh, yes. For Sam I learned to trust." She shrugged. "And to think a bit more of the way others saw the world, yes?"

"And Sam?"

Bella clucked her tongue at the braids wrapped around her head. "You cannot wear your hair like this."

"I always do."

"Then today is a good day to change. A new beginning. Besides, it will look much prettier under the mantilla flowing loose." She unwrapped the crown of braids around her head. Her hair spilled about her shoulders in a pale shimmer that picked up the silver embroidering in the dress. The dress made her eyes appear almost blue. Would Tucker like that?

Bella paused. "Do you hate it?"

"No." She was beginning to feel like a butterfly coming out of her cocoon, caught between the old and the new, facing a strange and wondrous world. "It's beautiful."

"For Sam it was much harder to adjust." Bella sighed, going back to their original topic as she resettled the mantilla on Sally Mae's head and fastened it with pins. "He had so much mistrust, so much anger."

She could see that. Sam of the easy surface charm had never let anyone close before Bella. "So what did you do?"

Bella's grin flashed. "I threw myself at him shamelessly."

Sally Mae had had a chance to see a bit of Bella in action. "From what I saw, he wasn't running away."

"With his body, no, but in his head?" She clucked her tongue. "I will marry a very stubborn man."

"So will I."

Bella stepped back. "Not only once, but twice. I think this makes you more foolish than I."

"Possibly." Sally Mae turned, checking the dress from every angle. She wasn't used to seeing herself like this, more frivolous than practical, more beautiful than modest, but she liked the thought of how Tucker would react. She smiled. "But it could be I'm just more determined."

She definitely had to be determined. Folding her arms across her chest, Sally Mae planted her feet while the organ music started for the third time. "No."

Sam tugged her toward the church aisle. "Now is not the time to be stubborn. We've got two days of hard riding between us and Hell's Eight."

They'd been going around like this for five minutes. Neither was budging. Sam wanted the wedding started. She refused to get married by a reverend with a gun pointed to his head.

"Tucker's going to think you've changed your mind."

"Tucker would not be wrong."

Sam, a master at negotiation, knew when it was time to change tactics. "The wagons are hitched, all ready to go. Just got to get you two married and we can be off."

She looked down the aisle to where Tracker stood, pistol drawn, pointed at a visibly shaking reverend with the most mutinous expression she'd ever seen on his face.

Why couldn't they understand? "He is a man of principle. A threat won't make him change his mind."

Sam smiled one of his cold smiles. "He'll change his mind."

"Because thee say so?"

"Damn straight. This is my first time out as a best man and I'm not pleased he's putting a tarnish on my image."

"He is not the one ruining this day."

"He is from my point of view."

Since his point of view was what had Tracker pulling a gun on a preacher who'd refused to perform a mixed marriage, she wasn't surprised. She picked up her skirts and marched past Sam. "This is ridiculous."

The organ music picked up in volume. The pews were full of Montoyas, their ranch hands, Hazel and Davey and, surprisingly, Alma Hitchell. The rest of the town had expressed their outrage at the union with their absence. It hurt after all she'd done for them, but it wasn't unexpected. She smiled at Alma when she passed. The woman, cripplingly shy, blushed and ducked her head. Sally Mae wondered if she'd get in trouble with her husband for being here. Dwight wasn't the most broad-minded of men. Guilt put a rein on her anger long enough for her to stop at the end of the woman's pew. "I thank thee for coming, Alma," she said softly. "It means a lot to have thee here sharing our joy."

The woman nodded, keeping her head down.

Since there wasn't anything else to say, she continued the last few feet down the aisle, anger growing with every step. This was not the wedding she'd wanted. Tucker watched her come, his gaze assessing as if through studying her body language he'd discern the best way to handle her. He was dressed in a black suit and looking very formal in the white dress shirt she'd sewn for him, complete with sleeves. She would have thought him very handsome if he wasn't armed to the teeth, looking as if he was headed to a gunfight rather than attending his own wedding. The tension in his shoulders didn't bode well for her reception. She didn't care. She was a little annoyed herself.

"I am not happy with thee, Tucker McCade," she whispered as soon as she got close enough.

He folded his arms across his massive chest. "Seems to me I just heard you call this a joyful occasion."

"It seems to me thee have very picky ears that only hear what they wish."

"Maybe. Or it could be I'm more interested in getting the job done than worrying about some pissant's sensibilities while doing it."

She closed her eyes. Pissant. He'd called a man of God a pissant. Taking a steadying breath, she opened her eyes, meeting the reverend's. "I'm terribly sorry for this—" she encompassed the men, the guns, the pistol pointed at his head, with a wave of her hand "—inconvenience."

Behind her, chortles of laughter rippled along the rows.

"That's one way to describe it," she heard someone say.

"Next she'll be calling a posse a wee get-together."

At least someone was getting amusement out of this. She glared at Tucker before reaching up and snatching the pistol from Tracker's hand. An explosion rocked the church. She screamed and jumped back only to scream again when Tucker snatched her up against him. The reverend swore and patted his chest, presumably looking for holes.

Tucker ran his hand over her from shoulder to knee. "You all right?"

Tracker reached over and took the gun back.

"Might want to be more careful about what you go to grabbing, Doc Lady."

"Doc Lady?"

"Got to call you something," Shadow said, "and 'moonbeam' just didn't seem right."

Dear heavens. They knew Tucker called her that? A blush heated her cheeks. "If thee can't see thy way to using my given name, Doc Lady will do."

Tucker's hand slid over her hip. She pushed it away. "I'm fine, Tucker, let me go."

He stood her up. She straightened her mantilla.

He grabbed her shoulders, giving her a little shake that sent the mantilla listing again. "You ever pull a fool stunt like that again, I'll paddle your butt. You could have killed the reverend."

She gave up and left the mantilla where it was. "I wasn't the one pointing a gun at—"

"Aw, hell, I was just offering him some persuasion," Tracker interrupted.

Her "watch thy language" coincided with the reverend's "Watch your mouth."

The reverend looked over at her, a slight lift to his brow. "Thank you."

She inclined her head. "Thee are welcome."

Tracker grumbled an apology.

"Now that you're here, we can get started," Tucker said.

The Reverend's "no" coincided with hers.

Again he gave her a look.

"What in hell is your problem?"

Sally Mae wasn't sure whether Tucker was talking to her

or the reverend, but when Reverend Schuller opened his mouth, she held up her hand, cutting him off. "Thee are in a church, Tucker McCade. It is not a place for gun or force."

"The son of a bitch won't marry us without some incentive."

"Then we will wait to be married."

His jaw set. "I promised you a wedding today."

"Thee cannot force a man past his principles to serve thy own."

"Seemed to be working fine until you stuck your oar in the water," Shadow pointed out.

"No, it wasn't."

"The level of his shakes told me different," Tucker countered.

"Then thee read him wrong."

The reverend wiped his brow. He was a small man who wore spectacles and dressed neatly. He might not have Tucker's size, but he had a will of iron. "Thank you."

"If you're so grateful to her, Schuller," Zacharias called, "start reciting the vows."

Reverend Schuler wiped his neck. "As I said. I cannot in good conscience marry this woman to this man without speaking to her first."

She turned on Tucker. "All this because the reverend wanted to talk to me?"

"No, all this because I don't take kindly to his implication that I'd drag you kicking and screaming to the altar."

She rolled her eyes. "Thee couldn't just let him ask?"

Tucker's mouth took on that stubborn set. "He should have taken my word for it."

"We're burning daylight," Sam called.

"Shut up, Sam, and let me handle this." It was the rudest thing she'd ever said. She expected gasps of horror. All she heard was another ripple of laughter. She straightened her skirt and faced the reverend. "Thee wanted to talk to me."

"In private."

"The hell you will."

She snapped at Tucker, "I am not married to thee yet, Tucker, do not push me." Then she turned back to the reverend with a hint more patience. "Why?"

"Well, I was going to say to keep you from being bullied…"

"As thee can see, I am not being intimidated."

"More's the pity," Tucker muttered.

She glared at him again. "He is just joking. He'd be horrified if I feared him."

"Don't bet the farm on that, moonbeam."

The reverend tucked his handkerchief back in his pocket. "Do you truly wish to marry this man?"

"Yes."

"Why?"

The first man to hear of her love was not going to be the virtual stranger Tucker had rustled up to marry them. She took her place beside Tucker and straightened the mantilla once again before yanking the veil back down. "I told thee we should have waited until we got to Hell's Eight."

Tucker watched her carefully. "So you did."

"Wait."

Bella came running up. With deft hands, she realigned the lace and the veil, rearranging them back into graceful folds. "There, once again, you are beautiful."

She cut Tucker a hard glance. "Do not mess with her clothing again."

"At least for a few hours," someone murmured just loud enough to be heard.

Bella blushed. So did Sally Mae. Good grief, her wedding was turning into a farce.

"I think you'd better get on with it, Reverend," Tucker suggested. "I think the crowd's getting restless."

The reverend looked around the pews filled with hard-eyed men with ammo strapped across their chests, knives in their belts and impatient expressions on their faces. He swallowed, shifted his glasses on his nose, opened his Bible and nodded. Sally Mae barely had time to take a breath before he got to the "I do's." While she was still trying to catch up, he pronounced them man and wife. Tucker lifted her veil. His hand cradled her face. His expression was somber while indescribable emotion darkened his eyes. She searched his gaze, wanting to know what it was, sensing it was important.

"Hell, kiss her, Tucker," Zacharias called. "You've kept her waiting long enough."

She couldn't look away as his thumb stroked over her lower lip. "Yes, I have."

He kissed her gently, sweetly and ever so tenderly. As he pulled back, letting their lips part in reluctant increments, he whispered, "Do you remember asking me once why I stayed in Lindos?"

"Yes."

He smoothed his thumbs across her cheeks. "I stayed for you."

Five hours later she wasn't feeling beautiful. She was hot, sweaty and irritable. The men were testy because they'd gotten a late start, and the wagon in which Tucker had insisted she and Bella ride had her rear end feeling permanently bruised. And they were only halfway to their stop for the night on the way to Hell's Eight. The wagon hit another rock. Bella groaned and grabbed for the side. Her face was shiny with sweat and she looked as miserable as Sally Mae felt.

"Thank goodness, the clouds cover the sun," Isabella said, letting go of the wagon with one hand to clutch her hat with the other.

Sally Mae grunted as the wagon lurched back to the right. "I cannot understand how riding in this is better for the baby than riding on horseback."

Bella nodded. "I think it is one of those old women legends."

Sally Mae had to think on that. "Old wives' tales?"

"Yes. One of those."

Zacharias laughed and clicked the reins against the team's back. The two horses picked up the pace a notch. Sally Mae exchanged a glance with Bella. More speed just meant harder bumps.

"I bet thee are reconsidering thy insistence on accompanying us."

"A little, maybe." She glared at their driver. "Especially when Zacharias aims for the bigger bumps."

"You should be home."

Bella rolled her eyes at Sally Mae. "Always Zacharias wants me off the horse, in the house, under guard."

"He just cares about thee."

"Too many care about me that way."

Zacharias said something to Bella in Spanish. She snapped something back. Sam dropped back until he was alongside. "Trouble?"

Bella glared at Zacharias. "You should have left Zach home. It is dangerous for him to be here."

Zach didn't look at Bella or Sam. He just snapped the reins. He was a tall man, whipcord lean with eyes that looked through everyone and saw everything. Sally Mae had no doubt that he was every bit as dangerous as Sam or Tucker. He had the same unnerving calm confidence. "*La patrona* should be at *el rancho* where she is safe."

"*La patrona* should be with her Sam, riding to meet his family."

"I made the decision she could come, Zach," Sam said.

"It was unwise."

"I would only have followed."

"Hush, Bella."

"It is not his place—"

Sam cut her off. "If trouble comes, his will be one of the bodies between you and the bullets, Bella, that gives him a right to his opinion."

Bella subsided back in her seat. "I do not like it when you are right so often, Sam."

He tipped his hat and smiled. "I'll make it up to you later we get to Hell's Eight."

"I do not see how you can make up to me for this wagon."

"Not even if I tell you there's a hidden pond for you to swim in at the Hell's Eight, and the water is always cold and refreshing?"

Just the thought had Sally Mae wanting to groan. She pulled her bodice away from her chest. "Any chance Tucker knows where this pond is?"

Tucker's deep laugh drifted back.

Sam leaned his arm on his saddle horn and chuckled. "You can take that as a yes."

She closed her eyes and imagined it. Cool water rippling around her overheated body. Tucker on the bank, watching with those incredible eyes. She opened hers. He was watching her and she knew he was imagining it, too. Sam was looking at Bella with the same heat. Sally Mae blushed. Tucker laughed again. So did Bella and Sam. Zacharias didn't. He stopped the wagon and reached under the seat, pulling out a rifle and settling it across his lap. "I don't like the look of that pass ahead."

"Tracker's checking it out."

Zach nodded. *"Bueno."*

It looked like any other pass they'd ridden through over the last day to Sally Mae. Beside the wagon, Crockett whined. The poor pup. The day was hot and his tongue was hanging out. She patted the wagon seat. He jumped, made it halfway and faltered. Leather creaked as Sam leaned over in his saddle, caught him by the scruff and hoisted him up.

The puppy scrambled across Bella, giving her a sloppy kiss on his way to Sally Mae. He landed in her lap, too big now and too gangly to fit comfortably. From there it was only a lean to get to Zacharias.

"Do not think it, *perro.*"

Whether it was the tone of Zach's voice or the canteen Sally Mae opened, Crockett didn't push his luck.

The attack came out of nowhere. Splinters of wood exploded by Sally Mae's feet followed quickly by short explosions of sound.

"Get down!" Sam and Tucker hollered.

Zach shoved her over as the horses reared.

Isabella screamed. So did Sally Mae. Everywhere, guns sounded, and men shouted until she couldn't tell whose voice belonged to whom. From the back where he was tied, Crockett barked and snarled. Sam spun his horse in a circle, firing at the ridge. Tucker stood in his stirrups, a big target backlit by the sun as he sighted up the ridge. A bullet whined past Sally Mae's ear.

"Get down." Bella grabbed her and dragged her to the back, swearing in Spanish as Sally Mae's skirt caught on the rim of the seat. She fell headfirst. Stunned, she lay dazed, blinking against the sun. Bella tugged on her arm. Zacharias shoved at her rear.

"Goddamn it, Bella, get your ass down," she heard Sam yell.

Bella yelled right back, "If you would not make me wear these skirts, it would be much easier."

Sally Mae shook her head and forced herself up on her elbows. Yards of material blocked her view. Bright red material. Bella's skirt. Bella was caught like her. She reached up, unhooking the folds from the metal rod across the back of the seat. There was the thud as Bella flopped into the back. The wagon jerked as Zach drove the horses forward to the rock ledge.

Bullets popped like corn over a hot fire, splatting into the wooden sides, pinging off rocks.

"Son of a bitch, they're shooting at the women."

That was Tucker.

With a suddenness that jarred her forward and freed her own skirt, the wagon stopped. Sally Mae struggled upright. A hand grabbed her arm with bruising strength, lifted her out and tossed her to the ground. She hit on her hands and knees. She heard a horse scream, Crockett bark, and then there was the thunder of hooves.

"Got to be they think she's Ari!" she heard Sam holler.

"Son of a bitch!"

That meant they'd be shooting to kill. She didn't know much about Ari, but she knew that about the men pursuing her. And they weren't nice.

"No!" A soft body landed on top of hers. Bella.

"Get off me."

"They shoot at you."

"All the more reason for thee to get off me!"

"No."

"Thee will be hurt."

Bella clung tighter. "No!"

"*Patrona,* over here. Now."

Bella muttered above her, but in a few seconds, Sally Mae was free of her weight. "All the men in my life are bossy."

Sally Mae couldn't laugh. As soon as Bella moved, she pushed to her hands and her knees. A bullet between her hands sprayed her face with dirt. Through a haze of tears, she saw Zacharias lifting on the wagon.

Catching her gaze, he snapped, *"Ahora. Ayuda me."*

She didn't need a translator to know he needed help. Heart pumping, breath rasping in her lungs, she ran, ignoring the bullets pelting the ground around her until they came so fast and hard she could only yank Bella back and cringe.

Please, Lord, give me the strength…

"Goddamn it, Sally Mae, I told you to get down!" Tucker shouted.

Yes, he had, but there was no place to hide. Tucker and Sam returned fire, covering the rest of her and Bella's dash toward Zach. As soon as they got near, Zach ordered, "Grab an edge and lift."

"See," Bella grunted, hefting up on the wagon. "Bossy."

"Very," Sally Mae agreed, striving to match Bella's calm.

The wagon groaned and shifted. She braced her hand under the side and pushed, adding her muscle to Zach's and Bella's. The wagon went over with a thud and a jangle of metal. Fire burned in her thigh as she scrambled behind. She screamed and grabbed for it.

"Sally Mae's hit," Zach yelled, snagging her around the waist before throwing up against the bed.

"How badly?" Tucker called, backing his horse up toward the wagon.

With efficiency that gave no thought to her modesty, Zach tossed up her skirts. "A graze." He shoved her down so hard that pebbles scraped her cheek. "Stay there."

She caught a glimpse of Tucker's face as he sighted his gun up the ridge. Cold angles. Deadly intent. A single shot rang out, followed immediately by a scream. She didn't need to see to know the bullet had found its mark or to know the man was probably dead. She wasn't as sickened as she should be. Tucker had been right when he'd said she didn't understand the necessity of killing, but she was seeing it now. It was kill or be killed here. She'd always thought of fighting or walking away as a choice, but there was no choice here. To do nothing was more than suicide for herself. It was also suicide for her husband and their unborn child. That wasn't an option. She huddled against the rim of the upturned wagon, keeping her face pressed to the ground, struggling with the reality, the fear.

The gunshots continued, thunder in her ears, joining the staccato chaos in her mind. The sound grew louder, overwhelming, echoing wildly as scenes flashed in her mind's eye. Past. Present. Past. Shouts. Wild cries. Horses running past. White billowy tops of wagons glowing red in the setting sun, screams, gunshots, more screams. Oh God, so many screams.

Mommy. Splinters jabbed her cheek as she pressed her face against the side of the wagon, just like before. She blinked at the flashes of memory. Her mother shoving her down into the secret compartment under the wagon, her blue eyes wide with fear. With an order to stay, she'd closed the lid.

Oh my God, she remembered that. Her mother had told her to stay hidden, no matter what. And she had, the gun her father had given her in her hand, almost too big to lift. She hadn't known what she was supposed to do with it, but she'd held it and she'd stayed, watching as the Indians slaughtered her family one by one. And she'd cowered, doing nothing as they'd died, clutching the gun she didn't know how to fire, screaming in her mind, *Mommy! Mommy!* as her mother's blood soaked her dress, the dirt…

"Sally Mae. Sally Mae."

She blinked. Bella was in front of her, holding her shoulders, shaking her. "Are you all right?"

She pushed the hair out of her eyes. "Yes."

Bella let her go and slowly leaned back. "You had me worried."

"I'm sorry."

Around her the present-day battle still waged. To the left she could just see Tucker's horse was lying on the ground. Behind him Tucker lay, gun propped on the well-trained horse's side, using him as a shield as he fired shot after shot.

"How many do you count, Sam?"

Sam's answer was lost in a volley of gunfire. She looked around. Two of the *vaqueros* were facedown, likely dead. That left eight. Six if she discounted the absent Shadow and Tracker. Six guns against, oh my God, she couldn't tell how many.

"How many are there?" she asked Zacharias as he reloaded.

He shook his head. She didn't for a minute believe he didn't know, which must mean the answer was too many.

"What are we going to do?"

Bella glanced over from where she rummaged in a wood box that had been in the back of the wagon. She pulled out two pistols. She shoved one into Sally Mae's hand. "Fight."

Sally Mae looked at the ridge around them. Everywhere she looked puffs of smoke indicated yet another gunman. "We can't win."

"Then we will do much damage before we call it lost." The other woman looked perfectly at home with the gun in her dainty hand. Beautiful, confident. Deadly. Capable of doing anything. Capable of committing murder. Sally Mae didn't take it. She couldn't. "I can't."

Bella said something in her own language. "It is your man out there taking the bullets for you."

She looked. Tucker was positioned between them and the ridge. Anyone trying to get to her would have to go through him. "I know."

"He is willing to die for you," Bella snapped, pushing the gun toward her. "What are you willing to do for him?"

She could very easily die for Tucker, but kill for him? She just shook her head, not able to explain a life's worth of beliefs. Zach swore and cut her a look of disgust. She wanted to rail at him, but then there was the sound of a horn that jerked all of their attention around. Crockett barked crazily, lunging against the rope that tied him to the wagon, turning back and snapping at it when it drew him up short. She looked up. Oh my God! Outlaws swarmed the ridge, coming out from behind the rocks. She quit counting at twenty. Twenty well-armed men. Killers. Every one. Rising out of the ground like Hades' minions, guns pointed at them.

"We only want the woman," one of them called.

They think she's Ari.

Her. They meant her. This was all about Ari. The sister to Caine's wife. And they thought she was this Ari. And they were trying to kill her? That didn't make sense.

From behind them came the sound of a hammer being cocked. Heart in her throat, Sally Mae scooted up on her knees and turned. Two men stood half-shielded by a boulder. Even half-hidden she could tell they were dirty and ill kept. And even with her inexperience she knew with their guns trained on Zach, Bella and herself, they were out of options. She nudged Zach's side. He swore. When prompted with a jerk of a rifle, he dropped his on the ground. Sally looked over her shoulder. She could just make out the leader's head over the toppled wagon bed. He was watching her. She had to think fast. She could only see one path.

"I'll come out if thee let the others go," she called to the leader.

"What you'll do is be quiet, Sally Mae."

She ignored Tucker. "But thee have to promise to let the others go."

The leader, a blond man with a big droopy mustache and a hat pulled low over his brow, flashed her rotten teeth in what she supposed was a smile. It was hard to tell with the mustache. "You have my word of honor."

Bella elbowed her in the side. "They have no honor."

She knew that.

"Then we'll have to hope that what I'm doing will give thee some time to get away."

"I can't let you go out there, ma'am."

She looked at Zach. "Thee can't stop me."

He grabbed her arm, his expression grim. "Watch me."

"Your first responsibility is to Bella."

"And I tell him to stop you."

She shook her head at Bella and jerked her arm free. "He won't. He doesn't have the right and thee need the chance."

"You step out and they will kill you."

She shook her head. That was one thing she was sure of. "No. If they'd been trying to kill me, about thirty of those bullets would have done their job by now."

"Maybe they are just lousy shots."

That defied logic. "Is anyone that bad in such large numbers?" she asked Zach.

Grimacing, he shook his head. "Damn hard to believe they could be."

"Then I'm going to gamble I'm worth more alive than dead."

"Gamble on what?"

"The fact that those two haven't shot me, either." She raised her hands and called, "I'm coming out."

"Goddamn it, Sally Mae, you stay where you are. No one is bargaining with anyone today."

She was. "It's not thy call, Tucker."

"The hell it's not."

"She's not who you think she is," Sam hollered to the bandit. "She's not Ari."

"Don't matter to me either way," came the discouraging response. "If it's decided she's not who she's supposed to be, then I'll sell her. A little scrawny, but that blond hair will get me a good price."

Sell her. Oh God. Sally Mae put a hand to her stomach.

"You'll never collect it," Tucker said with disconcerting calmness. Everything about him was calm, still, waiting, watching...

"I think I will. I think I will even take the little brunette, too."

"The hell you will."

"What will stop me?"

Sally Mae grabbed the pistol out of Bella's hands and put the muzzle under her own chin. "I will."

"Jesus."

"Damn."

"No!"

The last came from the leader. A heartening reaction. She focused her attention on him, blocking out all other distraction. "Thee need me alive, I believe."

"You won't do it."

The barrel burned her skin. Certainty burned in her gut. "I will not allow thee to use me to hurt them."

"I think she means it, boss."

She did.

"Do not do this, Sally Mae," Bella begged.

"I'll be all right." She took a step, knees quivering so badly she had to lock them to stay upright.

Zach grabbed her arm. She shook her head at him. "If I go with them, I'm expecting thee to come after me. Thee will tell Tucker I'll be waiting."

"*Señora,* there is not going to be a piece of me left if I let you go out there."

A gun clicked on the ridge behind them. She had no doubt it was trained on Zach and Bella. The wagon no longer even provided cover.

"Correct me if I'm wrong," she whispered, "but at this moment all their guns are trained on me?"

"Yes?"

"And as I move so does their attention?"

Zach nodded, frowning as he understood her intent. "It's not much of an advantage."

She licked her lips. They were dry as bone. So was her mouth, her throat, her whole being. This likely wasn't going to end well. "It's better than nothing."

"*Estas loca.*"

The shaking was so bad she wasn't sure she could even stand. "I prefer to think of myself as desperate."

Isabella reached into her skirts and pulled something out of the pocket before shoving it into Sally Mae's pocket under the guise of a hug. The object was heavy and she had little doubt what it was. Another gun. She who never wanted to carry a gun now had two.

"I will tell Tucker you wait," Bella vowed.

She nodded. "I thank thee."

She stepped around the edge of the wagon, for the first time having a clear view of everything. Behind her, Crockett barked wildly.

Tucker was on his feet, his gun trained on the leader, his finger on the trigger white-knuckled with tension.

She smiled at him. He didn't smile back. "I'm gonna tan your ass when this is over, Sally Mae McCade."

She took a shaky breath and forced an equally shaky smile. "I will not even consider that violence."

She was taking a terrible risk. She knew it. Tucker and Sam stood ready, as did the Montoya *vaqueros,* watching for any opportunity. Dear God, she didn't know how to provide it, but she had to.

"You married to the skinny one?" the leader asked.

Tucker looked at him. "This morning."

"Well, I'll have to enjoy your wedding night for you."

Tucker's response was a baring of his teeth that could nowhere near be called a smile. "You're already a dead man. You won't be enjoying anything."

The outlaw laughed. "What I am is going to be a very rich man." He motioned to Sally Mae. "Come here."

Sally Mae followed the abrupt jerk of his hand. What choice did she have? Her threat to kill herself would only carry so far.

One step, two steps, on the third the world spun. She had to stop, or fall down. Tucker made a move toward her. The bandit behind him brought his rifle down the middle of his back. He dropped to his knees. She lunged for him. A bullet between her feet stopped her dead. "Just keep coming the way you were."

She righted herself, closed her eyes and then opened them again. She still didn't see any choice so she kept walking. Her breath wheezed in and out of her lungs. And with every step she got a better look at her captor. And with every step the temptation to pull the trigger grew. Evil. He was so evil.

"No." Soft and low, Bella's voice reached her. "Not that way."

No. It wasn't the way. But there had to be one. She had to think a way to change the odds. If only she knew where Tracker was. Where Shadow hid. Were they dead? If not, why hadn't they done anything by now?

She reached the leader. Immediately, he grabbed her arm, ripping the gun from her grasp before jerking her up against him. "I have a long-standin' score with your husband. I'm gonna enjoy settling it."

"You promised."

"I lied. Though if you're real nice to me, I might keep my word with the others, but he's not going anywhere."

She turned her head. "Tucker."

"I told you, Sally Mae, to stay at the wagon."

Yes, he had, but staying in the wagon wouldn't have given her any leverage. She put her hand in her pocket. "I'm sorry."

"No need to be sorry, Ari. We'll keep you busy enough you won't miss the half-breed."

She shook her head. Out of the corner of her eye she could see the outlaw's finger tightening on the trigger of the pistol pointed at Tucker. Oh, why didn't he duck, run, do anything but stand there, daring the bandit to shoot him?

Please, Lord, give me the strength.

"Don't make me do this," she whispered.

The bandit laughed. "Don't worry, you'll enjoy it."

No, she wouldn't.

"But first, this needs to be handled."

Yes, it did. Pointing the gun through her skirt, she pulled the trigger.

The gun beside her head exploded in rapid succession to hers. The bandit stumbled back, clutching his stomach, staring at her in disbelief. Blood blossomed between his fingers, overflowing the constraint of his hands. Around her men dropped like flies, one after another to the rhythm of gunshots raining down from the ridge above.

"About damn time Tracker and Shadow got into position," she heard Sam call.

Around her the battle resumed, this time with the odds evened out, but for her the only battle that mattered was the one before her.

"You shot me," the leader gasped.

She nodded, unable to look away from the blood.

"Didn't think you had it in you," he groaned as his knees buckled. She caught him, easing him to the ground.

"Get the hell away from him, Sally Mae."

She ignored Tucker's order. "Neither did I."

His eyes narrowed and blood frothed on his lips. "Never read anyone wrong. My…first."

And last. Because of her.

"Thee should make thy peace with God."

"Too late." He coughed and choked. Blood coated his teeth, dribbled from the corner of his mouth.

"God always listens."

On a last choking cough, the life left his eyes. Around her the battle was fought with guns and bullets. Inside her, it raged with tears and recriminations. Past. Present. Inaction action. Her mother's screams. Tucker's curse. Blood. The ever-present blood. Damned if she did. Damned if she didn't. Damned. Reaching over, she closed the outlaw's eyes, before wrapping her hands around her stomach and vomiting.

Tucker dropped the three bandits closest to him as they turned to fire at Tracker before he could pick them off. The ones that had a shot at Sally Mae. Before the last one hit the ground, he was at Sally's side. "Goddamn it, moonbeam, you pull a stunt like that again and you won't sit for a week."

He could have saved himself the breath. She wasn't looking at him, just the dead man, her lips moving rhythmically. Was she praying?

He shook her gently, his voice a hell of a lot harsher than his grip. "Sally Mae!"

Tracker came racing down the ridge, rifle propped on his thigh. Hell, now what?

"Trouble's coming," Sam said, putting into words what everyone knew. Tracker didn't risk a horse for anything less.

Tucker shook Sally Mae again. "Moonbeam, snap out of it." She didn't respond to a direct order while in shock any better than she did in real life. She just kept staring at the man she'd killed. Her face pasty-white, her lips parted, her breath coming in shallow pants as she mumbled words he couldn't understand.

Tracker pulled his horse up. "Comanches three miles out."

"Shit."

Shadow rode out from around a rockfall. "No way they didn't hear the gunshots."

No, there wasn't.

Crockett came running up, jumping on Sally Mae and kissing her face. Tucker pushed him away. He turned on the dead outlaw, growling. Wood groaned and metal clanked as Zach and his men heaved the wagon back upright. Some curses in Spanish said all he needed to know about that situation.

"Axle's broke," Zach called.

"The wagons are too slow anyway," Shadow offered.

Tracker pulled his hat down. "We're going to need to ride fast to outdistance the Comanches."

"Comanches..." Bella reached out to Sam. He caught her hand in his and brought her fingers to his lips.

"No worries, Bella."

She bit her lip and nodded.

"We don't have time to coddle her," Shadow said, jerking his chin at Sally Mae.

Goddamn it. Tucker knew that, but he wanted to. He wanted to wrap Sally Mae in cotton wool and keep her safe forever. He didn't want—he looked around at the blood, violence, her pale face—this. He'd never wanted this for her.

"We'll take the women up ahead of us on the horses."

Zacharias walked over, his spurs clinking with every step. "My men and I will stay behind and greet our new friends."

It was a generous offer.

"Four *vaqueros* against—" he looked at Tracker "—how many are there?"

"Ten. Those aren't good odds."

Zach smiled. "*Sí,* the Comanches have much to fear."

And maybe they did. The Montoya Ranch was not only in the middle of Comanche country, it was also in the middle of the disputed area between Texas and Mexico. The area was filled with bandits, rattlesnakes, Indians and bad weather. And these men were at home with all four, had cut their teeth fighting just such odds. Maybe they'd survive. Running his finger down Sally Mae's cheek, Tucker sighed. Regardless, it was an offer he couldn't refuse.

"Thank you."

"De nada."

It wasn't nothing, it was a chance.

"Is the baby all right?" Bella asked, breaking into the moment.

Tucker hoped so, but how could he tell? Goddamn, it might be a good time to pick up that praying Sally Mae was fond of. He forced a smile. "Gonna take more than a little bit of a ruckus to jostle my son from his resting place."

Bella's laugh was as strained as his voice, but it was still a bit of normalcy in a tension-filled moment. She walked up to Zach, and to the man's horror, put her arms around him and hugged him. *"Hasta la vista, mi amigo."*

"Hell," Sam called from where he was gathering weapons. "I'm getting jealous over here, Bella."

Zach caught her hands and removed them from around his

waist. "You do as *el patron* says. None of your nonsense. And you ride as I taught you."

She bit her lip and nodded, tears in her eyes. "But I will see you again," she whispered fiercely.

Zach didn't answer.

It was time to go. Tucker picked up Sally Mae. She kept on mumbling. He kissed her lips, taking her prayers as his, hoping God would count it worth something, seeing as it passed through her. "Keep praying, moonbeam," he whispered. "We're going to need all the help we can get." To the others he called, "We'll leave the horses and guns."

"Scatter the ammo about," Tracker added.

"Good idea. Scatter it all about. Horses, too. Maybe gathering treasure will slow the Comanches down." Because if the Comanches followed immediately, they didn't have a prayer in hell of escaping. Comanches rode like the wind.

"Let us handle that." Zach stood with his three remaining men. A couple were bloody, all were dirty. All were armed to the teeth. All he might never see again. "You get the women to safety."

Tucker set Sally Mae down by Smoke and turned back. He shook Zach's hand.

"On behalf of Hell's Eight, thank you."

Zach met his gaze squarely. There was no fear in his eyes, no dampness to his grip. He had the assurance of a man who knew his skills, knew his purpose and was comfortable with both. Zach's gaze cut to Bella. "On behalf of *el rancho* Montoya, we thank you."

Tucker nodded. It was a bond, forged in battle, sealed in blood. If either side survived this, they'd be allies for life. Zach touched the brim of his hat before joining his men already busy scattering weapons and horses. Caine would be pleased. Hell's Eight could do worse than have the Montoya *vaqueros* as friends. They sure as shit couldn't do better.

"Let's go." Tucker tossed Sally Mae up on Smoke. Thankfully, even while in shock, some things the body just remembered. Her legs parted as she slid into the saddle. He tugged her skirt out from under her before swinging up behind her. Beside them, Sam mounted before putting a hand down for Bella.

"Hold on, Sally." He couldn't tell if she was listening. He kicked Smoke into a gallop. At least running, she wouldn't be able to look at what she'd done.

17

The screams pulled her out of her numbness. Full of strain, pain and horror, they didn't fit the pattern of the others. Sally Mae opened her eyes. She was lying in a bed. She ran her hand over the clean sheets, touched her thigh, felt the edge of a bandage, pressed and then winced at the immediate pain. Pushing the sheet back, she pulled up her nightgown. Around her thigh a strip of white linen was tied. There was no blood on the bandage. The wound wasn't fresh.

The scream came again, long and drawn out. She recognized that sound. It was the sound of a woman in labor. Swinging her legs over the edge of the bed, she stood. The room spun. Using the mattress as support, she braced herself until the dizziness passed. Her knees felt weak. Beside the bed was a plate of food. She lifted the napkin covering a bowl of soup and bread. She squeezed the bread. It was rock hard. It'd been here awhile. She closed her eyes and tried to remember what had happened. There'd been the ambush, the fight. She remembered holding a gun, pulling the trigger, but she couldn't remember anything else. Couldn't remember if she'd hit her target. Couldn't remember getting here, wherever here was. Couldn't remember anything except a soothing darkness that stretched comfortingly around her and the occasional murmur of Tucker's voice.

On the chair beside the bed was one of her dresses freshly pressed. She pulled it on over her head. Without her corset she couldn't button all the buttons, but enough fastened above and below the waist to keep her decent. On the table beside the bed lay her cap, also freshly starched. She put it on her head, feeling oddly uncomfortable as she pinned it in place. She didn't waste time wondering why, as a man yelled over the woman's next scream. "For Christ's sake, do something for her!"

Trouble. She didn't bother with shoes, just rushed out the door, following the murmur of voices and low moans of pain until she arrived at a bedroom. Inside, a man stood beside the birthing bed, holding a blonde woman's hand. Beside him stood Bella and an older woman of Mexican descent.

"There's nothing I can do."

"I won't accept that."

Bella shook her. "There's always something."

"You should not even be in here," the woman reprimanded. "A newly engaged woman who has never had children should not be in the birthing room."

"Let it go, Tia."

This was the infamous Tia who Tucker so loved. The woman who'd taken eight wild, lost, devastated teenage boys and given them the anchor they'd needed to forge Hell's Eight. If Tia was here, it must mean they'd made it to Hell's Eight. She offered a prayer of thanksgiving.

"Maybe I can help?" It came out more of a rasp than a confident statement.

Everyone turned at once. There was more shock in their stare than she'd expected. From Caine, there was even a bit of horror.

She put on her most I-am-competent-despite-your-disbelief smile. "I am a nurse and I trained under my husband for seven years. I've attended more than a hundred births."

"Tucker!" Caine bellowed.

"What?" came the faint response from beyond the open window.

Caine didn't take his eyes off her. "Get your ass up here now."

"Not on your life."

"Your woman is awake."

There was a curse. No one moved, just stood there, staring at her as if she had two heads. Two minutes later, a door banged open and there was the heavy tread of boots on the stairs. Tucker burst into the room, coming to a halt just inside the door. He took in the situation with a quick glance and then smiled a smile she'd never seen him use before.

"Good to see you finished your nap, Sally Mae."

"I thank thee."

"Get her out of here."

"Shut the hell up, Caine."

The woman on the bed moaned, and her head whipped from side to side as another contraction started. "Desi doesn't need this right now."

"Just what is this?" Sally Mae asked.

It was Bella who answered. "You went a little crazy on us, *amiga*."

"Caine," Desi said, reaching for him with her other hand. Even from here, Sally Mae could see the furrows already clawed into Caine's arm. Still without hesitation, he gave it to her again.

"How crazy?" Sally Mae asked, taking in the amount of blood saturating the towels piled on the floor, the size of Desi's belly, the pallor of Desi's complexion, the whiteness of her lips.

"It's been three days since the ambush."

Again there was that confusing jumble of images. A blond woman, Indians, herself as a child, screams, a man with a droopy mustache, herself as an adult, a gunshot...blood. "Three days?"

"You haven't spoken since then," Tucker inserted gently.

Because she couldn't think of anything better to say, she settled for, "I must have had a good reason. I don't usually skip meals."

Desi's moans grew louder. "Tucker, get my bag."

"Sally Mae."

"The only thing you need to get, Tucker, is her the hell out of here. The last thing I need is a crazy woman near my wife."

Sally Mae flinched at the vehemence in the statement. "I can help."

"Lady, if you force me to, I'll toss your ass out that window."

"Caine!" Tia gasped.

"The hell you will," Tucker snapped.

"Then thee had better toss thy wife right after me. It will save time." She squared her shoulders and matched him glare for glare. "I can help thy wife."

"You're nuts."

"I'm a doctor."

"That's not what I heard."

"I'm about as close as thee are going to get right now, and from the amount of blood thy wife is losing I'd say I'm the last chance thee have."

Caine blanched. Desi moaned. Tia crossed herself. Tucker stepped forward. "She's damned good, Caine. Better than any doctor I've ever seen. If she says she can help, then she will."

She looked at him, surprised.

He smiled at her. "I used to doubt the viability of your beliefs, but I've never doubted your dedication or your ability."

"I thank thee."

"She fainted at the sight of blood," Caine argued. "How the hell can she do anything but make things worse?"

"She fainted at the impact of taking a man's life. She's a pacifist, for Christ's sake."

"Do not blaspheme, Tucker McCade!"

Desi's scream filled the room. Sally Mae had had enough. She pushed past Tia and pulled the covers back.

Caine grabbed her arm. "What the hell do you think you're doing?"

A gun cocked in the silence. Bella's "Let her go," punctuated the end of Desi's scream with quiet resolve.

"You won't shoot."

Bella smiled, looking impossibly beautiful and sweet. "Everyone tells me that."

"I'm surrounded by crazies." Caine released her arm, and bellowed, "Sam!"

"What the hell did you do now, Bella?" came the immediate dry response through the window.

Caine said, "At least he knows you." His tone was equally dry.

Bella didn't flinch. "Yes. He knows me very well. He also knows Sally Mae, and I am certain when he gets here, he will tell you what a donkey's behind you are to question either Sally Mae or myself."

"He doesn't have to wait for Sam to hear that." Tucker

snapped, "Stop being a jackass, Caine. You know damned well I'd never suggest anything that would hurt Desi."

"Shit." Caine ran his fingers through his hair. "I don't know a goddamn thing right now."

Desi gripped his bloody forearm and gasped, "Please, Caine. Let her try."

"You sure? She could do more harm than good."

"Anything is better than the nothing I have now."

Caine nodded to Sally Mae. Bella uncocked the gun. Tia turned to Sally Mae. "I think the baby is stuck."

Oh, darn. "Breech?"

Tia nodded. "Sideways."

"Tucker, get my bag."

"I've got it here," Sam said. When she looked at him, he shrugged. "Figured even Bella couldn't create that much of a ruckus by herself."

Bella feigned a pout. "I am saddened you doubt me."

The attempt at humor fell flat. Sam brought the bag to Sally Mae. He glanced at the bed, the towels. Desi. The smile he gave the laboring woman was gentle. "Looks like Sally Mae woke up at a right opportune time, Desi."

"You recommend her?" Caine asked.

"Without reservation."

"Then for God's sake," Desi snapped, "Everyone get out!"

Sally Mae finished washing her hands. Tucker cast her a glance. She answered the question in his eyes with a nod of her head. She didn't know what had happened to her in the last three days, but this was familiar. This she could handle. All the men left the room except Caine. As she applied the special salve to her hand and arm, she asked Desi, "Do thee want him here?"

Desi bit her lip.

"It's all right if thee do and all right if thee don't, but things will get pretty intimate, and if thee are going to focus more on worrying about him than helping me, I'd suggest he step out. For just a bit."

Caine's response was an immediate planting of his feet. "I'm staying."

"Is he always this stubborn?" she asked with a smile. If his insistence on staying didn't say how much Caine loved his wife, it was obvious from the tender way he stroked his hand over her sweat-dampened hair and the tender kiss he pressed on her brow.

Desi smiled up at him. "This is one of his good days."

The joke was weak. Sally Mae laughed anyway.

"Then letting him stay will be easier than fighting him." She smiled at both of them. "If thee need to faint, please fall backward."

Caine eyed her hand. "What in hell are you going to do?"

"I'm going to try and turn the baby."

"How the hell—" Realization dawned. He turned pale beneath his tan. Tia grabbed his arm. "Maybe it is best you wait outside, *mi hijo*."

"No." He looked at Bella. "Make sure I don't fall on her."

Bella, a bit paler herself, nodded. "Done."

Sally Mae lifted the sheet and draped it over Desi's knees, giving the other woman some privacy. Soon it wouldn't matter, but right now she needed her calm.

"This will hurt, but it's necessary. Try to remember to breathe and relax."

Please don't let the baby be stuck. Please don't let it be too far gone. Please let Desi have enough strength left if I have to do the unthinkable.

Please, Lord, give me the strength.

"What are you looking for?" Caine asked.

She saw the desperateness with which Caine watched her every move, felt the faith in Desi's acceptance of her skills in her response to her direction. She smiled quietly at them both. "An answer to a prayer."

Her prayers went unanswered. Not only was the baby breech, it was stuck. Desi was bleeding badly and they didn't have much time. She washed her hands again in the fresh basin of water Bella had fetched, trying not to notice the way the blood stained the water first pink then red. Trying not to remember. She needed all her focus at this time.

As soon as Desi got her breath, she asked, "How bad is it?"

Stalling for time, Sally Mae dried her hands. "What makes you think it's bad?"

"I'm getting…weaker."

Sally Mae licked her lips, unsure how much to tell. How much Desi could take.

"Tell her," Caine ordered, his expression granite hard.

She licked her lips, the truth clogging in her throat. "It doesn't get much worse," she finally admitted.

"The baby?" Desi panted.

Caine shook his head, pinning Sally Mae with those green eyes of his that cut through pretense like the edge of a knife. "You save Desi."

Desi shook her head. "No."

Tia crossed herself and started praying. Bella joined in. All Sally Mae could do was give them the truth.

"You're built very small inside. The baby's stuck. The more you push the more you tear inside. That's why you're weak. You're losing blood."

"The baby?" Desi asked again.

"It's weak, too."

Caine brought Desi's hand to his lips, pressing a kiss to the back. "What can you do?"

Nothing was the first word that came to mind, but it wasn't true. There was an operation. She'd seen it done four times, only done it twice.

"I can use forceps." Just the thought sent crushing waves of inadequacy through her. What if she made a mistake?

"Do it."

She shook her head at Caine. "It's not that easy."

Desi panted with the onset of a fresh contraction.

"Whatever thee do, don't push."

Desi nodded and groaned. "Easy for you...to say."

No, it wasn't. None of this was easy.

"It can't be more complicated than this," Caine muttered.

It was. The hairs on the back of her neck tingled. She looked up. Tucker stood in the doorway, watching her. She licked her lips. These people were his world. He expected her to do something for them.

"The procedure is very dangerous. It can hurt the baby or the mother if not done just right."

"How dangerous?" Caine snapped.

Tucker came to her side.

There was no way to soften the truth. No time. "Even if it was a fully trained doctor who'd done the surgery a hundred times, things have gone so far the odds are high that both will die, but the baby's chances to survive are better."

Caine's response was immediate. "Forget it."

She licked her lips again. Tucker's hand settled on her shoulder, squeezed. She leaned into him, letting the comfort spread through her.

Desi worked up on her elbows, her big blue eyes dark with pain and...understanding? "What happens if you don't try?"

Sally Mae grabbed Tucker's fingers where they curled over her shoulder, clinging hard to his strength as she divulged the truth. "Thee both will die."

Caine swore long and viciously.

"You need to talk. I'm going to step out," Sally Mae said. Desi was already reaching for Caine. So much love flowed between the couple, it was palpable. Sally Mae stopped at the door, blinking back tears because there was another truth she had to reveal. "There isn't much time. Every minute that passes the odds go down."

There wasn't anything left to say. She closed the door.

Tucker immediately pulled her into his arms. His cheek pressed the top of her head. "Damn it, I missed you, woman."

She hugged him back, holding him close, wanting nothing more than to climb inside him and escape from the hell to which she'd awakened. "I'm sorry."

He tipped her head back with a hand in her hair. The strings of her cap brushed her cheek. "For keeping me waiting for your kiss? You'd damn well better be sorry."

Oh God, she needed his kiss. His mouth closed over hers, tender at first, but then harder as the hunger flared between them, as the fear and need of the past few days fought for an outlet and found it in passion. Against her, his cock pressed. She rubbed her belly over the hard ridge, delighting in his groan. He was the first to pull back, sprinkling kisses over her cheek, her eyelids, the corner of her mouth, each kiss punctuated with a new order.

"Don't ever put yourself in danger like that again. Don't

you ever go away from me like that again. Don't you ever, ever scare me like that again."

"No." She cupped his face in her palms as his mouth wandered down her neck, nipped at her throat, kissed her nipples through her dress, before working back up. "I won't."

His eyes were dark as they met hers. "I mean it, moonbeam. Because next time I won't be so nice. Next time, I'll climb right into the nightmare with you and drag your ass back whether you're ready to come or not."

It was a silly, nonsensical thing to say. The fact that her no-nonsense Tucker was saying it was proof as to just how much she'd scared him. Standing on tiptoe, she kissed his beautiful mouth, fitting the edges of hers to the edges of his the way he liked. "I can't afford to remember right now, but I promise when I do, we'll talk, all right."

His expression sobered. Through the door she could hear the murmur of voices. Desi's tight with resolve, Caine's hoarse with fear.

"You don't have to try this."

"I know." She could run away. No one would blame her. They'd probably applaud her common sense. She was, after all, just a woman. And as such had her limitations.

"But I think you should."

Except to Tucker. She blinked and looked up.

As always, he saw her as she was. Nothing more. Nothing less. Flaws and all, but always his equal. She leaned her cheek into his hand, too much between them for pretense.

"I'm not saying it will work," Tucker added. "I get the feeling there are too many opportunities for things to go wrong for anyone to say that, but I've seen you work, Sally Mae, seen you heal people when other doctors would have just walked away."

He lifted her hands to his mouth and pressed a kiss to the left. "There's magic here." Next he pressed a kiss on the right. "And here. And not just the sexual kind."

"Thee can't know...." How inadequate she felt to have just suggested this. How humbled she was that he thought she should.

"Yeah, I can." He brought her palms to his chest. "I know you, Sally Mae. I know how scared you are now, and I know how much you want to help. I know there's no one else I'd send in that room with as much confidence."

He reached around his neck and lifted the bullet over his head. The one that he wore as a talisman. The one that reminded him of where he came from and where he wanted to go. The one that gave him the incredible inner strength she so admired.

"I love you, Sally Mae. You're my wife, the mother of my child." He dropped the necklace over her head. "But you're also a damn fine doctor. And win or lose when you come out of that room, there's no one going to be prouder of you than me."

Oh God. She clutched the necklace in her hand, feeling the roughness of time etched on its surface, the warmth from his body.

The door opened. Caine stood there, head up, shoulders back, as if through sheer force of will he could control the outcome. She hoped he could.

"We want the procedure."

She wasn't surprised. There really hadn't been any other choice. She nodded and headed into the room. Caine touched her shoulder as she walked by, stopping her. His mouth tightened. His drawl was hoarse and low as he said, "I love her."

It was a declaration. A plea, maybe even a prayer. She nodded. "I know."

Caine made to close the door. Beyond it, Tucker watched, arms folded across his massive chest. On the outside, looking in. The bullet weighed around her neck.

She caught the door with her hand. "Wait."

At the cock of Tucker's brow she licked her lips. "Come with me."

"Why?"

He wasn't supposed to ask why. He was just supposed to say yay or nay. But he had, and she had to answer. It was easier than she expected. "Because I need thee."

Immediately, he was through the door and at her side.

"I thought you'd never ask."

18

Four hours later, he took her to the pond.

They sat on the bank, side by side as the arrival of twilight chased a bit of the day's heat away. It would have been an idyllic setting with the trees surrounding the water in cool green and the pond reflecting back the ruggedness of the mountain behind. Idyllic except for the fact Tucker had put a good foot of distance between them.

"I've got to tell you, moonbeam, I almost lost my stomach in there a few times." Picking up a rock, he lobbed it into the pond. The ripples spread outward, growing with the passage of time, distorting the reflection of the mount. "It was almost a sure thing when you went in with the forceps."

But he hadn't. From the time he'd walked through the door, he'd stood behind her, silently offering strength through the touch of his fingers on her spine. She'd asked God so many times to give her strength, but he'd done her one better. He'd given her a man who knew how to share his. "I'm glad thee didn't."

"You and me both." He laughed and chucked another stone. A tickle of unease crept up her spine. He had yet to look at her. "Caine would never let me live that down."

"Probably not. But he would have forgiven thee. He's very happy right now."

"Because of you."

She shook her head. "Because the operation worked."

Tucker shook his head and patted her knee. Patted her knee? "Because of you, he has both his wife and his son."

"It was sweet of them to remember Jonah that way."

"Well, they couldn't likely go around calling the kid Sally. Jonah seemed a decent compromise."

She smiled, eyed the distance between them again and frowned. "Can I ask thee a question?"

"Shoot."

She was too tired to prevaricate. "Is this distance between us because of me, too?"

He didn't immediately scoot over as she'd hoped, didn't tell her she was imagining things. But he did take a deep breath, and did answer.

"Yes."

Inside, her heart sank. Outside, she held on to her composure. Barely. "Why?"

He rested both forearms on his knees, letting his hands dangle, looking for all the world like nothing more important was being discussed between them except the weather. "You mentioned once that you worried you wouldn't have a place here. It occurred to me, watching you work miracles in there, that you're right." His right hand clenched to a fist. "You were meant for better things than being buried up here married to me."

"Bullshit."

The curse snapped his head up. "I'm tired of men telling me what I need, what I want. Do thee want to know what occurred to me while I was in there working miracles?"

"Not sure I do, judging by the look in your eyes."

She came up on her knees. "It occurred to me I never would have had the courage to try that if thee weren't there beside me. It occurred to me that while I'd been praying for years for God to give me strength, he did me one better. He gave me a man who knew how to share his strength with me. It occurred to me that after all these years of trying to find acceptance in all the wrong places, I finally had found it with thee. And I loved it."

He caught her hands and tumbled her into his lap. "You thought all that while working tongs into a woman's belly."

She nodded, the tears she'd been trying to hold back spilling over. "I thought all that. So please, if thee think I'm too un-feminine after watching me operate, just tell me, but don't lie and make up stories."

"Unfeminine? Where the hell did you get that idea?"

"I want to be more than a doctor, Tucker. I want to be a wife, a mother. I want to take care of you and our children as much as I take care of others."

He tipped her chin up and kissed her, soft and sweet the way he did when his heart was exposed. "For a smart woman, you have the strangest notions. Remember me, Sally mine? The man who haunted Lindos simply because you were there? The man who almost jumped over the moon when you said you were pregnant because he finally had an excuse to take what he wanted? The man who wants to teach you to kick a man's nuts up into his teeth? The man who wants to see your pretty face first thing every day when he gets up and every night before he goes to sleep?"

She couldn't help a watery laugh. "I think thee forgot to tell me all that."

"Well, must be because I was relying too much on your feminine intuition to pass on the news. Or maybe it was because I had some idiotic notion if I didn't say the words you'd be safer. Or maybe it was myself I was worried about, who knows, but I'm rectifying that right now."

With his hands on her hips he brought her closer. "Scoot on up here so I can say this right."

"I need to be on my knees for this to be right?"

His grin was the old Tucker full of confidence and sensuality as he eyed her breasts, which were even with his mouth. "It'll save time later."

Her nipples peaked and she shivered. His chuckle sent another shiver straight down her spine. His fingers went to work on the bodice of her dress, the backs rubbing in an erotic prelude. "I love you, Sally Mae McCade. I fell the moment I saw you standing so prissy in that saloon, taking grown men to task with a complete disregard for your personal safety, and I've never looked back."

He loved her. The knowledge skimmed her consciousness the way his fingers skimmed her bodice, lightly, experimentally before settling down through the barriers to find the core beneath. Happiness blossomed outward, blending with passion, burgeoning with joy. It was all she could do to keep her voice even. "Thee fell in love with me because I was prissy?"

He spread her dress wide and went to work on the ties of her nightdress, loosening them only enough so he would cup the material under her breasts, pressing them up and in. "Got to admit what that prissiness said about your wild side really caught my attention."

She smiled and dragged her nipple across his lips. They immediately closed around it, nipping the way she liked at first, sending those darts of sensation deep before nursing them back into the foreground with a gentle suction.

Threading her fingers through his hair, she held his mouth to her, rocking against him as the rhythm caught. "Oh!"

"I'm not hurting you, am I?"

"No, but it's so good." Better than before, sharper.

"Heard tell from Caine pregnancy can make a woman more sensitive. Shall we find out?"

He smiled and curled his tongue around one turgid peak, holding her gaze as he dragged it across. She fell against him, wanting more. He gave it to her, opening his mouth, taking as much of her breast as he could inside, letting her feel the roughness of his tongue, the edge of his teeth, the promise of pleasure.

He leaned back, touching one damp tip with his finger. "I'm thinking he may be right."

Definitely right. "Yes."

"Let's see how much, shall we?"

His fingers slipped between her thighs, rubbing gently as he sucked and nibbled at her breasts. She couldn't stifle a moan and, as he continued, didn't bother trying. "That's it, moonbeam. Feel good for me."

She wanted it to last, but he knew her too well. Within minutes she came, crying out as her body buckled under the joy.

He held her until the last shudder rippled through her, rolling her nipple across his tongue one last time before tugging her dress and nightdress over her head and laying her naked on the soft moss. Something fluttered to the ground as he tossed his clothes aside. He stood there like a pagan god of old, his eyes hot with desire, his cock heavy with need. For her. She licked her lips and spread her thighs. He laughed and came down beside her.

"We do have a slight problem, you know."

"We do?"

"Uh-huh." He traced her lips with the tip of his finger, making them tingle and pout. "I promised Sam I'd beat your butt black-and-blue for that stunt you pulled back there at the ambush."

"Thee did?"

"Yup. Don't see as I have any choice as he's already taken care of disciplining Bella."

"I heard." Bella's moans of pleasure had carried clearly through the hacienda walls.

Tucker smiled. "I think the boy's gone soft in his old age."

"Or maybe he just loves his wife."

"That's a distinct possibility."

"As the walls are thin at the hacienda. I think thee know it's more than a possibility."

"That's why I brought you down here and left strict no-trespass orders." He cut a glance at her from under his hat, a faint smile tugging at his lips. "I don't want any interference with my discipline."

She grabbed his hat and tossed it aside. Unfettered, his hair fell around her with the coolness of night. "Good idea."

His smile was very white in the shadows. "My wild woman."

She smiled back at him, sliding her hands around his neck, spreading her legs for him as naturally as she took her next breath. "My wild man."

He settled between, his cock pressing at the entrance of her body. His hands, behind her head, cushioned her skull from the ground. His body above hers sheltered her from the cooling breeze. "All yours, moonbeam."

"Good."

"But not tonight, baby."

"What?"

"Tonight's not going to be about wild."

"It's not?"

"No. It's going to be about love." His lips nuzzled her cheek, slid back to her ear as his body joined with hers, that first stretching riding the fine edge between pain and pleasure, causing her to tense. "Shh, relax, just relax. Let me in, Sally Mae, let me love you the way I want. Sweet and gentle. With everything I am."

He caught the lobe of her ear between her teeth, biting gently.

She cried out, tilting her head facilitating the caress the same way she struggled to facilitate his entry with a lift of her hips. "Yes, please. Love me like that. With nothing between us."

"Only love."

She relaxed. His cock slid smoothly along her channel, opening her for his possession. He groaned and shuddered. She sighed and quivered.

"That's it, just like that. Son of a bitch, you're so tight. So sweet."

His hand came under her thigh, lifting her leg until it draped over his shoulder. Turning his head, he kissed the inside of her knee. His fingers retraced a path down the inside of her thigh, finding the plump folds of her labia, slipping between until they settled on the hard nub of her clit. A shudder took her from head to toe as he squeezed just hard enough to bring about another quiver. "I like you like this, all open and accepting. Mine to do with as I will."

His thumb circled. Her hips bucked. Her pussy spasmed.

"And what's thy will?" she managed to gasp.

He smiled, those beautiful eyes of his studying every nuance of her reaction. "I already told you. To love you."

He leaned in, pushing his cock deeper, spreading her farther until every nerve, every tendon was stretched on the rack of anticipation.

"Look at us, Sally Mae."

"I can't."

She couldn't move for fear of losing the exquisite pleasure.

"Yes, you can." His thumb circled her clit, stoking her desire, her belief that nothing between them was impossible. "Just lean up."

The move stretched her farther, tightened her around him until the slightest move created the most delicious friction. "Look how beautiful you are."

His cock slid out, one perfect inch at a time, teasing her, thrilling her. It wasn't she who was beautiful, but them. His cock, thick and dark, magnificent, glistening in the faint light, looked huge against the small pink opening to her body. Dark to light. Male to female. Passion to desire.

"Tucker," she moaned as he began the dance all over again, pressing in, demanding she make room for him, answering the hungry flex of her pussy with more pressure.

"Don't look away, Sally mine. Watch it happen. See how perfectly we fit."

She did, absorbing with her mind the beauty of them. Together. Perfect. In and out, over and over, he drove the point home, loving her with slow, steady insistence, looking for something, demanding something she'd gladly give if she only understood. The pleasure spiraled as he lifted her leg higher, drove his cock deeper. Her clit ached with unrelenting need. Her pussy spasmed and quivered, every muscle trembling as she watched his cock sink deep, always so deep. She was close, so close.

"Tucker!"

"What, baby?"

His thumb circled, his cock pressed a fraction of an inch further, touching a place she had not known existed, bringing her that much nearer to the maelstrom…

"Tell me."

Lightning flashed outward from her core, and her body convulsed in an agony of pleasure. Her back arched and emotion welled until she couldn't hold it back anymore. "Oh, Tucker. I love thee!"

"Thank the Lord!" He dropped to his elbows above her, giving her what she needed in a wild drive for completion that caught on the remnants of her first orgasm and stretched it into a second. As her pussy milked frantically at his cock, he thrust deep one last time, sealing his groin to hers. His cock jerked within the tight confines of her sensitive flesh, sending ripples of joy outward as he filled her with the hot splash of his seed.

She held him tightly, whispering against his cheek, not able to say it enough, get close enough. "I love thee. I love thee. I love thee."

He held her tightly, his big body shuddering against hers. He turned his head and pressed a kiss so sweet against her lips, she felt the burn of tears. Oh, heavens, how she loved him.

"About damn time you admitted that, woman."

She blinked, shivering as he flexed within her. "I haven't said it before?"

"No, you have not." Another kiss, another flex. "Trust me, I'd have remembered."

She pushed his hair away from his face, needing to see his expression. He was serious. "It seems I say that to thee all the time in a hundred different ways every day. Thee had to know."

He flicked her nose with his finger. "A man likes to hear the words."

Yes, her Tucker would. "I'll love thee, forever, Tucker."

"Good."

She pinched him for the complacency in that "good."

He feigned pain. "Thought you didn't believe in violence?"

"One of the things I was doing while I napped those three days was reconciling my beliefs with who I am."

"How's that going?"

"I'm not sure. I think it's going to take me a while to figure out what that means."

He pushed her hair off her face. "You know I'll be right here loving you no matter how it works out, right?"

"Yes. I thank thee for that."

"You're welcome, but I'll always love you, no matter what."

"Good."

He smiled back, acknowledging her point as he withdrew from her body. His smile spread with her mew of disappointment. "As a matter of fact, there's only about one thing I'd love more than you right now."

She wasn't worried. She tried to copy the arch of his brow and failed. "And what would that be?"

"A dip in the pond." He got to his feet and took her hand. "C'mon, woman. We stink."

"Speak for thyself."

His answer was a laugh and a dash to the pond. She watched

as he dove in, his perfect body silhouetted for one moment in the setting rays. She smiled and whistled. He came up chuckling, slicking his hair back from his face. "Hurry up, slowpoke."

She was in no hurry. She was warm and languid from their loving and the water was no doubt cold. Something rustled under her foot. She picked it up. The paper unfolded in her hands. The salutation caught her eye.

April 5, 1858
Dear Ari:

Ari was the woman Tucker had been searching for, the one the outlaws had mistaken her for. She read on.

I don't know how to start this letter, except to say, "Thank God you're alive."

So much has happened in the last year. Not all of it good, but some of it so special there aren't words to describe it. I'm married. Happily so to a man of whom Papa would never have approved. He doesn't have money, doesn't have social position and doesn't care a fig about mine, but he is everything I never dreamed big enough to desire when we used to sit under the apple tree, imagining the perfect husband. A heart that knows no limits, a sense of honor that can't be compromised, and a love for me so rich, I'll never be poor. He's Hell's Eight, and if you're still living in the Texas territory when this letter finds you, you know what that means. If not, you're in for a treat. The men of Hell's Eight are a breed apart. A standard on which to build legends, for all they'll scoff at you if you tell them so.

My husband's name is Caine Allen, and he's the one insisting I write this letter. He believes in family and in my intuition.

Though everyone says you're dead, he says my gut feeling is good enough for him, and he's promised finding you will be Hell's Eight's number-one priority. He can be high-handed at times, but in the best ways.

I'm sorry I can't introduce you to the man handing you this letter, but you see, I've made seven copies and entrusted them to seven different men with the hope they'll find you: Tucker, Sam, Tracker, Shadow, Luke, Caden and Ace. Like your soon-to-be niece or nephew, my husband and yourself, (though you don't know it yet), they're Hell's Eight, and I'm asking you, Ari, to put yourself in their care because each one of them has made a promise to me, one they've sworn to uphold.

You see, they've promised to bring you home, Ari. Home to Hell's Eight, where there's no past, no recriminations, no judgment; just peace and a place where you can breathe easily. After what we've been through, I know it sounds like a preacher's description of heaven, illusive and unreal, but I promise you, there is a way out of hell and if you haven't already found it, I'll help you.

Trust no one but them, Ari, because father's solicitor, Harold Amboy is the one who arranged for us to be attacked initially, and he has men hunting for you, too. He intends to control Father's money through one of us. But you can trust any of these men. Absolutely and completely with everything you hold dear.

I'm crying as I write this. I can't imagine what you've been through. I can't forget how we parted, my nightmares, which must have been your reality, the sense of helplessness as I stare at the night sky, wondering if you can see the same stars, wondering if you're healthy, happy and, most of all, safe.

Do you remember the game we used to play at the summer house as children when things didn't go our way? How we'd go find a patch of daisies dappled in sunlight, link our hands in our special way and then just spin until we didn't care about anything else? I just want to see you again, Ari, find a patch of daisies, grab hands and spin until laughter takes over and all the bad falls away. Though it's irrational because I have no idea how long it will take the men to find you—days, months years—I have to say this.

Hurry home, Ari. I've planted a patch of daisies and it's waiting.

"I'd have been annoyed to have lost that."

Sally Mae looked up, tears in her eyes. Desi's heart was on this page.

Tucker took the paper from her hand.

"Thee have to find her."

He hooked his arm behind her neck, pulling her against his chest where she always felt so cherished. Despite the dampness, she still did. "We will."

The bullet caught between them, pressing into her breast. She reached to take it off. Tucker stopped her before she got it over her head.

"You keep it."

"It's thy lucky charm."

He shook his head. "I don't need it anymore."

"But…"

He placed his finger over her lips, cutting off her protest. "It's time for it to have a different meaning."

And standing in the fall of evening, seeing the love in his eyes as he looked at her, feeling the contentment in his touch as he cradled the prospect of their child against his palm, she understood. The time for looking backward was over.

She stood on tiptoe, pulling his mouth down to hers, shivering when his water-cooled body met hers.

His lips brushed the corner of her mouth. "You were right, moonbeam, when you said I needed a new path."

"I was?"

He kissed her nose "Yup. Right when you said this was magic."

His mouth came back to hers, nibbled at the outer edge. "Right when you said I had a choice."

She snuggled tighter against him, tilting her head back, facilitating the caress as she studied his eyes. Those beautiful, wonderful, expressive eyes that were so full of love. For her. His teeth nipped, caught and tugged. Her knees buckled. He caught her the way he always did, holding her when her strength gave out. Joy welled in a breathless rush. She needed to hear it again. Cupping his face in her hands, she asked, as he took her breath as his, her love as his, "And what do thee choose?"

He didn't flinch, didn't hesitate, just held her close and gave her back everything in a kiss so intimate its promise resonated in her soul. "With every breath, I'll always choose you."

★ ★ ★ ★ ★

The Hell's Eight is the only family he's ever needed,
until he meets the only woman he's ever wanted...

SARAH McCARTY

Caine's Reckoning

When Caine Allen rescues a kidnapped woman and returns her to town, the
preacher calls in a favor. One Caine's honor won't let him refuse.

From the moment he beds Desi, Caine knows turmoil will follow. Caine
wants all Desi has to offer. Her screams, her moans...everything. Yet there's
a bounty on Desi's head, and keeping her sexually satisfied is proving easier
than keeping her alive.

Available wherever
trade paperback books
are sold!

Spice

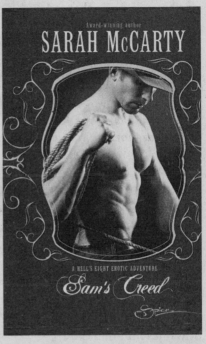

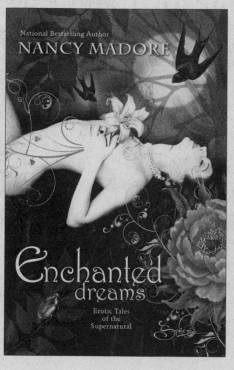

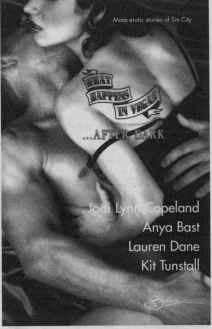

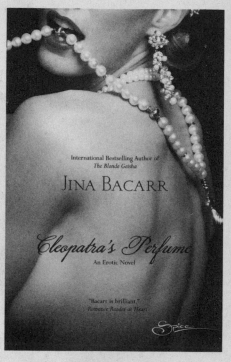